"Truly scary … a fabulous dive into the mind of a classic, self-justifying psychopath … A fantastic book." BARBARA NADEL

"With stylish economy and a remorseless eye for detail, Iain Maitland's Mr Todd lures us in to his moral abyss. The banality of evil … drip feeds us its shockingly tense story of unending horror … Riveting, terrifying." PAUL RITTER

"Hurls you through the secret underground tunnels of an insane mind bent on destruction … phenomenally dark and utterly compelling." CHRIS DOLAN

Praise for Iain Maitland's previous books:

"A compassionate novel imbued with a deep knowledge of mental health issues … Tense and insightful … A heart-stopping thriller with a powerful denouement." PAUL BURKE, NUDGE BOOKS

"Extremely well written and very frightening." BARBARA NADEL

"A breathless journey through fear and love, that explores how interdependent those two extreme emotions are." EWAN MORRISON

"Enthralling … makes us cold to our bones … a stunning novel." BURIED UNDER BOOKS

"Tense … astounding … dark and chilling … and shockingly realistic. Gripping and immersive … an intelligently written thriller that deals with the intricacies of the human brain, mixed up with the emotional ties of the family." ANNE CATER, RANDOM THINGS THROUGH MY LETTERBOX

"Taut, darkly humorous and heartbreaking, with an unforgettable narrator, *Sweet William* packs a real emotional punch." LISA GRAY, DAILY RECORD

"A dark, rocket-paced thriller." JON WISE, SUNDAY SPORT

"A story of danger, delirium and devastation … absolutely electrifying." ALIX LONG, DELIGHTFUL BOOK REVIEWS

Also by Iain Maitland:

Sweet William

Out of the Madhouse (with Michael Maitland)

Dear Michael, Love Dad

MR TODD'S
RECKONING

Iain Maitland

CONTRABAND &

Contraband is an imprint of Saraband
Published by Saraband
Digital World Centre
1 Lowry Plaza, The Quays
Salford, M50 3UB

www.saraband.net

ISBN: 9781912235452
ebook: 9781912235469

Printed and bound in Great Britain by Clays Ltd, Elcograf S.p.A.

10 9 8 7 6 5 4 3 2 1

This is a work of fiction.
All characters are a product of the author's imagination.

For Bernard, my pal.

Part One

THE BUNGALOW

SUNDAY 23 JULY, 7.22PM

Snip.

Snip, snip.

Snip.

It's still close to 80 degrees even at this time of the evening. It's been like this for weeks now and they say it will last all summer. It's going to be the longest, hottest summer since records began. I can do without it; what with everything else as well.

Snip, snip.

Snip.

Snip, snip.

Adrian stands tight and tense at the side of the kitchen, hunched over, snip-snip-snipping away at the vegetables he's laid out carefully, almost symmetrically, in a rainbow of colours, in the wok on a back ring of the oven.

Snip.

Snip.

Snip.

He does this every evening, cutting all of the ingredients down over and over again. By the time he has finished, and it will be a while yet, the wok will be filled with a mass of multi-coloured slivers.

Snip.

Snip, snip.

I sit here, at the kitchen table by the back door, trying to write my diary, to record my thoughts and feelings, to work things through, drenched in sweat and listening to him slashing and stripping and trimming every single vegetable down as far as he can. It's a wonder he does not cut himself.

Snip.

This endless snipping is something that would irritate many people, anger them even. I often wonder what would happen if someone with what might be termed a 'hair-trigger' temperament had to listen to this time and again. And again. And again. And again. There would be some sort of violent incident for sure.

Snip.

I do not say anything, no matter what. I am a calm man. There is very little that troubles me. I am in control.

Snip, snip, snip.

He is my son. He is 25. He still lives at home. He always has. I think he always will.

Snip, snip, snip, snip, snip, snip. Snip.

He is unemployed. I believe he is probably unemployable. He has what are called 'issues'. He is on medication.

Snip, snip.

Snip.

Sometimes, there is a long pause, an agonising wait before he carries on or stops, finally satisfied with his relentless shredding. But that will not be now. Not yet. He still has much to do. He still has to go on. And on. And on. And on.

Snip.

Snip, snip.

We live in a small two-bedroom bungalow. It is on a busy main road between Felixstowe and Ipswich. I have the back door open tonight, yet again, as the heat is unbearable when it is shut. Having the door open means I have to listen to the noise from the road and the pavements and the neighbours and the children in the gardens to either side of me and all along.

Snip.

The children should be indoors by now, having had their tea and getting ready for bed. But they are not. They are left out all through the evening to shriek and yell as they please. To do whatever they want.

Snip.

One of them has something wrong with it and just grunts and screams at intermittent intervals. Grunt (pause), scream (long pause), scream (slight pause), grunt, grunt, grunt. That noise and its randomness are almost as unbearable as the heat. Night after night after night.

Snip.

Snip.

The bungalow is too small for two grown men living on top of each other like this, while trying to lead separate lives, especially with the eternal heat. Two bedrooms at the front, a bathroom to one side in the middle and a living room and a kitchen-cum-dining room at the back. The hallway, from the front to the back of the bungalow, is no more than twelve strides. I have measured it out. There is room for a little storage in the loft and a garage too, just to the side of the bungalow at the end of the driveway. Even so, there is not enough space for everything.

No matter where I go, I can always hear Adrian. Each cough and wretched sniffle. Every visit to the bathroom, both short and long.

Snip.

I do not mind what I call the humdrum noise of everyday matters, however unpleasant. That does not trouble me unduly. It is the unnecessary noise, and the non-stop repetition of it, on-off, stop-start, on-off, stop-start, that I am constantly aware of.

Snip.

Snip.

Snip.

Having eaten my main meal at lunchtime, with a sandwich and a piece of fruit at six o'clock, and having been polite to Adrian for just about as long as I can bear, I have now gone into my bedroom to finish my diary.

It is no cooler even with the window open. There is no breeze. There has not been one for days and I can smell the bins from here. A rancid, decaying smell, however much I sprinkle carpet freshener over the rubbish. I can always smell it. It's even worse than the pig farm and the fields of cauliflowers and cabbages over the way. And I can still hear Adrian, no matter what, my ears somehow straining for the sound of that endless snipping.

Snip.

Snip.

Snip.

Snip.

I am 55 years old this autumn and I have stopped work. I am at home almost all of the time other than my morning and afternoon visits to the local shops for fresh air and groceries and, as often as not, to choose a microwave meal for my lunch.

I write throughout the day – letters to people, little notes to officialdom, jokes and bons mots for myself; all to keep busy. I have my diary to fill in the gaps. I am not yet so old or befuddled as to watch daytime television with its endless procession of life's flotsam and jetsam.

Adrian has been at home for most of the time since I stopped working; other than when he has to go into town to sign whatever forms he has to fill in for his benefits. But he has been going out more lately, during the days, and I have been wondering what he's been doing. It worries me. More than I can say.

I should not have to put up with all of this at my age, really I shouldn't.

Snip, snip.

(50, 51.)

My diary is a hobby, of sorts, which I hope will keep me busy during these long summer weeks ahead. I think about things, some serious, others amusing, and write something every day, sometimes several times. I try to write at least two or three pages; it's a home-made notebook, so I can write as much as I want when I want. I am not limited to a single page as other diarists are forced to do with an A4 desk diary. I write about what I have done, along with my musings on life.

Snip.

I will write more now.

Snip.

Some of what I write, my general thoughts, is thought-provoking and would make people stop and think if I were to read it out loud to them. Other entries would, when I am 'on form' as it were, make them laugh heartily. I can be most amusing when I put my mind to it.

I have kept a diary regularly for a while now. The GP I see for my blood pressure said that it is good for me as it is a way of staying calm and lowering my stress levels. He is about my age, perhaps a year or two older, and I feel he understands me better than the young female GP I used to see. She would sit there looking down her nose at me (when she could bring herself to look my way). I did not like her very much. Little Ms High and Mighty. Nor her me, truth be told.

Snip.

(Was that 53 or 54?)

He also told me I should use my diary to go over those events of the past that have troubled or upset me in some way, to 'work through them', the GP says, so I can understand things more clearly and feel more at ease about what has happened. What has been done to me. How I have come to this.

The GP has emphasised that writing everything down along with my thoughts and feelings is therapeutic and that I must do it regularly and come back to 'the main issues' as he calls them, at something like three-monthly intervals. Sometimes, the way he speaks to me makes it sound like an order. As though I have to do it.

Snip.

(I think that was 55.)

I do go back to the events that have upset me and write about them again. The GP says it will help me if I look back over previous entries to 'compare notes' and to see how far I have progressed with my feelings and how well I am now compared to how I used to be. To see how I am coping with the stress of everything.

Snip, snip.

(55, 56?)

Things have not been at all easy for me for some time and they have taken another downturn recently. I lost my job. 'Made redundant' was the phrase used formally. That and, occasionally, 'early retirement' (although I am not old enough for that to be strictly correct).

I do not think either description is accurate, but I do not like to make a fuss, even when I feel extremely angry about something.

I will say I lost my job; 'taken away from me' is a more accurate description, though.

Snip, snip.

Snip.

Living with someone like Adrian is not easy. He is a fully grown man and he does not do any sort of work at all. He does not do anything as such. When he is in, he sits somewhere or other tap-tapping away and knock-knock-knocking and get-get-getting on my bloody nerves.

When he is out, I wonder what he is doing, making trouble and being a nuisance, bothering people, and more. I feel sick at the thought of him and what he gets up to. Up to no good.

It's a wonder I can stand it all.

I did not see my life turning out like this. By Christ, I didn't.

I deserve better.

I do not know what will happen next nor what will become of us this long summer.

I am beginning to wonder how this will end.

It's so hot and cramped and noisy and frustrating all the time. I cannot bear it.

Really, I can't stand it much longer. I feel as though I am going stark staring mad.

SUNDAY 23 JULY, 7.36PM

I am going to work through how I came to have my job taken away from me. I will then compare what I write now with what I wrote last time when, I have to admit, I was angry (with full and complete justification, it has to be stated). I am calm now.

*I worked, for almost 30 years, for Her Majesty, HM Revenue &
Customs as it is known these days. I had a variety of roles, mostly
as a tax inspector, at different grades. A great many people among
the general public do not understand the difference between a tax
inspector and a tax collector. They often think they are one and the
same. They are not. They are different. I always take the opportunity
to correct people whenever I can. It is really quite simple and easy
to remember.*

(Adrian has stopped his snipping. I cannot hear anything.
Waiting to discover what he's doing next sets my nerves on edge.
But I will ignore the nagging silence and carry on writing.)

*A tax inspector, as the name suggests, inspects tax returns. They
check to see that all is correct and in order. That Mr and Mrs John
and Joan Smith – and Mrs and Mrs Lesbian and Mr N'gog these
days, of course – are paying exactly what they should be paying.
"Not one penny more, not one penny less," as I used to say to taxpayers with a little smile as they sat opposite me at my desk.*

*A tax collector, as the name implies, collects tax. They have to
make sure that everything, including fines and interest, is all gathered up and paid in full and on time or as soon as possible thereafter.
The difference is distinct. I liken the former to forensic work and the
latter to manual work. One uses a scalpel. The other works with a
sledgehammer.*

(I think Adrian must be eating now. What a drama he makes
of it all with his sniffs and twitches and endless routines. I cannot
bear to watch or even hear him at times. I must focus instead on
my writing. I have lots to write.)

*I am not being immodest if I state now that I was a very good
tax inspector, if not an excellent one. I had what I like to consider
a 'nose' for it – I had something of a sixth sense for spotting returns
that didn't quite add up in some way. And those higher up in the*

Inland Revenue, as it used to be known, recognised that.

(Adrian has to have everything a certain way when he eats, all 'just so'. I sit calmly through it all, regardless.)

I was, in later years, an investigator. I did that for almost 15 years; 37 days short, in actual fact. Whenever I was asked what I did for a living, I would, of course, always say "the civil service", suggesting some bland administrative-type work. A pen-pusher! That is what is known as a non-confrontational statement. It, or something much like it, is what should be said by all Revenue & Customs employees to members of the public at all times when 'off duty'.

(I hear beeping. Adrian's mobile phone. Beep. Beep. Beep. Beep. Beep. Beep. Beep. Beep. Beep.)

I had to look at what was presented in tax returns. I needed to do my research to see if what was in front of me was likely to be true. Most often, it was not. Those who work in 'cash' businesses, for example, and there are very many, almost always under-declare what they earn. It can be by as much as half on occasions, I have found.

It is the same with tips. "This is not free money," I once stated to a man who seemed to think any tips he received were all for his back pocket. He feigned deafness. I raised my voice to get his full and immediate attention. "Money is due to the Crown."

(Beep. Beep. Beep. Beep. Beep. Beep. Beep. Beep. Beep. For God's sake, answer it.)

As part of my job, I would often have to interview taxpayers, usually several times, until they would, under my mild but persistent questioning, admit to some wrong-doing or other. I would always uncover something eventually.

"Is there anything you would like to add," I would ask, turning over a page in their file and looking at the next one carefully. I would then look up and smile at them (although few would meet my steady

gaze). That was a very effective tactic. Everyone who sat in front of me had something to hide. That is a fact. My job was to find out what it was.

On occasions, I would have to drive by a taxpayer's house to see if their lifestyle was consistent with what they said they earned. You might be surprised to learn that some people who claimed to make very little money would have two cars on the driveway, both with relatively new registration plates, and perhaps even a boat.

I recall once, walking by a taxpayer's house and seeing, with the lights on, that she had had a brand-new kitchen just fitted that she could not have managed to buy based on what she had put in her tax return. I made a careful note to do one or two checks when I got back to the office the next morning. It was something we would have a little chat about later.

Now and then, I would have to follow a taxpayer to see what they were up to 'behind the scenes'. I do remember having no end of trouble with one Pakistani gentleman who simply would not come clean about matters. If he had been honest immediately, it would have been better for him. But no, he was not. I followed him by car one morning to see him taking his daughters, three of them, to a private school some way away. That is not something he could afford, based on his tax return, and it needed to be investigated further. His lies and deceit ruined him in the end. He had only himself to blame.

(Adrian's mobile phone has gone quiet. That beeping will be something or nothing. A reminder, most likely, that he needs to take his medication.)

I would always find something in every return I looked at. I was renowned for it in the office. One of the young ladies called me 'Sherlock' for a while before she moved on. I think her comment was meant to be a little joke, but it had a ring of truth to it and I believe everyone recognised that.

I, being a jolly sort, reciprocated in kind by always referring to her as 'Watson', which was very amusing all round. "Ah Watson, good morning" and "What do you think, my dear Watson?" were two of my favourite 'one-liners'. We certainly had a good few chuckles.

(Adrian is up and moving about the bungalow. To his room. Back into the hallway. I hear the front door being opened. I wait for him to say what he is doing. The door slams shut. He's gone. Why? He never goes out in the evenings. Never.)

Despite all that I did, the dishonesty I uncovered, the unpaid tax I recovered for Her Majesty's Revenue & Customs, I have been 'let go'. It was a dismissal. And I can see, as I think back over things and write these words down again, where it all began.

I stop my writing, at a convenient point in my story, to slip to the front of the bungalow and into the porch, to see where Adrian is going. He is out there, a little way up the road, waiting at the bus stop to Ipswich. Where is he going at this time of night? What on earth is he going to do? The thought sickens me.

MONDAY 24 JULY, 7.57AM

We are in the living room, Adrian and I, getting ready for breakfast. It is still stiflingly hot. The air outside is hazy. Adrian always wants to have the windows shut in case he gets hay fever. He never has. But he thinks he might if he is not careful. I am sweating again, partly due to the heat, but mostly because of Adrian.

The way he is.

What he is doing.

Where he was last night.

Breakfast, at 8.00am every morning, is a ritual for Adrian and, although I never show it, another ordeal for me. It is not something we enjoy. Not for us the amiable conversation, the sharing of news and thoughts and the occasional but companionable silence of a father and son at ease with each other. I do not know why we still do it. Breakfast. Habit, I suppose. There is little more than that between us.

I tried to be a good father in my own way.

He is not a nice person. He is not normal. He is not decent.

I have been ashamed by him, embarrassed – and now I am fearful.

Adrian fusses around as ever. I sit quietly in the corner as always, waiting endlessly. He has to have the fold-out table just so and I have learned that it is best to keep out of his way while he arranges everything. He lifts up one side of the gateleg table, securing it by swinging the leg below into position. He checks the leg, once-twice, once-twice, to make sure it is safe and well.

I turn on the radio on the side of the table.

We listen to the Radio 4 news and the weather every morning.

Like ordinary people do.

At the 8.00am pips, he stops for an instant, as if standing to attention for a two-minute silence. He then spreads the tablecloth and lays place mats, one each, plus another one for a pot of tea and another two for racks of toast, butter and a jar of marmalade with a teaspoon. We have a mix of brown and white toast and he likes to put these in separate racks. He brings two chairs out from the kitchen and places one at either side of the table.

It is at this point that I move to the table and sit down, my back to the garden window.

Adrian carries the breakfast things through on a tray.

We will sit, opposite each other, for no more than ten minutes, hardly saying a word.

There is a moment or two's silence as he pours tea for me and then himself, before shaking his head and scolding himself quietly because he has forgotten the milk. He hurries back to the kitchen. I hear him opening the cupboard to get the jug, pulling at the fridge door for the milk carton, pouring milk into the jug, putting the milk carton back into the fridge. Checking the door is shut. Once-twice, once-twice. Every time.

I repeat the headline news, calling out to him. Echoing the newsreader word for word.

The latest dramas from Westminster.

It's something to say. I might as well be talking to myself.

He returns to the table, settles back down and then realises he has also forgotten the little pack of sweeteners. This time, he shakes his head and stands up sharply. For a moment, I think he is going to cry.

I do not say a word about this. We have shared the moment and others like it many times and I know it is best not to react at all, to show irritation or anger. It is better if I stay quiet as he returns to the kitchen and repeats the process.

There have been occasions when he has done this four or five times in rapid succession for one thing or another. I sit here unblinking, never moving a muscle. My eyes gaze calmly into the middle distance.

I then call out again, telling him what the weather will be like today.

Hot.

As if it has been anything else for days, weeks, forever.

Now he has sat down and has fussed his way through sweet-eners and milk and is stirring his tea. I let him reach for the toast first, to smear the butter, add a teaspoon of marmalade, spread it across with his knife. Then back again, and so on, and so forth, to have it thin and even. He waits for me to prepare my toast too. Not because he is polite, caring, thoughtful. I have been drawn into his obsessive routine. I have to play my part in it.

He bites into his toast, a look of pleasure on his face as he moves the buttery marmalade mess around his mouth. He opens his mouth as if to show me the churning food. He makes an 'ahh' noise. As if it is the nicest thing he has ever eaten. That, and the endless, swirling, chopping, clacking noise of his teeth, would set most people on edge.

I take deep breaths.

For I am a relaxed man.

Nothing troubles me.

I do not know whether we will ever have a normal conversation. Sometimes, I want to ask if or when he is going to try and get another job. Perhaps he could pick up where he left off, five or so years ago, with old friends. Now and then, I think I should suggest he gets out and about to a church, a charity shop, somewhere to meet people. But it is pointless. He is what he is.

Odd.

Friendless.

A bloody menace.

I stay silent and we listen to the radio and an interview with someone from the Met Office about heatwaves. She drones on, saying there's no official definition of a 'heatwave', it's just a term to describe an extended period of hot weather that's higher than usual for the time of year.

If I ask Adrian a question, anything personal, he does not like it.

He gets angry and defensive. Says I am 'getting at him'. Again. As if I constantly badger him, causing him stress and 'grief', as he puts it.

Anything I say must be neutral and vague, parroting the radio without thought or opinion.

The woman on the radio is now interviewing someone or other from the ambulance service. A know-all who loves the sound of his own voice. The man repeats what are obviously carefully prepared comments. It sounds as though he is reading answers from a card.

They are talking about a heat-health watch service, which is some sort of alert system for medical and emergency services when temperatures are high for a sustained period of time. There are various different levels, apparently.

Adrian stops eating and tilts his head upwards.

He is listening and thinking about whatever it is he is going to say.

I know better than to interrupt him, to ask him what is on his mind.

Level one, says the know-all with the robotic voice, is in place through the summer weeks and medical and emergency services need to be aware that something called the temperature threshold may be reached during this time. Level two is when it's expected that the threshold – an average of 30 degrees by day and 15 degrees at night for two consecutive days or more – will be exceeded soon.

Adrian pauses, as if he is having second thoughts.

About speaking, starting a conversation, about being normal.

He dips his head down and we continue to listen to the radio in silence.

Level three of this health alert, and the know-all chuckles as if it is something very funny, is when that temperature has been exceeded for more than two days, and level four, he laughs again, is when a prolonged hot spell means it is severe. I do not know why he thinks this is funny. People die in hot weather. Someone needs to say something. He should be reprimanded. A letter needs to be written by a community-minded member of the public.

Adrian smiles. To himself.

As if he has thought of something very amusing but does not want to share it.

Not just yet anyway.

I know what it is. I am not stupid. He is thinking that this is not a heatwave, even though I have said over recent days and weeks that it is. Although it has been hot for so long now – level four – the weather may not have exceeded 30 degrees for two successive days. It has, I think, dipped above and below that mark. Above one day. A touch below the next. Up again the day after. And on and on. Relentlessly hot day after day after day. But not, strictly speaking, a heatwave.

I can hear Adrian in my head saying, "So, technically, this is not a heatwave… whatever anyone says." The pause being for my benefit. The 'anyone' being a little dig at me. He'd then smirk and start clearing away the breakfast things.

"Um," he goes, and then brings his cup up to take a mouthful of tea. He slurps it. Loudly.

"Er." He takes another bite of his toast, pulling at it with his teeth before wolfing it into his mouth with a wet and sloppy noise.

He stares into space for a moment or two, thinking, his mouth chomping up and down on his toast.

I know what is coming. The sly glance at me. To check I am listening. To hear what he is about to say. To laugh at and belittle me without doing it directly. Repeating what we have heard on the radio. In direct contradiction to what I have been saying. That this is becoming the hottest and longest-hottest summer ever.

He makes a noise somewhere in the back of his throat.

A pleasurable noise.

It sounds almost sexual, which makes me feel uncomfortable.

The radio has moved on now. From the weather. To a train accident in India. A shooting in America. Endless death and misery. We carry on, sipping our tea and eating our toast, but Adrian and I are still thinking about the weather. He is deciding what he is going to say and how he is going to say it. I am waiting, ready.

Then he's chewing, chomping and clackety-clacking and clearing his throat repeatedly.

I sit and wait. He edges his way towards what he's going to say. His nasty little dig at me.

He looks over at last. Our eyes meet, I hold his gaze. And then, as he is about to speak, I get up and walk away, shutting the living room door carefully behind me.

MONDAY 24 JULY, 9.49AM

Having put together a 'to do' list for today – a letter to the BBC, various notes to attend to, a shopping list, a small package to put in the post box to a neighbour – I am now going to write my first entry of the day in my diary. I will work through what I will describe as 'the first incident' that led to me having my job taken away from me. I should add that the word 'incident' makes much more of it than it actually was; something and nothing.

The incident, at the start of the year, was in relation to a young trainee in my section who I will not, out of respect, name, not even providing her initials, although I know not only her first and last names, of course, but also her middle name, which is rather amusing.

Her parents chose an unusual name quite out of keeping with the young woman's appearance and demeanour. I will say no more on the matter other than to suggest the lady in question has the manner of a librarian about her and the middle name of what might be described as a burlesque dancer (to put it politely). I will, as I have done before, simply refer to her as 'the young woman'.

(Adrian is outside. I can hear him opening the garage door, a screech as he lifts it up and over. I do not know what he wants in there.)

The incident – as I suggest, the word is something of an exaggeration for what happened – occurred when we were resting in the staff room, enjoying a mug of piping hot coffee after a very busy afternoon going through the papers to bring ourselves up to date on all matters regarding outstanding taxpayer files. We were sitting opposite each other in easy chairs with a small table separating us. (I say they are easy chairs but, in reality, they were rather straight-backed and forced one to sit up in a most uncomfortable manner.)

We had talked over various issues until we came to a recent enquiry – not to be confused with a more formal and detailed investigation – where it transpired that the young woman lived close to the taxpayer in question. She had, without reference to me, or anyone else, taken it upon herself to make some additional checks, walking by the gentleman's house, seeing what type of car he drove and so on. She had done this quite thoroughly, going there on various separate occasions and, so as to be less likely to be spotted, in different ways (on foot, by car, etcetera).

It was while we were drinking our coffee that she revealed this information to me, starting off hesitantly and shyly, glancing and smiling at me for encouragement, as she explained what she had done. She seemed, if I may say, rather servile in manner (unlike many girls of today who can be quite full of themselves and 'uppity', to use mother's apt expression). I was, frankly, rather taken aback by this revelation but I have been trained not to show emotion, nor to give anything away as to what I was thinking at any given time.

(Adrian is now in the garage, rummaging about among the packed-away accumulation of many years. I hear random noises. A clonk. A clang. A thud. I don't know what he is up to.)

As an investigator, I should explain that there are times when you do make a conscious decision to express surprise, but this is often done as a subtle way of encouraging a taxpayer to tell you more. I have found that there are certain types, 'white van man' for example, and to use a popular expression, who like to boast about their 'enterprising ways' and, with only a little encouragement, will talk freely of their exploits and reveal, inadvertently, all manner of lines of further enquiry that can lead to a full-scale investigation into their affairs.

In this instance, though, as she sat back, I could tell that she had summarised matters and concluded what she had to say so I did not feel it necessary to press for further information. However, although I was obliged to admonish her, more of a gentle chiding, about what she did, I had to admire not only her initiative, which one does not see in young people at all these days, but the way in which she had gathered her information and described her findings so succinctly. ("A taxpayer living beyond his declared means," she summed up accurately with a firm nod). I was encouraged by her.

I could not tell, from the look on her face, quite what she made of my chiding, which I felt I had to do, as per my job specification rather than by my personal inclination. I have found in the past that some of the ladies, especially the younger ones, can be brought easily to tears by even the mildest of criticisms, perhaps about an unfortunate new hairstyle or a rather promiscuous application of make-up or bright red lipstick. I have learned, sometimes the hard way, to be very mild in what I say and how I put it to them.

(Lo-oo-oo-ng scrape.)

I would have been especially gentle with this young woman as I had something of an admiration for her and the work she did. I had been with her for only a short time, working one-to-one, mentoring her for some six weeks or so at this point.

(Sudden bang.)

She had been in the department for a year or two prior to that and I had noticed her as we went about our work and we smiled as we passed and, occasionally, while we were waiting for the lift, we would exchange a few words about the weather and such like. I do recall an extended and quite animated conversation about a Wimbledon tennis match on one occasion.

(Adrian is searching for something. I hear dragging noises as things are pulled out. Bumps as they are pushed back.)

During our six weeks together, she had shown a considerable work ethic and commitment and I believe we had struck up something of a rapport. She had, if I might say, something of a twinkle about her at times when she was with me.

(Another loud bang.)

As I ended my gentle chiding, she leaned forward and ducked her head down in front of me. I could not tell if she was upset with what I had said or was merely reaching for her cup of coffee on the table. It was at this moment that, quite inexplicably, the incident took place. I looked down at her head of smooth brown hair, clean and shiny, and had an overwhelming urge to smell it. Before I could resist, my head dipped down too and I found myself taking in a breath of the sweet lemon scent of her hair.

(Sudden knock.)

I think, at this moment, that might have been the end of it. Had I simply pulled back, she would have assumed that I had leaned forward to pick up my cup of coffee at the same instant and our heads had bumped together by accident.

Unfortunately, she did not move for two or three seconds or longer – as a normal person would have done when heads collided – and I took more breaths, two, three, perhaps four even, as was stated later.

It was then, as I moved to sit up, that I made an involuntary noise, somewhere between a sigh and a groan, at the back of my throat and she reared back – it is the only way to describe it – with a look of anger on her face.

(Heavy crash.)

Before I could speak, to calm her down over the obvious mis-understanding, she was gathering up her things in what might be described as a tizzy. She was, of course, only a young thing and I have found on occasions that they can be more emotional and hot-headed, especially at certain times of the month, shall we say. As she stood, I looked up at her blandly (so as not to encourage further over-reaction), and she stared back at me with a strange expression on her face. I could not tell if it was a kind or a nasty look. It was at this moment that I smiled nicely at her, as slight encouragement, and she spoke at last.

"You sad little man," is what she said. Those were her exact words.

You.

Sad.

Little.

Man.

I really could not believe what I was hearing. It was a shocking thing to say.

It would be fanciful to state that she spat out each word in turn while staring furiously at me. That would sound melodramatic over a matter that was, when all's said and done, something and nothing. But I can say with certainty that she looked at me as she spoke and said it with some irrational vehemence.

As any ordinary person would be, I was enraged by this, although, as per my training, I did not show it other than to stand up sharply to signal that our meeting was at an end. I have to state, here and now, that I thought her reaction was, and I use the word after very careful thought and consideration, unhinged. It revealed much about her.

(Silence from the garage.)

She then turned and left the room in a hurry, pulling the door to behind her. I could tell she was trying to slam it shut, to make a dramatic point, as the ladies are inclined to do, but it was a door that closed very slowly at its own pace – a fire-related safety device was fitted, I believe – and so the effect was somewhat lost.

(Still no noise from Adrian.)

I stood waiting for a few minutes, hearing her clackety-clack march down the corridor, hoping she would not see anyone while she was such in a state. I heard her opening another door and then one more some way off in the distance. It sounded as though she were exiting the building itself, going down the stairs rather than taking the lift. (I assume she did not want her colleagues to see her in such a state of agitation.)

It was, strictly speaking, 45 minutes before she was due to finish work and she should not have done this. I moved over to the window as, from there, I could see the car park and, to my astonishment, she was walking across this towards her car. As she got to it, she turned and looked back up at me. I could not, from that distance, make out her expression, nor what she was mouthing at me, but her hand gesture left little room for doubt. Clearly, she was still in something of an irrational mood.

I stepped back from the window and hoped that, by not responding to her silly anger, as I have been trained for so long not to do, it would quickly blow over. I went about my business, filing and such like – and humming and whistling to myself as I often do when I am cheerful – for the remainder of the day as if nothing had happened. I hoped that would be the last I would hear of the matter.

(Scr-ee-ee-ch of garage door.)

Sad to say, it was not. There were, over the next few days, accusing looks and stares, not only from the young woman but other feminist-lesbian types on the third floor with whom she'd obviously colluded. One strident woman, with a short-back-and sides haircut, with whom I'd never really got along, despite my early efforts, gave me a withering look and shook her head in a pitying manner when I walked by the next afternoon. (Not that I cared about her. Not one little bit!)

There were then quiet words with line managers and notes on files and the stupid young woman was moved to the fifth floor. (It served her jolly well right.) This whole episode upset me greatly, and I wanted to put it behind me as quickly as possible. It was, however, and without wishing to be over-dramatic, the beginning of the end for me at the Revenue.

It is quiet outside. Adrian has been in and out of the garage. Taken something. I don't know what. He has not come back into the bungalow. He has gone out. I do not know where or why or for how long. I am worried more than I can say. It is bad enough that he keeps disappearing, but there are things in the garage, so many things, that can be used for wrong-doing. This is my fear. That he has taken something that will cause great harm to someone.

MONDAY 24 JULY, 10.30AM

I lie here, having put my diary to one side for the moment, thinking about what I should do next. I have a letter to write to the council that needs my attention. And a report that has to be filled in online, which I will do on a computer at the local library. I have a little bit of research to do online too. I have other mundane chores and tasks to complete as well; routine matters but nonetheless important for the smooth running of life.

But these must all wait their turn.

Adrian invades my thoughts.

And what it is he is doing.

Adrian is a creature of habit, trapped by his twitches and ever-repeating rounds of behaviour. Whatever's going on must be something important, life-changing, for him to be able to break his relentless patterns.

I think Adrian is doing something bad.

It will not be the first time.

He has 'previous', as we used to say at HMRC, and an offender always re-offends.

I get up off my bed. Go to the door. Listen. Double-check he is not in the bungalow. All quiet. I slip into the hallway down to the kitchen and to the back door. Opening it, I move into the garden and go towards the side door of the garage that opens into the garden. To see what he has been doing in there. Moving things about. Taking something. Uncovering things that are none of his business.

Not so long ago, maybe two or three years before he turned into what he is now, there was some trouble in the neighbourhood. Clothes were going missing from washing lines. Women's things. A bright polka-dot bikini. Other items. It was reported in the local paper; something of a joke story really, an old cliché. Itsy bitsy teenie weenie. Who stole the polka-dot bikini? A bit of fun to fill the pages. Not so funny really.

I open the garage door.

Look around.

Everything seems to be as it should be.

Women's clothes, though, never men's or children's. Not

children's, not intentionally anyway. Women's things, that's all. It started in the May and went on every day or two until the end of June. Then it ended for a while. What the locals called the 'knicker nicker', as if the whole business were amusing, something to chuckle over, a little bit of 'Carry On' smut, no more than that. Good old British saucy fun. A laugh, as they'd say around here.

The back wall of the garage is full of shelving, pots of screws and nails, half-empty tins of paint. Tools and accessories for gardening and other work. It's all as it should be. Neat and tidy. Just as I left it.

Further down, against the bottom half of the back wall, is an old Formica kitchen table with boxes and tubs underneath, hand-yman items that might come in useful one day. A big spanner. Old rope. A container of acid. Rolls of black gaffer tape. A tub of screen wash. A pot of Polyfilla. A watering can.

There are other items. A steel step-ladder. Lawnmower. A rake. A half-empty bag of cement. Two spades. A saw. A fork. A torch. A leaf blower. An axe. Adrian's old bicycle. A pile of plant pots. Bricks. Spare roof tiles. All there? No, something is missing. I just don't know what.

Then he got caught. Adrian. He'd taken a handful of items from a line, a woman's and a little girl's too. Hard to tell the difference between them sometimes when these 20-something women wear tiny strips of this and frilly bits of that. Put those next to a little girl's fuller cotton pants and they'd look much the same.

I stand there thinking.

My mind half on Adrian, half on what's missing.

Something dangerous in the wrong hands. Threatening.

The father saw Adrian as he dipped inside the back gate. Watched and waited as Adrian unpegged and took the clothes off the line – leaving the tops and trousers and towels behind – and then chased Adrian down the road. He caught up with him and grabbed hold of his arm by the local parade of shops, spun him around. There was some pushing and shoving – Adrian angry and tearful – and the manager of the local Co-op called the police.

I look along the shelves, pot by pot, tin by tin, one at a time, almost ticking them off in my head. Then see what's what on the Formica table.

I look over the lawnmower and other bits and pieces. Add them up. Do it again. They seem to be all present and correct.

I count the boxes and tubs in front of me. Seven there. I think there have always been seven. I think he's taken something from one of these. I have to look, one by one.

There were visits from a policeman and woman and then social workers; nasty, grubby busybodies. And checks where they looked around Adrian's room and on his computer. Adrian shouted and sobbed and claimed he was dared to do it by a friend, unnamed and then ever-changing, no more than that, and that the father has assaulted him, bruised his arm, cut his knee when he pushed him to the floor.

I felt ashamed.

Knew something was wrong with him.

Some twisted thing.

It was this 'assault' – little more than a mark and a scratch in truth – that saved Adrian. The police, most likely not wanting the hassle and the costs and the time spent on it all, persuaded the father to accept a warning, as did Adrian. The matter was put to one side. Left on file, though. For another time. The next time. There is always a next time.

I step out from the garage side door. Close it. Walk back into the garden where I look around. It's a longish garden, out of all proportion with the size of the bungalow. High-fenced to either side for privacy, it stretches down to the train line that runs across the bottom, taking passengers to and from the town to the coast. Containers too, back and forth to the port of Felixstowe, rumbling through at night, all night, every night, even on Sundays. Beyond that, fields and farms.

He's definitely taken something.

Adrian.

I'm not sure what, but I know it's something significant I should have spotted.

There is little between me and the wired-off train tracks except for the patio at this end, rougher and readier than I had hoped, that I built a while back. I did not do a good job, truth be told. It has sunk slightly to one side.

And there is an old Second World War shelter halfway down and in the middle of the garden. Its dome protrudes up into the garden and is now covered with grass and moss. There are steps down to the door that leads to the underground shelter; no more than a small, cramped room really. I boarded the door up a while back. I don't want anyone going in there. It would be dangerous.

There are tree stumps at the far end of the garden, close to the railway line. Rotten apple trees. I cut them down with an axe and then a saw. Tried, unsuccessfully, to leverage out the main stump with rope. Burned it away instead, most of it anyway, with acid.

And then it comes to me, all of a sudden. What Adrian has taken. From one of the shelves.

An ornate, bejewelled paper knife from mother and father's cruise to Madeira in 1967. Originally used for opening letters by mother. Now old and battered, I'd kept it in the garage to cut string and such like.

He's taken mother's knife. What on Earth would he want with that?

MONDAY 24 JULY, 1.25PM

I have been busy. I have gone to the library to use the computer and then to the post office to send my letter to the council's Chief Executive and the parcel to the neighbour. I then went on to the shops and picked up some groceries and a pre-packed sandwich and a banana for my lunch from the Co-op. I will have a hot meal at teatime.

I have eaten my lunch with a cold glass of semi-skimmed milk and am now going to try to write in some detail about the second event – perhaps I should say events or series of events – that led to what I will call my dismissal.

The first incident with that young woman – 'incident' being an exaggeration, really – was next to nothing; a moment, no more. A misunderstanding. Something that, although discussed and noted, should have been waved away as being of little or no real conse-quence to anyone. Not so the second, let us say, sequence, although even now I would stress, as I had to do through several meetings and reports, that I was the innocent party.

The section of HMRC that I worked in had changed in recent months, if not years, looking back – and not for the better, I might add. There was a time when older members of staff retired and were not replaced, their workload being spread out among the rest of us. It soon reached an intolerable state of affairs and, eventually, when we were all feeling the strain and the section and indeed the department were at breaking point, some new employees were recruited.

Although these were generally welcomed at first, they were, almost uniformly, young people with little know-how or training and, rather than easing the workload of us 'senior folk', just added to it because we had to explain everything to them as they went along and then had to check what they were doing was completed properly. Often it was not: 'slapdash' and 'lacking in cross-references' were two of my regular feedback comments.

(It's hell living here, this bungalow, this road. It's killing me slowly, bit by bit. There is no peace no matter where I sit or lie down. Whether I have the windows open or closed. Endless and also sudden noises all the time. From either side. I can't think to write.)

At one point, after a particularly difficult day correcting the work of several 'juniors', I did put a note, anonymously and in a slightly different hand, in one of the feedback boxes to this effect and how it meant our workload had doubled and everyone had jolly well had enough of it! I wrote in quite a light-hearted, almost jovial, manner, wishing to put over the (slight) criticism in the nicest possible way.

I had, not unreasonably, also mentioned as an aside that two of the new recruits, young men in their early 20s whom I shall refer to by their initials, FD and RP, were simply not up to scratch. I should say that most HMRC employees are, almost without exception, cut from the same cloth – quiet, measured, thoughtful and hard-working types like myself. 'Good sorts.' Not so these two, who seemed to have wandered into the office from a nearby building site. All they lacked were the helmets and high-vis jackets!

They often arrived late, sometimes together, and seemed to do very little work that I could see as they effed and blinded their way through the day, talking about football and drinking and, as often as not, women in the basest manner. They had no respect for their elders and betters. I had never met anyone like them at work and felt obliged to alert HMRC that we had 'two bad eggs' among us. I think, being kind, I had used the phrase 'rotten apples' who are 'upsetting the apple cart', which seemed to be a rather clever way of making a valid point.

(My mind is forever distracted by thoughts of Adrian. Going

into town on the bus. With a knife inside his pocket. Why would he want a knife? And such an ornate one at that? He is a constant worry. One day, I know, there will be a knock at the door and the police will be standing there, one man, one woman, to break some terrible, shameful news to me.)

Somehow or other, my 'rotten apples' comment came out and it worked its way back to FD and RP that I had made such observations. I know not how. This became apparent a day or two later when they started to refer to me as 'Doris' between themselves and in front of me (but not when others were about).

I recall the moment I first overheard their conversation, quiet but just loud enough for me to hear, about someone called Doris and they spoke of this "old woman" in derogatory tones "sticking her nose into other people's business" and saying later, "Doris needs to be careful she's not taught a lesson".

I should stress here that these were not the exact words but as close as I remember them, excluding, of course, the language that seemed to pepper every conversation. As a brief example, it was not "old woman" but "f___ing old b____". I am not someone who swears – perhaps the odd "bloody!" – except under the most extreme provocation and so I will not use the full word here. Bad language is the preserve of the ill-educated and the uncouth sectors of society.

(To the left of the bungalow, as you face it from the road, there is a single mother, 24 years old I have discovered, with two girls of six and eight years. You do not need to be an HMRC tax inspector – ex or not – to do the maths on that young madam. There is a man who visits now and then, a boyfriend, the most recent of several she's had this past year. She lets the children play outdoors all the time. Throwing balls about. Being a nuisance. They are outside now. They have a paddling pool. And a hose. And a radio. I hear their screams, high-pitched and sudden. It goes quiet for a moment or two and there's another bout of screaming. I have to wait until it's all quiet again before I can continue my writing.)

I felt, given that these sounded like offensive comments about an elderly lady who may perhaps have been part of an HMRC random enquiry, that I should speak up and ask FD and RP who they were talking about. There was, at this point, quite a lot of sniggering between themselves, rather like naughty schoolboys who had been caught out by a teacher when they were smoking behind the bike sheds, but neither of them would say that it was what they were now calling me.

I had to put up with all sorts of nonsense – such as them shouting "Doris" out of the windows when I was arriving and leaving – over the following days and weeks. Much of it was childish. I came back from lunch one day to find a pile of papers I was working through had been separated into two piles and shuffled into a different order.

On another occasion, two cups of coffee had been placed next to each other, one on each pile of papers, so that the stains bore a striking resemblance to a pair of bosoms. Any doubts I might have had about this were quashed by the drawing of nipples in the middle of each circular brown ring. I made no comment regarding this, deciding instead to rise above such puerile antics.

(What worries me most about Adrian is that he is secretive and sneaky and underhand. There have been so many instances over the years where he has kept things hidden from me. A poor report at school. The reason why he stopped seeing his best friend, Christopher. The time I saw him in town with a sobbing, angry girl. Whatever it is that's happening, I will have to go and find out about it.)

With FD and RP, I did prepare a few what might be called choice 'ad libs' so that, if or when more bosoms were to appear unexpectedly, I could make a light-hearted comment to show to the wider office that I was a 'good sport'. These ad libs would seem jolly enough to my fellow workers but would have a hidden 'sting in the tail' for the perpetrators.

One, upon uncovering bosoms, would have me looking at the papers and then looking up and out of the window where I would say, "I'm a keen bird-watcher but I don't see any great tits OUT THERE", upon which the office would have a very nice chuckle while I would turn towards the two young men with a winning smile.

I have to say now that no more bosoms appeared and I was, in my own quiet way, a little disappointed by this as I had a number of quick-fire ripostes ready. For a few days, perhaps one week, the matter seemed to have resolved itself. Sadly, though, this was not the end of it. Almost inevitably, the bosoms were followed by the drawing of various penises, across several official documents, in assorted sizes and, shall we say, states; from flaccid to ejaculatory. I found these increasingly distasteful but nonetheless ignored them as best I could.

I did again prepare a few more spontaneous reactions with a little more of a cutting edge to them, a bite shall we say, but I only managed to start one of them, beginning with, "I see someone's a little li... limp today", before stumbling over my words somewhat to the amusement of the two men. I did, in fact, start to repeat the comment with a little more confidence – I was clearly under-rehearsed – but by that time everyone in the office had resumed what they were doing and my words tailed off to the smirks of the young men in question.

I have to stop again. To change my shirt. It is so hot. The shirt soaks in. Sticks to me. Absorbs cotton into skin. I peel it off. Dry myself down with a towel. Put on a fresh shirt. Return to my diary.

I have a fan. A desktop one. It is meant to be cooling. I cannot have it on and facing me while I write – the pages of the diary lift up, distract me, make it impossible to write. It is of little use anyway.

I have to have the windows closed to soften the noise outside.

The fan just blows stale air round and round. It gives me a headache, but I will complete what I have set out to write. About how things turned more sinister.

MONDAY 24 JULY, 1.53PM

I have so much to worry about. It is not just the heat that exhausts me.

Adrian and what he is doing. Other things too. Things I don't want to write about.

I have to focus my attention on what happened at HMRC.

Eventually, it all turned more serious at work, most likely because I did not react as FD and RP wanted me to do by getting visibly angry or upset. Much of this, of course, had to do with my training – to present a neutral face at all times, even when you feel like exploding inside!

I did not complain up the line either because I regretted the consequences of my earlier note and thought I could 'ride things out' rather than risk escalating matters. I did keep the pictures of bosoms and ejaculating penises as evidence of what happened. But, at some point, they vanished from my desk. That, I am sorry to say, was not the end of it.

What happened next was that, quite simply, some of the papers in the files I used when interviewing recalcitrant taxpayers began to, shall we say, 'go missing'. This was a very serious matter indeed. Files would typically comprise taxpayers' returns, information from different sources and taxpayers' submissions such as accounts, invoices, receipts etc.; a cornucopia of information, some of vital significance to an investigator seeking to prove wrong-doing.

There can be, as you may imagine, a quietly satisfying moment in an interview when a taxpayer might deny, say, the existence of undeclared earnings and you open a file, pause for a moment while you (pretend to) look for something, and then take out and slide a piece of paper slowly across the desk with a slight cough and the words, "Would you like to explain this then, please?"

(To the right of the bungalow lives a sluttish middle-aged woman and her slob of a husband, who has been made redundant from his job according to my files. At times, there are shouts and rows and screams and effing-this and effing-that fights; mostly at night when they have been drinking.)

(I can hear them now in their back garden, him singing along to a Beatles CD and her joining in, drunkenly and out of tune, whenever a song takes her fancy. I've heard, and tried to ignore, Ringo Starr singing 'Octopus's Garden' five times so far. I cannot bear it much longer. I have to wait until it finishes and they finally move on to another song before I can write more. I hope to God it is not 'Yellow Submarine' next. I doubt I could listen to that more than once without cracking.)

I should state here that most HMRC files would often be quite bulky and I might not need to refer to or cross-reference all of the papers in a particular file during an interview. This is why I may not have noticed at first that items were missing. There were then occasions, two or three perhaps, when, faced with an especially thick bundle of papers, I could not find what I was looking for and assumed I had temporarily misplaced it.

As a quick thinker, I would often put the taxpayer on the spot in a different way when this took place. "Do you," I would ask, while flicking through the files as if searching for something... pause... stop... look up... make eye contact... "have an overseas bank account?" I would then smile. This would be a very interesting moment indeed.

My smile was a very effective weapon – it unsettled them.

(There are times when I do not know if Adrian is the victim or the perpetrator of his damaged life. He has the manner and the voice of the victim; as though things happen to him, that it is not his fault he has ended up like this. That he has suffered.)

Inevitably, there was the one occasion when it suddenly dawned on me what FD and RP were doing – taking vital evidence out of files just prior to interviews – to embarrass me to the point of humiliation. I will speak frankly here, the absence of key documents at this one interview made a fool of me and, therefore, Her Majesty's Revenue & Customs. Indeed, it shamed Her Majesty herself since I represented her in my duties.

I was dealing with a man who had, in simple terms, been earning money that had been going, in cash, into an account that was not listed on his tax return. I had pressed and probed him and had papers at the top of the file, so I thought, that proved both the long-standing undeclared income stream and the savings account.

This man denied everything both categorically and vehemently over and again, no matter how many times I came back to it from different angles. As I opened the file, ready to produce the two key documents to present to him, I saw that they were not there. I floundered somewhat and, in my confusion, dropped the file on the floor, the papers scattering everywhere. As I picked them up and returned to the desk, I stuttered over my words, then saying, as I often did to unsettle someone, "We will have a l… l… little chat about that l… later."

The man, having watched this, laughed out loud at me long and hard in a braying, mocking tone. I felt my face reddening as I realised I had been made a complete fool of by FD and RP. My natural surge of sudden anger was directed at them but I can tell you now that it still took all of my training not to lean across and slap the taxpayer's stupid pig face.

I kept my temper in check, as I have been trained to do, for the remaining minutes of the interview, cutting it a little short by scheduling a follow-up meeting at the taxpayer's place of work a week later. Of course, the impetus of the interview would be lost by then and the break would give the taxpayer time to prepare himself and bring in, as these rogues so often do at this stage, a lawyer or some bleeding-heart charity do-gooder. He would, no doubt, wriggle his way out of a prosecution with the usual sob story of mental ill-health somehow leading to poor record-keeping and heaven knows what.

(The road, in front of the bungalow, is constantly busy during the day. For the most part, it is a relentless hum I can ignore but, being on a slight hill, there are crunching gear-changes and revving noises to live with at unexpected moments. The train track, at the bottom of the garden, is busy too, with so many containers rolling endlessly by throughout the day, as there are now. There are times when it seems busier at night and I sleep fitfully, what with the endless rumbling and the heat. I am exhausted before the day even begins.)

Livid, but with my emotions in check as always, I returned to the office to be confronted by the sight of these two morons on their own for once, lolling about in their chairs, silly smirks across their faces, as if waiting for me. One of them looked at me and sneered, "aww-wight?" in a cocky manner. The other had his feet up on the desk and his chair tipped back at a sharp angle. He just laughed.

At this, I grabbed his feet with my left hand as I walked by, lifting them up high and fast so that he unbalanced and tipped back out of his chair, banging his head on the wall. He sat there for a moment, stunned. As he then rose to his feet, his friend – his 'maaa-aaa-te' – launched himself up out of his chair too, coming within inches of me, jostling me and knocking the file out of my right hand, the papers flying everywhere.

I responded by pressing him back firmly against the desk whereupon there was something of a pushing and shoving match between the three of us. It was only halted, with me sweating and blood from RP's neck all over my fingernails and running down my fingers, by the arrival of our next-in-line manager Ms – Mssss – Thompson coming into the office.

(Adrian may be the perpetrator, though. He has a temper. I remember things from his childhood. The stampings. Complaints about him from friends' parents after a sleepover. So many things that reveal his true self.)

There were a number of meetings the next morning followed by a rearrangement of desks on the third floor. I was, as I stressed with increasing emphasis time and time again, the innocent party in all of this but, without the (stolen-back) drawings and any recollection of 'Doris' comments from any (cowardly) colleagues who sat a little further away, plus the absence of missing papers from my interview, I did feel my defence was somewhat compromised. Things were 'fudged' over as they often are internally at HMRC, with all parties having to accept warnings to put the matter to bed.

I will leave matters there and write no more about this series of events other than to say that FD and RP both moved to other offices at the end of the month when, I believe, their probationary periods ended. I stayed on where I was, at least on the same floor, but I was moved into the main part of the office where everyone could see me at all times. This made me angry. It made me feel like a naughty schoolboy. But I did not say anything. No one would have noticed my fury. I have been well trained in disguising that at all times.

This has been, on and off, a long session and a stressful one, with the noise from all around and my thoughts on Adrian continually invading my mind.

I lie down, knowing I should really do something, maybe tidy the garden. But it is so hot and I am so tired and I do not think I will do that today. It can wait until tomorrow.

I will just lie here, ignoring everything, and wait until Adrian gets in and we can resume our awkward tea-time shuffles around each other. Him with his dreadful secrets. Me with my terrible suspicions.

MONDAY 24 JULY, 2.43PM

The noise – to either side of the house, the road in front and the railway line behind – makes it impossible for me to relax at all. To lie here. To think. To drift away.

I sit and wait and sweat and worry. My mind turns over and over. Round and round. Here, there and always, relentlessly, back to Adrian.

And then it occurs to me. All of a sudden. I have, if Adrian repeats his most recent patterns of behaviour, about two hours before he returns home.

Enough time.

To check his room.

To uncover the truth.

The business with the stolen underwear was not, I'm sorry to say, the end of the troubles with Adrian. A while later, he joined the local leisure centre. A free trial. Swim and sauna. A month, maybe two. Not that he lasted that long. Something took place. In the sauna. A mother and her 16-year-old daughter.

There was a knock on the door.

An older policewoman and a young policeman, a special, 20, 22 at most, who looked half-scared to death.

A word, she said, with Adrian, if you please.

He went outside and sat in the police car with them. I stood and watched from behind the blinds in the bedroom. I could see Adrian sitting in the passenger seat, next to the policewoman. The young policeman sat behind, taking notes I think. I could see Adrian shake his head, once, twice, three times. Watched him getting angry. Frustrated. Inarticulate in his rage.

He looked towards the bungalow. Saw me, I think, watching from the window. When he looked up and over, I stood still, not moving at all. The movement would give me away. Motionless, I don't think he could be sure I was there, standing back, slightly in the shadows. Three, four times he looked across. Held his gaze steady. Looked away. I could see, or at least imagine, him trying to stop himself crying, to avoid making a fool of himself. He did not succeed.

After five, maybe ten, minutes, he got out of the car. Tearful. Ashamed. Cowed. She, the policewoman, said something to him before he pushed the door shut. He listened for a moment. Nodded. Once. Twice. The second more forcefully. Yes, yes. I heard you. I understand. He then walked up the pathway as the young policeman watched him before turning and saying something to the policewoman.

Adrian opened the front door. I was in the hallway.

I looked at him. "Well, Adrian...?" I said in a carefully measured tone. He glanced downwards.

Then shook his head, pushed by me angrily, slammed his bedroom door. A shameful conversation delayed until another day. Even then, brief and defiant, my cautiously phrased questions rebuffed.

Now, I stand in front of his bedroom door, ready to open it, while he is out, to search for clues; to uncover what it is he is doing.

I put my fingers on the handle, push it down, open the door and step inside. It is a small room, maybe 10 feet by 12 feet, with one window that opens on to the driveway; the bins, my old Renault Megane and the garage just behind at the end of the driveway. The room has soft-grey painted walls, a dark-but-faded swirly carpet and off-white IKEA furniture. All old, 10, 15 years, but perfectly clean and presentable.

It looks like a hospital room and even smells faintly of the disinfectant Adrian uses to clean the furniture surfaces once a week. There is nothing on the walls: no posters, or photos; never have been. The surfaces of the units – a desk, a three-drawer-chest and a five-drawer chest – are empty. The wardrobe is shut. The waste-paper basket has scraps of paper in it; a screwed-up, out-of-date voucher for a new cereal bar, a small, colourful piece of cardboard, torn in two, advertising a nightclub opening in town. The foil and green wrapping of a packet of Polo mints. Scraps emptied from his coat pocket.

I move to the single bed, pull back his duvet, look at the sheet, run my hand under the pillow, lift the mattress. Check below. There is nothing there.

One by one, I open the drawers of the five-drawer chest. Lift and run my fingers through sheets and towels and blankets and, lower down, I flick through old books and CDs, mementoes of school days and years gone by. I thumb each carefully, checking for something, I know not what.

I work my way down the three-drawer chest, his socks and underwear, pyjamas, rolled-up T-shirts, a dressing gown filling up the bottom drawer. I check, open, run my fingers over everything without success, not sure what I expect to find.

To the wardrobe, all neat and tidy, a few old paperbacks, Alistair MacLean and Desmond Bagley adventure stories mostly, on the shelf at the top. Hanging up, there are jackets, shirts and trousers from left to right, dark to light, with three pairs of shoes at the bottom. I slip fingers into pockets, pushing into corners, finding nothing.

Except one thing. Two really. Two, torn-in-half, pieces of a drawing.

A pencil sketch on a postcard-sized piece of stiffish paper.

In the pocket of a lightweight jacket he wore when going out last night.

It is a drawing of a small girl's face. She is perhaps four or five. She is fair-skinned. Soft-featured. Lots of hair. Cute. She seems to be smiling. It is a head and shoulders drawing. And she is bare-shouldered, perhaps she is naked. Her smile is not quite right though, as if Adrian has struggled with it, first having her showing her teeth and then not; the change, several heavier-drawn lines and some shading-in, creating the effect of a mild disfigurement. A simple mistake but enough for him to tear the drawing in half in anger.

But he has not thrown it away.

He has kept it for some reason.

I don't know why, but the keeping of it worries me.

I slip the pieces back into the pocket and then lift up the sleeve to smell it. I am not sure what I am expecting; the scent of a young girl, I fear. Sugar and spice and all things nice. But I smell nothing except the fabric. I take the jacket out and put my nose to it properly as if examining the evidence; I smell sweat and dirt, or maybe that's my imagination. I turn the jacket to look inside and I see what looks like grass and mud marks on it; as if the jacket has been on the ground and been pushed into it back and forth.

I catch my breath, terrible thoughts running through my mind.

Look around the room searching for something, I'm still not

sure what; it's all too neat, too careful, even by Adrian's obsessive-compulsive standards.

As if the truth has been disguised, hidden away, put somewhere else.

Adrian does not now have a computer. He did have. But there was another incident, following the one in the sauna. This time in a lavatory in a department store in town. The toilets, male and female, shared the same entrance, the closets back to back, a thin wall between them. The men's, so Adrian said, were, filthy: they'd not been cleaned. Or flooded, he sometimes said. As if he'd forgotten his original story. He'd popped into the ladies, no one there he said, sat down and realised there was no paper. Looked over into the next cubicle; a young girl was sitting there. Younger, pre-teens.

The police came again. Several of them.

Took away his computer.

Found nothing. At least, nothing that would convict him in a court of law.

Adrian did not want it back. The computer. Said he felt invaded. Dirty. An innocent boy – man really – and an honest-to-goodness mistake. I don't think anyone believed it. I didn't. But he was adamant. And the mother of the girl – a widowed young mother, wanting to protect her child's sweet innocence – did not wish to take things further. Again, the matter was left to lie.

And now Adrian has nothing in his bedroom to be uncovered, no magazines beneath the mattress, no letters or notes or reminders of loves, real or imagined, at the bottom of drawers. It is an empty room, stripped bare of personality. Devoid of life. Of heart and soul.

But he has a mobile phone. In his back pocket. He carries it with him all of the time; to the bathroom, to the toilet, to bed. I hear it beep at night as he receives messages, glimpse the light beneath the door and imagine him sitting there quietly watching the movements of bodies on the small, illuminated screen.

Adrian has everything on his phone. His messages, his searches, his pictures, his downloaded videos, his secrets, his life, whatever it is he wants to hide. It is the phone that I need to see to discover what is going on. But I have no idea how I am going to get it without him knowing. But I must. No matter what.

MONDAY 24 JULY, 7.55pm

Adrian came home, empty-handed, in the late afternoon. I greeted him in the hallway. Then waited, to see if he might talk, volunteer what was going on.

He answered my greeting with a brisk hello without making eye contact, moving into his room and shutting the door carefully behind him. Silence, as if he were lying down.

I had my tea at 6.00 and retired to my room while he went through his snip-snip-snip routine again. He has now, at long last, finished and I can write more of my diary.

I will now write about the final incident – another series of events, really – that was totally misconstrued by everyone both inside and outside HMRC. Indeed, it was what happened outside of HMRC that led to my demise. Again, this was wholly unfair – the whole matter should have been dismissed as something and nothing. HMRC should have dealt with it and made a note on file, no more than that.

A young lady joined HMRC on what was called a fast-track apprenticeship; this is, or at least was, an alternative to university and a way of learning on the job. I did not work one-on-one with her at the beginning; I think that the previous incident I wrote about was something of a 'black mark' against me, although nothing was put in writing to that effect, of course, nor said out loud. It was my investigator's sixth sense – my antennae, if you like – that told me I was being kept away from young women when on my own, 'just in case'. Outrageous really. Disgraceful. But I said nothing despite my understandable anger.

(Adrian is at the garage again. I hear the scr-ee-ee-ee-ch of the up-and-over door being raised.)

The young lady was assigned to the same team of investigators as me, sharing files and workloads, visits and interviews. She was, as part of her training, shadowing random enquiries and investigations with a handful of extra returns being chosen for her to work on as part of her training. Over a few weeks, a month or two, our arms-length relationship, nods and smiles, business conversations, chit-chats over coffees, turned into something more than just being good work colleagues.

As an aside, I should say that random enquiries – where a number of taxpayers' returns are chosen at random to be checked in more detail – can be most fruitful in the hands of an experienced investigator. What starts as an enquiry – a relatively gentle checking of one aspect of a return (typically, something that doesn't quite 'add up') – can often widen into a full-blown investigation that generates significant unpaid taxes for the Crown.

I can say now that, over the last two and a half years of my time at HMRC, I saw three of my random enquiries turn into investigations and on to, in turn, a bankruptcy, a company in receivership and one male suicide leaving behind a wife and two small children. I state this without any particular satisfaction, simply to illustrate that I have, on several occasions, turned a random enquiry into something else, the discovery of substantial unpaid taxes, through my expertise and diligence. But I am not a boastful type so I will leave the matter there.

(I stop and listen for a minute, to hear more bangs and clonks from the garage but there are none. It is all quiet.)

Our platonic relationship – friendly colleagues working together as part of a team – turned into something more one day. We had worked late one Friday evening, some three or four of us, sharing out some of my files on various taxpayers whom I had earmarked for visits the following week.

I have to say I was in good cheer that evening. Three or four of the taxpayers had funny surnames when put together; something I have watched out for over the years to amuse myself. Wanamaker was one, Love was another – and I made the off-the-cuff remark that I hoped for their children's sake that they didn't marry and have a double-barrelled surname! She found this most amusing once I repeated it more slowly and her tinkling laughter rather spurred me on to further tomfoolery.

The two female colleagues with us, both dreary lesbian sorts with hatchet faces, were not 'in on the joke'. We, however, the two of us, had a very jovial time as I was, shall we say, 'on form' and made lots of spontaneous jokes one after the other that she found very amusing. Her laughter drove me on to more and more harmless silliness. We finished the evening quite exhausted with merriment.

Early the next morning, when I have to be honest and say I had been thinking about her all night, I received a text from her on my work mobile phone. I should say that I am not a fan of the 'modern world' and have always resisted a mobile phone and other paraphernalia in my private life but was obliged to keep up-to-date and 'in touch' at work. The text, and I shall 'translate' it from teenage to proper English, read, and I will never forget it: 'Loved last night. Good to see you again over the weekend if you're free.' I could barely believe it. This lovely young girl and a middle-aged chap like myself.

I thought long and hard about this text and how I should respond to it (if at all, as personal messages on work phones are frowned upon). I drafted several replies, from the formal to the funny to that of a lovestruck teenager (I soon deleted that one – she may have been just out of her teens but I was 30 years older!).

Eventually, and it took me a good hour, I decided what to do. As an investigator, I am a man who finds things out and is aware of what is going on 'behind the scenes' without people realising it. I know things that most people don't know. I knew, for example, from overhearing a conversation in a booth close to me, that the young lady helped out in her family's delicatessen in town on Saturdays. So I decided to 'bump' into her as she came out for her lunch break. We could have a chat and see how things went from there.

(I hear the sudden scr-ee-ee-ee-ch of the up-and-over garage door closing and the clanging of metal on metal as Adrian walks away, carrying something; I'm not sure what.)

The delicatessen was easy enough to find, being on a side road leading towards the main shopping area. By good fortune, just along the other side of the road there was, a little way along, a bench on which I could sit and wait. I had, on my way in, walked by the delicatessen – very busy, it was – and saw that she was working in there. It was simply a matter of taking my place on the bench at 12.00, the earliest I thought she might have her lunch, and waiting patiently. I did not mind sitting there for I was in high spirits; more than I had been for as long as I could remember.

It was a fine day, and a good job too, as it was close to 1.20 before she appeared at the shop entrance and headed into town. She rather caught me dozing and I had to almost break into a run to catch her up to see where she was going. As I got closer, I saw she had some wrapped food in one hand, a bottle of water in the other, and her handbag over her shoulder. From the direction she was heading I assumed she was going to sit by the town hall and watch the world go by. And so, four or five minutes on, with me walking some yards behind, I was proven correct. She arrived in the town hall square and sat down on the first bench there.

It was at this point that I hesitated. Like many a lovelorn chap before me – yes, I was smitten – I wasn't sure how best to approach the young lady. I decided to stroll by as if I were a regular visitor out for a walk, and then do a rather amusing 'double-take' as I saw her – as if she were the last person I'd expect to be sitting there. She seemed surprised to see me – she clearly had no idea I had been walking behind her for the past five to ten minutes – but then smiled quite brightly while looking around, as if to check whether any other HMRC colleagues were with me!

We had a very pleasant chat about all sorts of things – the sunny weather, the frisky pigeons trying to 'do it' in the square and so on – rather than work-related matters. It was the weekend, after all. I said I often took a walk to the square at lunchtimes when I was in town on Saturdays (a little white lie) and she said the same and I said "snap" when she said that and this made her laugh and I did too. We sat there for a moment or two in comfortable silence. I thought that she might rest her head on my shoulder but she was shy and I did not want to force the issue (although I did edge a little closer to her just in case).

As she finished her vegetable wrap – her mother, who owned the delicatessen with her stepfather, had made it for her – she got up to head back. I gently admonished her at this point for not taking her full 60 minutes but she said they were very busy, which I had seen, and had to be back by 2 o'clock. I insisted on walking her to the shop despite her polite protestations. When we got there, I did think of kissing her goodbye on the cheek but the shop was full and the man *behind the counter was watching us, so I hesitated and she hurried in to serve the next customer. I went home and laid on my bed in a state of some excitement. Suffice to say, I felt like a young boy of 16 again. But I have nothing to add to that!*

(I can hear Adrian in the hallway. Clang. Clang. Clang. Clang. He drives me to the edge, he really does. Clang. Clang. Clang. Clang. I've worked out what it is, though. The only thing it can be).

Adrian has got the step-ladder from the garage.

He has bought it into the bungalow. To go into the loft. I wait a while and listen. I am correct. That is what he is doing.

I wonder what it is he is going to get down from the loft. Something dangerous in the wrong hands. Adrian's hands.

MONDAY 24 JULY, 8.26PM

I wish I had left the matter of the young lady there with that silly lunchtime get-together and my dreamy imaginings on my bed.

Had I done, my life would have been very different. I would not now be living in a constant state of suppressed fear.

But I did not. I went on. I am not ashamed to say it was a mistake.

The next week passed in something of a blur, partly because I was in and out of the office on so many investigation-related visits but mostly because I could not stop thinking about the young lady. I was very careful, when at work, not to show that there was anything between us. Personal relationships, in terms of intimacy, shall we say, were discouraged at HMRC. And I would not have wanted her to feel I was rushing things too quickly.

Our paths crossed only a few times face-to-face, when I would give her a little smile and say some nice words of encouragement about her work; on the third occasion, when I had a moment or two alone with her as we waited for a lift, I patted her on her arm (fighting the natural instinct to put my arm around her) and said "chin up" as she looked a little down and worried.

I also texted her, on the work phone, with one or two news snippets relating to enquiries and investigations of mutual interest. I made one or two friendly comments too, little jokes between the two of us, so she would know that my 'distance' from her at work was only a front for others.

(Adrian is unfolding the metal step-ladder that he has taken from the garage. I hear it clang. Again. Clang. As he puts it up. Once more, clang. He is definitely going into the loft. Clang. What does he want there, for Christ's sake?)

The next Saturday, a day I had been looking forward to all week, could not come fast enough. I again waited on the same bench as the week before. I was fortunate that I was a little earlier this time, arriving before noon, as the young lady came out just after that and stood at the entrance looking around as though she was not sure where to go to eat her lunch.

I stood up and waved and hurried across to her in my delight. This time, I had prepared a little packed lunch of my own so that we could sit and eat them together in the square. It was a lovely sunny day and I was looking forward to spending what I hoped would be a full hour with her. I was thinking perhaps that I might suggest our relationship moved on a little at this time and ask whether she might like to join me for an out-of-town meal that evening.

Sadly, however, as I approached the young lady, I saw an older woman, her mother, bang on the window and gesture emphatically at her to come back into the shop. The young girl, before we could speak, turned and went inside. I hesitated outside for a moment or two, watching through the window as the mother and daughter disappeared into a room at the back of the shop. The shop itself was empty and I could only assume that the mother wanted her daughter's assistance to unload a fresh delivery of goods from out the back.

As I waited, three young women – giggling among themselves – brushed by me and went into the delicatessen. I watched for a moment or two more as the mother came back out followed by the young lady, who had put her work overall back on and started serving the stupid young women. So much for a long and leisurely lunch! I sat on my bench until 2.30, feeling more and more frustrated with that thoughtless, selfish mother. I came close to going in and giving her a piece of my mind, but I knew that would embarrass my young lady. Instead, I went home and had a vigorous tidy round of the garden before doing anything else.

(I hear Adrian above my head, walking slowly about, moving each foot carefully from joist to joist. It is dark in the loft. There is no light. It must be unbearably hot. I do not like him rummaging about, digging into corners, finding things. It makes me uneasy.)

The next week was an agony for me as I was away on a course and had no opportunity to see my young lady at all. This was a residential course in Wales to do with online fraud and money laundering and such like – one of many I have attended over the years with gritted teeth as I loathe the endless lectures and need for small-talk with people I don't know and will never meet again.

Invariably, some of the younger men, down from Liverpool or Manchester, go off to a bar to drink and watch a football match and start chanting for one side or the other while some sad old spinster type stays at the hotel bar drinking too much and making a spectacle of herself with the nearest, half-interested man. I, overwhelmed at times with loneliness, spent my evenings, and eventually nights and mornings, texting my young lady about what was happening

and then, as the time passed and I became increasingly maudlin, my
thoughts and feelings for her.

(I am thinking about what he is looking for. There is little there.
I rack my brains. Papers and notes from years gone by? A few
items from his childhood he did not want to let go? Yes. That's it. I
cannot help but sigh. Toys, games. He is looking for something to
entice a young child. The thought sickens me.)

The next – the final – Saturday could not come soon enough for
me. I left Wales early Friday evening and well recall my almost bub-
bling-over excitement as I drove the long five to six hours home along
the M4, around the top of the M25 and up the A12. I went straight
to bed, slept fitfully and woke early, pacing about the little bungalow
by 6.00am. The agony of waiting until noon had me almost beside
myself as I cleaned and tidied the bungalow, putting things straight
and so on, keeping busy, distracting myself.

At last, I went into town and sat down on the bench close to
where my young lady worked. I arrived again at noon, give or take
a minute, and sat back to watch the comings and goings in the shop.
Within a moment or two, I could see there was something of a com-
motion behind the counter where, from what I could make out, the
mother and the young lady – my lovely cuddly girl – seemed to be
having an argument with a big, I have to say fat, middle-aged man.
I got to my feet, thinking for a minute that he was an angry customer
but I soon realised that this was my young girl's stepfather and she
and her mother were trying to calm him down.

What happened next was this. Fatso stormed out of the delicates-
sen, looked left and right as he crossed the road and started running
towards me. As I stated later to the police – and I was advised to
use the exact words he said and so feel I should repeat them here –
he shouted, "You fucking old pervert" as he reached my side of the
pavement and "Leave my fucking daughter alone" as he punched me

on the side of the head.

Taken by surprise, and as he was considerably larger than me, his blow knocked me to the ground. As I sat there slightly stunned listening to him effing and blinding away over me I noticed that, while one or two people had looked up and across as he came running and shouting, they soon looked away again after that and hurried on their way. That is what people are like.

I had expected a long and sustained assault from the man, a variety of kicks and blows as I was on the floor struggling to get to my feet. But he stood there, bent aggressively towards me shouting all the words under the sun. The young lady and her mother had come out of the shop and chased after him by this time, both grabbing an arm and holding him back in a rather theatrical manner.

As the three of them stood there, the man twisting and turning with words of anger and fury and dramatic screams and shouts from them, I got to my feet, took a biro from my jacket pocket and went to jab him in the eye with it. He was fortunate that he turned his head at the last moment as he would otherwise have been blinded by it and serve him right. He would only have had himself to blame. As it was, the pen simply caught the edge of his ear lobe and drew a black line across it.

As I explained later, my gesture was purely and simply in self-defence and had the desired effect of quietening him down until the police arrived, alerted to the incident by a passer-by presumably, a few minutes later. I do not wish to add anything to that; it was an unfortunate matter from beginning to end and I do not want to dwell on it further, thank you.

It is getting late now. Adrian has been in the loft, found whatever it is he was looking for and gone back to the garage and packed the step-ladder away before retiring to bed.

It is dark outside.

And still hot.

And I feel as tense as ever.

I will make my way to the bathroom and wash myself down before lying on my bed for another endless night of heat and noise and wondering what it is that Adrian is doing. I assume the worst and it preys on my mind and worries me to death.

TUESDAY 25 JULY, 9.10AM

We have had breakfast – the same endless 'round and round we go' routine as yesterday and every other day for as long as I have been at home. I now lie here on my bed, the window open and a slight breeze (at last) cooling my sweating skin. I can smell the pig farm today, which is even riper than usual in the heat, but makes a change from cabbages and cauliflowers. I think it must be close to 80 degrees already. I can feel my shirt sticking to the small of my back.

I am listening to Adrian as he packs away the breakfast things. It is easier for both of us if he does it alone. He has his routine. His ways. His order. His places. Once he has done that, and worked through all of his other 'to do' things, he will go out again, I think, disappearing for hours as he has been doing lately.

I do not know what he does.

It worries me.

I fear for him – and me.

He has finished in the kitchen now. I hear him moving to the bathroom. He shuts the door. I listen to the tap running as he washes his fingers. Squirts soap from his little dispenser. Once. Twice. Three times. Making sure. He dries his hands on his towel. Another clean one today; as every day. I hear the toilet seat creak up. A long pause. An endless sound. Coughing. Coughing. Coughing. I hear the flush. Pulls it twice, making certain; then once more, so hard I think the handle must break. Opens the door, shuts it quietly.

The endlessness of it all drives me mad.

I keep it all inside me, as deep down as I can.

I cannot let his madness overwhelm me, take me over.

Now Adrian is in his room. I hear the click as he opens his wardrobe. He is taking a shirt out. All quiet. He is looking at himself in the mirror, full length. He checks first this way. Then that. Not happy. A rustle and another click. He pulls the next shirt from his wardrobe. Takes one off. Puts one on. Checks himself again in the mirror on the wardrobe door. First this way. Then that again. All quiet. He stops. Starts. Tries on more shirts. Trousers. Socks. Shoes. Each time, this way, then that. Taking things out. Putting them back. Agonising over every single item.

I have to listen to this all the time.

The rustle, the bang, the creak, the irrational knocking.

God help me, it drags me in, tears at my nerves as I lie here waiting. And waiting. And waiting.

Now he has turned on his music on his phone, quietly, but I can still hear it. Boom boom boom. Boom. Boom Boom. I cannot hear the song. Nor the singer. No tune at all. Just the endless bass. Boom. Boom boom boom. Boom. No rhythm. No logic. The endless, never-quite-the-same repetitive noise. No pattern. No sense. On and on it goes.

My nerves are torn and jagged. The sweat runs off me. I could just lie here and scream from deep down inside my lungs.

I thought he was going out. Not listening to music.

I don't know what he is doing.

I wait, stay calm. Count to 10, 20, 30 and 40 and more, just focusing on the numbers, nothing else. On and on I go. 50. 100. 200, then 300.

Now there is silence. Sudden. Unexpected. He has turned the music off. I strain to listen, to hear him moving about. The tread of his foot on the floorboard as he rises from the bed. Footsteps as he crosses to the door. Pause. More footsteps in the hallway. The turn of the handle, the signal that he is leaving the bungalow. But I am imagining all of this, of course. It is in my head. My mind is full of his madness. My head is turned, skewed towards his insanity. There is no noise. It is all quiet. He is lying on the bed. Not moving. At least, not moving enough to make a sound for me to hear. I don't like to think what he is doing.

The silence is as bad as the noise.

I feel my back arching with tension.

Strained and damp, it is all I can do to stop my scream.

I wonder sometimes what he would do, Adrian, if I were to scream. To shout. To push and shake him. To knock some sense into him. To display my frustration. My anger. My complete and utter fury. My helplessness to change any of this relentless, ever-twitching tedium.

I do not know what he would do. Cower? Strike back? He has strong emotions. I know that. A temper too. The thought of what he is capable of frightens me. So I contain my feelings. Push them deep down inside. Subdue them. Squash them. Make them so small that I can lie here without feeling tense and shaking.

The silence goes on.

I cannot bear it.

But I must wait, hold myself together somehow.

I lie here for what seems an age in this unbearable silence. I think of Adrian as he used to be. Before he turned, became what he is today. I remember him as a small child. In a park. Climbing a tree. Running ahead of me. Laughing. Happy days. When did he last laugh? I cannot remember. It is so long ago that it has slipped away into the mists of our life.

I could not have imagined then what lay ahead of us, what he would become. The sour joke of the knicker-nicker. The obscenity of the sauna. The seediness of the department store lavatory. The filth of it all. I will lie here and wait for as long I have to, listening to his endless nip, nip, nip of noise. Until, eventually, I hear him moving about, walking into the hallway, out of the front door.

This time I am going to follow him. See what he is up to.

I am going to uncover exactly what it is he is doing.

I have to deal with this myself. I have no choice. I cannot call the police. I cannot have them here. Not now. I have to do what I need to do. God help me.

TUESDAY 25 JULY, 10.15AM

Adrian is on the bus, on his way into town. I am in the car, following two or three cars behind. I waited for ages. Listening to the silence. Then heard him moving. When he eventually left the bungalow, I went into the porch, pretending to be busy tidying away shoes, with half an eye on him up at the bus stop. As he got onto the bus and it finally pulled away, I held back a minute or two and then slipped out of the front door to the car on the driveway in front of the garage. I then followed the bus.

Adrian will never notice me.

He would never think of it.

Adrian is completely self-absorbed.

It is not easy following a bus. It does not drive smoothly and steadily from here to there, A to Z, so that you can stay five or six cars behind and follow it at your leisure. When it stops, to drop off or collect people, one or two of the cars in front overtake and carry on. I have to pull over, being beeped by the cars behind, so that I do not get too close. If I were the car immediately behind the bus, Adrian may look out and then spot me.

He would think that peculiar.

He may put two and two together.

He might change his plans, cover his tracks.

At temporary traffic lights, as workmen stand about with shovels by an open trench, the bus moves on into the single traffic lane and I speed up to slip through behind the three cars in front of me before the lights change. One goes through. The lights start to change. The next car accelerates and races through too. One car left in front of me. Go on. Go on. It slows, quite illogically, and stops. Had it kept going, it could have gone through and I could have done too. I shout in sudden frustration as the bus pulls away over the hill in front of me and the long line of cars on the other side of the road starts filing through.

I know where the bus goes. Its route into town.

But he may get off earlier.

At a stop before I can catch up. I may lose him.

He was normal once, Adrian. Not so very long ago. Did his GCSEs. Nine. 'C' grades and above. Decent enough. He was good at maths, I remember. Could have joined HMRC. I suggested it once. He shook his head. Dismissed it without proper discussion. A Levels, three of them, not great but good enough grades to get into a proper university, not one of these feeble polytechnics renamed as universities. Off he went to study a business management course in Yorkshire and then, no more than half a term or so later, or whatever they call it, he came home.

Not for him, he said, almost tearfully. The university. The course. The student life. Yorkshire. Something had happened there, I'm sure. I don't know what. It must have been something serious, something bad. He seemed angry. Confused. Defiant too. Defensive. Always defensive. I did not press him beyond cursory conversation. I did not want to ask. He did not want to say. There was vague and occasional talk of a gap year, maybe doing another course somewhere else at some other time. I don't think either of us ever really believed it.

He got a part-time job. At a fast-food place. For two or three months. He left. Didn't like working nights. Spent some time at home umming and aahing about. Then a cafe in town. Open only during the day. Four months there, maybe five. The longest spell. Then he left under another cloud. Something or other. A falling-out with a colleague, the female manager. More time at home.

Then a sales assistant in a furniture store in an out-of-town shopping centre. Next, a kennels or a cattery, I forget which. Each job coming and going in no more than two or three months. A growing awareness there was something not quite right about him. His time at home in between getting longer until at last he was there all the time. Benefits. Signing on. Interviews for jobs he'd never get, nor wanted. Endless meandering his way through life. A wretched existence.

I am being hooted.

Several cars, one with a man leaning out of the window and shouting.

I pull away, racing after the bus now.

His madness, for that is what I believe it has become, came on slowly; like the hour hand on a watch, I never saw it moving forwards. The normal boy – the one who was quiet and loved books and drawing and who would have lived an ordinary, clean and decent life – somehow changed, little by little over the years, to the nervous, twitching, endlessly fiddling wreck of the man he is today. I hate what he has become and fear what he is doing.

I am a car or two back behind the bus now as it approaches the town. Four or five bus stops to the town centre.

I do not know if Adrian is still on the bus. I think he is.

If he goes into the town centre itself, I will have to find somewhere to park as close by as I can and then try to track him down from there. I suddenly realise I have no coins on me for a car park.

I do not know what Adrian has been doing, is doing now. I had thought the theft of women's clothing was an isolated matter. That was bad enough, bringing the police and social workers to our door, into our home, rummaging and ferreting about. The others were worse in their way. The sauna at the local leisure centre. Sleazy. The toilets at the store. Seedy. There are things about my son – that side of him, the intimate part of him – that I don't want to know about. No father does.

He is close, I think, to something else this time; something horrific. There will be charges, a court case, a custodial sentence. The last time the police came round, I was taken aside. Warned. Told that he was on the police radar. "Next time." Next time, they said. The words left hanging in the air.

The bus pulls in, two or three stops from the town centre. Close to a park.

I hold back, watching, as Adrian gets off and, without glancing around, strolls slowly towards the park gates as if he has all the time in the world.

If I am quick, I can turn into a road, 20, 30 yards further down to the right and park there.

I must be quick, I dare not lose him.

TUESDAY 25 JULY, 10.30AM

I am standing, sweating, drenched as ever in the heat, trying to catch my breath by the park gates. I parked the car easily enough down the side road, then walked back as fast I could, close to running.

I can just see Adrian.

In the distance.

On the main path, going up the hill.

At the top, he can go one of three ways. I hope he goes straight on, follows the main path that meanders down the other side of the hill through gardens and trees and shrubs to a little boating lake and beyond to a café and other ways in and out of the park. He'd spend a few minutes strolling round the lake before wandering out and into town, round the shops, a few errands, and then back home. No harm done.

That's what I hope.

But I fear it will be to the left.

Or, worse, to the right.

To the left are the toilets. For many years, as long as I can remember, these were run-down and dirty; meeting places for sad old men and scared young boys, hiding away in corners. Fumbling and fiddling. Thrusts and sudden cries. Now renovated, I ask myself if this is where they still meet in secret and whether Adrian at heart is one of them. This wretched, virginal man-child with his dreadful secrets.

I don't think so. Not really.

Adrian is not that way, I'm sure.

I think he is another way. Something much worse.

So, to the right then, and what will be another turning point, another downturn, in his miserable life. I feel sick to my stomach if that's where he's heading. I think it is. It has to be. To the right and the children's play area.

Young mothers.

Pushchairs.

Sturdy boys and pretty girls.

I walk slowly – I do not want to do this, do not want to know the truth – up the path, following Adrian. At the top of the hill, just before he goes over the brow and disappears, he stops walking. As if undecided what to do. Fighting his demons, maybe. His better self, that long-lost part of him, encouraging him to carry on walking down the path and away and out of the other side of the park.

If he turns, looks back from where he's come, he will see me. Some way off. Near the foot of the hill. But clearly, unmistakably me. There is nothing I can do about that but hope and pray – if I believed in anything to pray to. There are people dotted about, single men and women, one or two couples, sunbathing, sitting around, talking, laughing. But there is no one else on the path between us I can hide behind. There are no trees or bushes close enough that I can move across and use as cover.

I drop to my knees, dip my head down, as if tying my shoelaces. If he looks this way, he may not notice, will not realise the hunched-over figure so far down the hill is his father following him. I untie my left shoelace. Make a show of re-tying it. Shift knees. Repeat the elaborate nonsense with the right shoelace.

Wait.

Has he turned, moved, disappeared out of sight?

Or is he there, looking at me?

I hold my breath, a moment or two. I have to do something. I cannot kneel here like this much longer. It looks odd. I take a fleeting look upwards, fearing he will be coming down the hill towards me, striding, his face contorted with fury. His shameful secret so close to being exposed.

But he is not there.

He has gone over the hill.

I must hurry to see which way he went, what he is doing.

I follow his footsteps up the hill, walking faster now, as if by doing that I might somehow stop him. Dreading what I am going to see. And what I will do when I see him for what he is. What, deep down, I have always known he has been. Not odd. Not strange. A pervert. Little things. Signs. Things he's said and done over the years. That all now fall into place.

100 yards.

I still have time to turn around.

To go home and ignore this horror.

I slow down; it's too hot to walk this fast. And bizarre too; people will look up and across and notice. He will be there when I arrive anyway. Wherever he is. To the left. To the right. In the distance, going down the hill, fading away into the trees and bushes. But I know the truth now. Inside. It won't be a shock to me when it is finally revealed.

Fifty yards.

I should stop, think what I am doing.

Leave it, ignore it, pretend it's not so.

I'm walking slowly now, almost slowing to a halt. One step. Two steps. A slow and reluctant shuffle. Not wanting to see what I am going to be confronted by. The truth about Adrian. What will I do? What can I do? I cannot call the police, have them at the bungalow, looking, exploring, digging about. I know what must be done. By me.

Twenty-five yards now, almost there.

I am close to the top of the hill.

And the moment of truth.

I have to go on, I have to know, to see – and then I have to stop it; maybe even prevent it happening. I cannot let him do what I believe he is doing; or is going to do. With a sweet boy. Or a cute girl. I don't know which. Does it matter? What will he do, how far will he go? The thought sickens me. Makes me feel nauseous.

I am at the top of the hill. I look ahead, down the slope – nothing. I turn to the right. Towards the play area.

And I see Adrian straightaway. And what he is doing.

TUESDAY 25 JULY, 12.10PM

I am back at the bungalow. In my room. Trying to stay calm. To think over what I saw, and what I must now do. My mind races, never settling, always going back to Adrian, focusing on something else for a second or two, something practical, something mundane, and then returning to Adrian once more, time and again. What I saw him doing. What he may have already done. What he is likely to do next.

What I should do now.

What I have to do.

I do not know how I can bring myself to do it.

I am angry. I feel frenzied inside. Beside myself after what I saw. I need to let it go for the moment. To steady myself. Be calm. In control. Be prepared. For when he comes home. I fear I must confront him. Talk to him. Stop things. Before it's too late. I have to do this alone.

He has to stop.

I have to stop him.

No matter what.

For the time being, I shall return, as best I can, to my diary, to finish my recollections of my final days at HMRC. This will calm me a little. The thinking of what to write. The phrasing of it. The working it out in my head before I put the words down on the page. The carefulness of it all. I have to be in control when Adrian comes home, puts his key in the lock, steps into the porch, kicks off his shoes and enters the hallway. Where I will be standing waiting.

The matter with the young lady all came out, inevitably. Her original text to me had been meant for another work colleague, the same age as her. A girl. A ms-ss-ss. She should not have been texting anyone in that way on her work phone. It was a misunderstanding of mine, a foolish fancy and, had it not been for that bully of a step-father of hers, no harm would have been done.

But the police were called and the fat stepfather and I were driven away to the station. And there were statements and interviews and DNA was taken, which worries me more than I can say and, finally, the matter was put to bed by both sides accepting a police caution.

That was not the end of the matter as the young lady and her family complained to HMRC with quotes from some of my texts being provided. Some of these, when written down and read aloud, showed me in an unflattering, albeit misleading, light.

(When I turned to the right I saw the play area. Two slides. Swings. Three climbing frames. Young mothers on benches. Smiling, talking, laughing. Pushchairs galore. Children every-where. Running, tumbling over, getting up again. And big, lanky, stupid Adrian.)

My employment with HMRC, although the paperwork and forms to sign will pile up for some time yet, ended swiftly.

Ms Williams – she pronounced the Ms with a long ssss when I called her Mrs in error – called me into an office and opened a file, read down the front page and then closed the file and looked away with a sigh. (Much as I used to do with taxpayers.)

She would not meet my steady gaze.

She would not say why, as such, I was being dismissed (for that was what it was, we both knew).

I do not think she even shook my hand at the beginning or the end of the meeting. Nor did she, as others had done before it was passed to her, make particular reference to the various incidents, which I could have explained given a proper opportunity.

(Adrian had his shirt off. He was on the far side of the play area. So much, and so many children, between us that I could not see him clearly. Bare-chested. Snatches, sudden glimpses. A clear view of his upper body. Standing there, clapping his hands in delight, this curious, freakish man-sized child.)

Mssss Williams made vague references to centralisation and deregionalisation and said I could transfer somewhere or other up north if I "really wanted to" (the implication being that it would all be an awful nuisance if I did).

When I made a tentatively positive noise to suggest I might be interested in doing that, she shook her head and said, with a thin-lipped smile, that this was "for the best… your pension will not be ungenerous… for the government".

(I studied Adrian for a minute or two. Saw him clapping. Shuffling about. No one seemed to think it was anything out of the ordinary. I could not see any young mother looking at him, admonishing him or pulling her child away. I turned away in disgust, as I saw Adrian, his head down, concentrating, starting to dance a little Scottish Highland jig. I came home, I am not ashamed to say, close to tears. At what he has become. At what I have to do.)

Mssss Williams did not look at me as she smiled, would not meet my eye. I think I was meant to smile back, but I did not. I simply got up and left without a word.

I cleared my desk that same day – within minutes actually – and have not been back nor seen or spoken to anyone there since I left.

These are the facts of the matter. I have moved on and I have now put it all completely behind me. I will not write of it again. Not ever.

I have now completed my diary, going back over all of the incidents that led to my dismissal and me being here in the bungalow all of the time.

I cannot say I feel any the better for having written it all down again. Nor can I state in all honesty that I am any more accepting of what has been done to me.

But I cannot think straight right now. My mind is racing, returning always to Adrian and what he is, what he has turned into, and what I have to do when he returns home later today. Before that, I need to try to relax and think about how I am going to do it.

TUESDAY 25 JULY, 1.35PM

I am stretched out on the sofa in the living room, trying to still my darting mind; I need to think and plan and work through the mechanics of what I am going to do before Adrian returns. But my mind is never at peace. It hasn't been for so long. Losing my job. Adrian. What I must do next, later today. And other things. There are things I don't want to talk about or write down. Not now. Not yet anyway. Maybe never.

My mind always goes back over everything.

It rarely gets a chance to rest.

There are times when I think I am going mad with it all.

And there is always so much noise here, constant, endless noise, from all around. I think this must have been a nice bungalow once, back when it was built in the 1920s and the road wasn't what it is today. No cars, I'd imagine. Maybe the clip-clop of hooves as horse-drawn carts made their way into town. I would have liked that noise, the gentle, natural sounds of days gone by.

This room needs cleaning properly. I have only just noticed. There are cobwebs; I can see them quite clearly from here with the light streaming in, across three of the four corners of the ceiling. I must, at some point later today, once I have dealt with Adrian, get up on a chair and wipe those over with a damp cloth. I am a clean and tidy man, but it is not easy to keep on top of everything I have to do.

There is a pile of post on the sideboard over by the window. Much of it has been stacking up for a while. Most of it is from HMRC, full of letters and forms to sign in triplicate to return to secure my 'package', such as it is. Stuff I don't want to read, to address at all. Not now. Not at all.

I have not been treated fairly and that's a fact.

I try not to think about it as it upsets me. I try to blot it out.

I will have to deal with it soon, though. I have no earnings and my savings are running low.

There are times when, almost with a flash of light, we suddenly see things as they really are. And so it is the case now when I look around. Once, freshly decorated and with new furniture, saved for and bought properly, this was a simple and attractive room. Now, my gaze takes it all in.

The dated, flowery wallpaper, curling in places at top and bottom. The tired brown-cord sofa and chairs, covered top, back and sides with throws, which I forget to wash as often as I should. The curls and swirls of the carpet, its darkness concealing goodness knows what.

The fact of the matter is that it is tired and run-down.

That bothers me more than I can say.

I should not have to live like this.

Adrian makes things ten times worse. He is what I call 'a fiddler'. He cannot leave things alone. He has to twiddle, to interfere, to make a wretched nuisance of himself.

If he sees a flake of limescale at the bottom of the kettle he will, even though the kettle has a perfectly good filter, have to clean it out. Noisily, scouring away at it with a brush.

If he finds a mark on a teaspoon, he will pull an anguished face or, worse, make a gagging noise and I will have to listen while he rubs at it with a cloth, making little grunting noises as he does so. It is all too much for me.

Even now, in the middle of the day, this is a noisy place.

And just so hot too. I have the windows open, I have to. Pig smells or not.

Otherwise, I believe I would simply melt away.

I can hear traffic on the road, boys revving engines as this is at the start of a long, clear stretch up a hill. The putt-putt-putter of a car's exhaust. The roar of a motorcycle. The high-pitched screams of little girls playing in the next garden. The idiot child grunting on one side. The endless drone of Ringo Starr's voice on the other. His greatest hits CD, whatever they might be, on endless repeat. I ignore it all. I have to. If I give in, I will be done for.

So I lie here.

Sweating and shaking.

The tension of it.

I hear the gate being opened. The latch being lifted off. The slight screech as the bottom of the gate scrapes on the path. It is too early to be Adrian. It is the postman and he is late.

He has been the postman for over 15 years now. When he started he would deliver the post between 7.00 and 7.30am. His round changed and got bigger as other postmen – and women, I suppose – retired and weren't replaced.

Lately, he has been delivering my post at close to midday. It is not ideal. Like milkmen and paperboys, postmen should all be done before the start of the working day.

I hear the postman's footsteps on the path and wonder why he is later than usual. A round of junk mail to deliver to every house and flat and bungalow, I imagine. I hear him shuffling his feet on the step up to the porch door. I wait for the clatter of the letter box and the flutter of a letter or the thump of a catalogue.

I hear him cough and clear his throat. He is standing there waiting. He must have rung the doorbell. But there is no jingle-jangle sound in the hallway. I must have forgotten to change the batteries. I make a mental note to get some batteries when I next go to the shops and then replace them. I can't remember when the postman last came to the door like this. He has not rung the doorbell for years.

I struggle to my feet. Do up my trousers, which I had loosened when I lay down. Run my fingers through my sweat-dampened hair to cover my bald patch.

Walk along the corridor to the door, twelve steps in all. I reach for the lock, twist and open the door. It's not the postman.

I know who it is, though.

As I swallow and clear my throat, he speaks. Shouts, actually.

"Where's Dawn? Where is she? What have you done to your wife?"

Part Two

THE HEATWAVE

TUESDAY 25 JULY, 10.01PM

It's been a horribly long day today, and rather harrowing, what with one thing and another. Adrian this morning. Him at lunch-time. Then Adrian again.

All I had to do, straining and sweating in the heat.

I have now gone to bed.

And it has just occurred to me that I have not eaten a single thing.

No food since my lunchtime meal. But I have been drinking. Drinking and drinking. Lots and lots of water.

I ponder whether I might be diabetic. I should not be. You find that most diabetics are easy to spot. I had one such tub of lard in front of me once at the Revenue. A tax dodger. He babbled and burbled away about why he had not submitted returns, nor kept any records. Full of nonsense.

He then leaned forward and spoke with such unexpected urgency that I thought he was about to say he was having a heart attack. But no, he declared he was a diabetic, as though that explained and excused everything. He slapped the palm of his hand on the desk between us not once but twice, as if to emphasise the seriousness of what he was saying.

What his diabetes had to do with anything I do not know. The sheer stupidity of the man. As I said to him by reply, "Ignorance of the law is not an excuse." (And I thought, but did not add, "nor is being a big thick lump".)

He just sat there staring at me, scratching his huge barrel of a belly and sniffing. (He had, I think, a blocked nostril as there was a faint whistling noise when he breathed in but not when he breathed out, which I found most peculiar, and rather irritating.) I will be blunt now; diabetics are fat slobs, mostly, with their womanly sagging chests and their undone buttons on their trousers.

I am not like that. I am a smart and dapper man, well turned out. I always carry a handkerchief.

I weigh the same now as I did 30 years ago: 10 stone, 7 pounds, 'in old money', if I might be a little humorous for a moment.

Of course, someone in their 50s does not look the same as they do in their 20s. But, other than a little balding of the pate and the wearing of glasses, horn-rimmed and fashionable, my appearance has stood the test of time. There are one or two streaks of grey in my hair, which add a distinguished air. I do not dye it like so many sad middle-aged men with their gingery shades and tell-tale white tufts by their ears.

Some old woman at work once said I reminded her of Napoleon. It is always difficult to see yourself as others do, but, in pictures of him when he was older, there is a similarity around the eyes. I am the same height as the Great Boney too, just shy of 5 feet 7 inches using the British measuring system. This is a nice height for those ladies who do not want a hulking great beast standing next to them. Or lying by them in bed!

I'm not too tall.

I'm not too heavy.

I'm 'just right'.

I had a stand-up shower in the bath this afternoon – it took ages to rinse it all out – followed by a proper sit-down bath.

Then I rinsed the bath out again.

I repeated the process, to be honest, both the shower and the bath, twice more, into the evening. I could not get myself clean.

These lard-laden diabetics are a burden on the NHS and the state. We all subsidise them one way or the other. They are a drain on society and its finances. I have, of late, noticed that there is a family of fatties living up near the parade of local shops.

I have seen them standing at the front of the 7-Eleven, Tizer and jumbo-sized packs of cheese curls in their hands, him and her, gorged and bloated on their endless state benefits, and two children of indeterminate age in tow, Tweedledum and Tweedledee. They both have dummies, the one in the pushchair and the one standing next to him (or possibly her, as its fatness disguises its sex). I've stood and watched as they all wobbled off. We all pay for these through our taxes!

I have, in actual fact, put something in the letter box to them recently. (I had, while having an hour or two to idle away one afternoon the week before last, casually followed them home – an end-of-terrace council house painted pink with a broken-down car jacked-up at the front and the usual debris of bin bags and dead flowers in broken pots all around.)

I posted a sheaf of paperwork, statistics on obesity and the cost to the nation, along with a short, some might say pithy, note on a postcard, encouraging them to lose weight. ASAP. I put it in a rather amusing way so that the message might be put across both effectively and nicely.

I cannot sleep. Even when I let my mind wander over nonsense.

Thinking about my little triumphs, relaying them in my mind with the bons mots I said or should have said usually helps. I sometimes re-imagine scenes in my mind for my own amusement.

But not now. Maybe not ever again. I think I am done for.

It is still hot, even at this late hour. But it is not the ferocious heat of earlier in the day. Of this afternoon, when I should really have laid down and stopped what I was doing. When I should not have exerted myself so much. Not that I had much choice.

I don't need to go into all the ins and outs. The this and that. The why and wherefore of it all. Things had to be done. There and then. And I did what I had to do. I am like that. When something has to be sorted. As a matter of urgency. I get the bit between my teeth. And I do it, come what may.

And now I am in my room and I should be asleep. But sleep will not come and embrace me, taking me off and easing my pain and agony. It is so very far away and I must lie here a while and search it out and wait for it to accept me.

If it will.

If I will ever sleep again.

I don't know that I will, not properly.

I am trapped. Here in this bungalow. In this sweltering heat. With all of the noise to the front, never-ending, getting ever worse as each year rolls slowly by and there is more and more traffic on the road. To the sides, the idiot neighbours might as well stand outside my windows day and night banging wooden spoons on saucepans and screeching at the top of their voices. And the endless to-ing and fro-ing of freight trains on the line behind me makes me want to scream.

And the worst thing is that I can never go, cannot ever sell this bungalow and walk away and leave everything behind and forget about it all. I have to sit, here in this horrid little box, and wait until the knock at the door, the day they come to take me away. And they will. One day soon. I know they will. It might even be in the morning, first thing.

WEDNESDAY 26 JULY, 2.57AM

It is in the early hours, these nights I cannot sleep for the heat and my tortured mind, that I go back over the turning points in my life. Those events, moments sometimes, that led me to where I am now.

I see things more clearly in these long minutes as they turn slowly into hours and I finally fall asleep for a short while. How things were. What happened and why. How it came to this.

I think it is time now, as I am still awake and cannot sleep, that I write about what I've kept hidden, deep inside me, for a while. It – she – poisoned me from within my heart and inside my mind.

I have only talked about my wife with one person. The GP. He asked me directly about her during one of our talks and I could not ignore the question. I had to answer him. I simply said she had left me. No more. No less. He paused and I could see his mind thinking things through. He had a pen in his right hand and he clicked the top of it over and over again, in and out, in and out, five, six, seven times in all.

He then asked if I thought she might come back. I said no, never. He paused and thought again – and clicked, eight, nine, ten – as I screamed silently inside. He asked me a final question, whether I wanted her back. I shrugged my shoulders. "Bit late now," I answered and could not help but smile as I said the words.

He looked at me – 'putting on a brave face' – for a while. Then suggested I should write about our relationship and what led to what he called, "the marriage break-up". I said we'd been together for almost 30 years and it would be hard to remember every little thing. "So many," I said, almost jovially. He said I should write about those things that led to "the end of the marriage", to list them and mull them over. I just smiled and nodded at this, as if agreeing.

He then turned to the subject of medication, which I declined, thank you very much. I certainly don't need pills. Never have done. Never will. He also made one or two vague references to group meetings where everyone sits around in a circle wailing about their woes and wringing their hands.

No, I said firmly, not for me. He then talked about one-on-one meetings with a psycho-something-or-other. I shook my head firmly. The cheek of it. And then I think he ever-so-slightly shook his head and I had the sense that he sighed as he agreed to my suggestion that I would come back in again some time soon.

Adrian came back later than expected in the afternoon. He did not take me by surprise. I had been listening out for his arrival either at the front door or at the side gate. I had come in from the garden when I heard a rat-a-tat-tat knocking on the glass of the front door. And then a louder banging. He wanted to know why the front door was locked and the side gate bolted. I said I had done it without thinking, an instinct when I'm on my own. "Can't be too careful," I said.

He asked what I had been doing. Gardening, I replied, things to be done. He said that it was too hot to be working outside and gave me one of his sly, sideways looks. I added nothing, other than to say I was going to shower and that I wanted to talk to him later.

He answered that he was going out, had just come back for his things. When pressed, he said he was staying at a friend's. I could not help but stare at him with incredulity. The thought of Adrian having a friend, let alone staying with one. He gave me a funny little smile, part-embarrassed, part-triumphant, and went into his room.

I waited as he came back out and went to the kitchen to get a carrier bag from under the sink for his clothes. I observed him as he went to the bathroom to collect toiletries. As he stuffed everything into the bag as he walked to the front door, I asked when he would be back. I said again, more firmly this time, that I wanted to talk to him. "Later... in the morning," he said, and I could hear a laugh in his voice, as he closed the door behind him.

I do not know where he is now, what he is doing, or when he will return. I should be worried, I know, I should really alert the police, but I dare not do that. I must sort it out myself. And I have other, more pressing, things on my mind right now. Adrian and whatever it is he is doing can wait until the morning. I will be ready for when he returns.

What do I write about my wife, the marriage, the end of it; in summary, in just a few paragraphs? Thirty years compressed into a page or two? I do not want to write in detail, not now, not yet. Maybe never.

We met as 21-year-olds at the Inland Revenue, both in desk jobs. Went out in a group one night a few weeks later, to see a film, some silly romance, and I somehow found myself walking her home as she lived near me. It was not planned. At least, not by me.

Young and inexperienced, we seemed to drift into being a couple. I don't know why but I had never had much luck with girls and she was tidy enough and always readily available, at least in the early years.

We went out for two years, became engaged for one and then got married at the local registry office. Her father looked daggers at me all through the reception. I don't know why. I think he felt she could do better.

We had a baby early on, not long after our marriage. By then, I knew all of it, everything, was a mistake. I was steady, reliable, regular. She was not; she paid me little attention and was more interested in her artwork. She saw herself as creative.

There were many times when she would rebuff me, drawing her legs and knees up into a tight little bundle and saying "not now" over and again. "When?" I would ask but she would not say. I would always ask, most nights for a while. Sometimes, she would relent, giving me what I wanted.

The baby died at three months. At night. The wife screamed when she found it. Thought it had slept through. In her sleep, they decided in the end. Sudden infant death syndrome is what they call it these days. One of those things that happens. It was a girl.

She didn't pay me any more attention, closed in on herself, shutting me out. Eventually, she seemed to get a little better, talking to counsellors and what have you, and our marriage, such as it was, continued. She made herself more available to me for a while, although having her staring into space most of the time was offputting to me. I took to calling her a slab of meat, my jokey way of trying to gee her into life, but it made no difference.

There was another baby. A boy. He died the same way. Unexplained. No reason. Our relationship was all but broken by this time, but then she became pregnant with Adrian and we tried to make another go of things.

She did not want me physically though after that, saying I had forced myself upon her once too often. But she stayed, not having much choice as her mother had died and her father had remarried soon after and they, her and his new wife, did not get along.

She held Adrian tight, watched him, stayed with him for hours, shutting me out, locking themselves away in the other bedroom as they slept. And he survived. When she finally came back into the bedroom, it was to separate beds and lives. A façade of a marriage, not much else. We muddled along and, after a while, after years and years, it became tolerable. You get used to things, however awful they may seem to outsiders, finding something in routine and familiarity. Habit, that's the word. Not much else.

Stay at home, that's what she wanted to do, painting and what not, while I went out to work. Not much of a salary at the Revenue, never is in public service, so she got a part-time job as a teaching assistant at a primary school to keep our heads above water, looking after Adrian and doing her art around that.

She never amounted to much, exhibiting and selling one or two paintings at local amateur exhibitions. Bought by friends and friends of friends mostly. She wrote poetry too and had a few published in a local group's pamphlet, 'Cabbages & Things'. I think she had a photograph in the local paper once. And she sketched and did lino-cutting, searching for success, the recognition that always eluded her. She never found it.

She always said she was an artist, but just didn't know what type exactly. We did not find out for years until, in her 40s, as ambition and hope gave way to regrets and failure, she drank more than she should so that, finally, I used to tell her that she had found her forte. As a piss artist. She never laughed.

A great yawning expanse of years followed where we stayed together; out of habit, a lack of money and no other choices. Living together, but largely separate lives, me with my books and crosswords, her with her sketches and photography and evening classes. We soldiered on in our passive misery.

And then she met someone. Him. At work. Another useless teaching assistant spending his days cleaning up after dirty children. And everything changed. I think it is this – this affair – that I need to write about really. This is the thing that I have to set down, to get things clear in my head, before I take the words and sentences and paragraphs and pages and burn them all.

I have kept this to myself – inside me – for too long. I think it was this – my marriage, the long ending of it, and what happened – that made me do what I did at work.

Looking for love. Solace. Comfort. And the anger and frustration. The arguments. The ill-feeling. The fighting. It was not me, not really. It was out of character.

She made me what I am today and where I know, at some stage or other, this will all now end. There is no turning back for me. No way to avoid the ending I know is coming.

WEDNESDAY 26 JULY, 11.07AM

I do not know how long I have been in this bed. It must by now be 20 hours since Adrian came and went. He has not yet returned. I wonder where he is. What he is doing. I have been lying here for so long, nodding on and off, in an uneasy, fractured, sweating sleep. I have written some of my diary. That calms me a touch. Steadies me a little. I have been to the toilet twice to urinate. I lie here now but know I must get up soon and go about my usual daily routine. Be ready when Adrian returns. Have it out with him. Whatever it may be. Sort it out once and for all.

Get up. Wash and wear fresh clothes.

Eat.

Be normal. Get out and about.

But I am in pain. I feel safe in bed. And, although the heat still torments me, all about me is quiet. It has been the quietest I have ever known it through the later part of the night and into the morning. Or perhaps I've just not noticed any noise. I have more important things to worry about. I could lie here forever. On my own. Not troubling anyone any more. No one bothering me. I could just turn my face to the wall and stare into space until the day I die.

And then I jump, startled. A knock at the door. Two.

Brisk. Authoritative. Not Adrian.

Expecting, demanding to be answered.

I sit up. Check my blinds are closed. Shift them carefully, reaching out to slowly close the window. Adjust them back again. I slip out of bed. Reach for my glasses. Settle my hair. Put on my shirt from the chair by the side of the bed. I feel vulnerable in sweat-dampened pyjama bottoms. Don't want to be discovered like this. I have my dignity.

I move to the bedroom door, listening carefully. I hear the murmur of voices. The police? I wait for the porch door to be opened, to hear them step into the porch, the knock on the main front door becoming a loud, repetitive bang and then, as I hold my breath, the turning of the handle that opens the door into the bungalow. I'd be standing there, stained and ramshackle in my appearance.

But there is silence.

Whoever they were, they have gone away. Jehovah's Witnesses? Gypsies wanting to cut the trees? Charity-tin rattlers? The police?

I am not sure if – or when – they will come back. When, I think, not if.

After a few minutes, to be sure they've gone, I open my door slowly, check the hallway and walk to the bathroom. Urinate again. I then wash my hands, rough and grazed from yesterday afternoon, at the sink. The side of my left hand is badly bruised and may need wrapping – I am left-handed, what used to be known as a southpaw in boxing terms.

As I wash my face, I look at myself in the mirror. Old now. Lines criss-crossed across the forehead, deeper than I've seen them. My cheeks sagging. The white of my stubble showing as I turn my face from one side to the other. When did I get so old and wretched? How did I not notice until now?

I walk slowly into the bedroom, looking out to the road. Waiting for Adrian to return, to tell me where he has been, what he has been doing. I fear for him and me, bringing trouble, police, to the door. I have to stop him before it is too late. If it's not already. There is no sign of him. I turn to the left; further up and across the road, there is a cul-de-sac. I step back. Then move forward, pressing my face close to the blinds, peering through.

I see a blue Honda Civic parked, facing this way.

His car.

It is there, no more than 30 yards away from my bungalow.

Should I stay here, ignore it? Pretend I have not seen it? That it has nothing to do with me. Just carry on as I am. But for how long can I do that? Before there is a knock at the door. Was that the knocking and banging earlier? Or should I go out to the car? Striding across? Deal with it?

I do not know what to do.

Have to think.

Decide on a plan.

As I stand here, torn by indecision, and the minutes pass, I suddenly see Adrian appear, from the right, where he must have got off the bus further down the road and then crossed and worked his way back up. He looks tired and dishevelled, with his carrier bag bulging with clothes and toiletries. He looks strangely happy, smiling to himself and swinging the bag backwards and forwards.

I open the front door. Step back.

He enters. We face each other in the hallway.

"What's going on?" I say straightaway.

He drops his bag on the floor, glances at me and looks away. He's always been like this. Never been able to look someone straight in the eye for more than a moment or two.

He looks up.

Down.

To the sides.

Anywhere but meeting your eye. He might as well throw his head back and roll his eyes around. Look at me! I'm mad, I am! I have told him, when he was younger, that it makes him look shifty and dishonest. In fact, it makes him look insane. There are times when I think he does it to annoy me. It angers me so much.

"Well?" By God, I could shake this out of him. And I will. If I have to.

He says nothing, looks down again, turns away, tries to brush by me. I move sharply to the wall so he cannot pass. We are going to have this out now. He has something awful to hide, I know.

Something wicked.

Evil.

I think of all that he has done.

Stealing from washing lines. The sauna. The business in the department store toilets. Yesterday, at the children's playground. It's all been building up to this point.

"What's going on then?" I can hear the anger rising in my voice. I must try to subdue it, stay calm for the moment.

"I've met someone," he replies, looking at me at last, holding my gaze, defiant. He hurries on, "I was about to tell you, ask you. Later. A woman… Josie she's called… she likes me. A lot," he adds for emphasis.

We both look at each other, and I don't quite know what to say. I had expected to have to press him, push him hard against the wall, force him to talk until he admitted to visits to playgrounds, dancing around, grooming, playing with little girls, following them until he got one alone. Yesterday. Last night. And then I would deal with it. But I did not expect this.

I am taken aback.

I had decided what to do with him.

I now have to think again.

He carries on as I look at him. "She's the same age as me, Josie." He swallows. "We were at school together. But different classes. She was the year above, born in August, she was. We met in town and we got talking. She talked to me first. She's my girlfriend now… my proper girlfriend."

"So, what, you were with her last night, at her place?" (Dear God, wonders will never cease.)

He nods, confirming, "She's staying in a women's hostel for a few nights while she sorts her housing stuff out." He then goes on, growing in confidence, "She's my girlfriend. We love each other. We want to be together." He says this bit as if he has rehearsed it, getting the words and the phrasing and the nuances just so in his head. As if I will be impressed by this stupidity.

"Be together," I echo, thinking, what to say next to the ridiculousness of it all. "What, where? Here? We've no room for her here. It's barely big enough for the two of us. No room for anyone else." I pause. "I suppose you could get a job and move out. Try and be normal for once."

"She has her own place, rented from the council, it's just that…" He tails off as I stare him down, him and his five-minute wonder of a girlfriend. Like everything else in his life, it won't last. He will mess it up somehow. He always does. He ruins everything. That's why he's still here. At home. A fully grown man. All 6 foot 3 of him.

"What does she see in you anyway?" I say, louder than I mean to. "You've not got much to offer, have you, no prospects, no job, nothing. What will you give her, a 50-50 share of your benefits?" I feel the anger surging again, at the madness of it all. A girlfriend. Really. I step back, trying to stay calm. "What's the bloody point?"

He leans against the wall, his bubble burst. I see him struggling for words, close to tears, but still defiant, standing up to me. "She says… I'm kind…"

I snort, I cannot stop myself, the folly of it. "Well, that will pay the bills, won't it? Your kindness. That'll go a long way, that will."

We stand there.

Both of us lost for words, momentarily.

And then he speaks up, gulping slightly between each sentence.

"I wanted to ask you… to say to you… if she could come for tea this afternoon, four o'clock. She'd like to meet you… you could get to know her. She's a nice person, you'll like her. She's gentle… and funny… and…" His words tail off again.

I look at him, shaking my head in disbelief at this nonsense. Yet I find myself saying, "Yes, okay, she can come for tea." I do not want her here. No, not at all. For so many reasons. But I cannot say no. I dare not. It would seem wrong somehow. And Adrian would not let it be; he would worry at it, keep coming back to it until, eventually giving in, it would be more of an ordeal that it needs to be.

So I agree. Let's have her in. Feed her. Get her out. See her gone. She'll soon be out of his life anyway, once she finds out what he's like. The twitching and the fiddling. The endless repetition. The dreary conversation about something and nothing. Round and round. Never-bloody-ending nonsense and drivel.

He smiles at last. I have not seen him smile properly for ever such a long time. "I'll text her," he says, getting his phone out of his back pocket as he turns towards his bedroom. He seems to stand upright, tall for a moment, instead of walking in his usual bent-over crouch. Because he is so tall, he stoops, so that he does not stand out.

"Oh," he adds, as if it has just occurred to him. As if it is an afterthought. "She's got a little daughter, Lily, she's coming up to four."

I watch him as he opens his bedroom door, picks up his bag, and gives me an awkward half-smile as he goes into the room.

So there we are. What it's all about. The daughter. Lily. Aged almost four.

It takes all of my power of self-control not to go into his room and sort this matter out for once and for all. But Josie and Lily will be at the door at four o'clock. And what would they do if they expected someone to answer and nobody did?

WEDNESDAY 26 JULY, 12.01PM

I am lying down again in my room. Before I leave to go to the shops to buy some fancy foods for our afternoon tea. Really, afternoon tea. I am still hot and sticky but it is slightly cooler, if that is the right word, in here than it is in other parts of the bungalow.

Adrian has already gone back to "fetch them" as he put it, to bring them back for four o'clock. I do not want to dwell on this matter now. I will meet them, make a judgement, and decide what to do from there. I have other matters on my mind at present. Her. Him. A letter. The letter that triggered the unfolding of everything.

Letters have always been an integral part of my working life, at least in recent years. People are always writing in, or used to do so, to tell us taxmen (and lovely ladies, of course) about rogues and ne'er-do-wells in the community. Some are more accurate than others, but all offer a line of enquiry. Many lead to full investigations. I would not have expected that I would find out about her and him in just the same way: via an anonymous letter.

I would not like to estimate exactly how many tax investigations I carried out nor how much extra tax I uncovered for Her Majesty.

Over time, I prepared an amusing 'ad-lib' for those members of the public who asked such inane questions. "Lots and pots," I would say and, for those simple sorts who looked confused, would add, with a chuckle, "Lots of investigations and pots of money!"

I was a careful and thorough investigator.

The best.

Truly, the best of all. I am not being immodest.

From cheats and liars to the mentally ill and half-witted, I had a 100 per cent strike rate. I always found something, somewhere. Always.

Most people knew what they were doing. Under-declaring income. Missing it out altogether. Pretending they did not think it was taxable. Simple 'errors' (but always in their favour, of course). Pocketing cash was a favourite for many. That is easy to identify. You simply trawl bank and card statements for outgoings and cash withdrawals to see what their average spend is in a week, a month, a quarter, a year. If they are pocketing cash now and then, that average spend can suddenly dip by hundreds a week, thousands a month.

"So, Mr Plumber (or whatever)," I would ask nicely with a warm smile and emphasis on the long, drawn-out, ever-so-polite mister, "I see from your bank statements that, over the past year, you withdrew an average of £2,000 a month in cash for personal spending... (pause)... except in June and September where the figures were, let me see now... (another agonising – for him! – pause)... £100 and £250. Would you tell me about these drawings please?" Of course, he would bumble about with his ers and ums, not wanting to tell me that he'd obviously had some cash-in-hand jobs in those months that went straight into his back pocket.

A better question to be asked by members of the public would be how many crooked taxpayers did you expose?

How many prosecutions?

How many businesses closed?

How many marriages broke up?

How many cheating scum, once discovered and shamed, took their own miserable lives?

I know the answers to those questions. Yes I do!

Investigations begin for many reasons. There are various HMRC systems, balances and checks that flag up possible lines of enquiry. There is also the random enquiry that covers a multitude of reasons, everything from a tax investigator noticing neighbours running businesses on the quiet (something I have seen myself no fewer than five times) to a trainee picking cases genuinely at random as part of their training.

Then there are the letters. I say letters because, in the old days, that is how people would notify Her Majesty's, at that time, Inland Revenue; a plethora of indignation and anger about ex-partners, family, former friends and neighbours who were, one way or the other, cheating the state.

There would always be letters coming in to local offices. Ex-partners, wives mostly, can be very bitter and revealing. They would always 'spill the beans', their little acts of revenge. I always made a joke to any husbands I was investigating that if they split up from the wives and had some tax money hidden away they had better either pay up ASAP or shut the ex up ASAP! These days most of it comes via online forms, of course, to be sorted and sifted and weighed centrally; not so effective, some might say.

People don't write letters so much these days.

One woman did, though. To me. She spilt the beans alright.

About her and what she was doing. With him.

I remember seeing the letter for the first time. Placed upright, in the middle of two or three other letters, junk mail really, on the little shelf above the shoe rack in the porch. Either she or maybe Adrian put it there without realising what it was, its significance. I picked it up as I came in from work. It was a Thursday evening and she was out at a night class and Adrian was in his room. It was a slim brown envelope with my initial and surname printed carefully on it by hand followed by the address. Second-class stamp. Smudged but definitely a local postmark.

I was intrigued as I do not usually receive post that looks like that. For some reason, despite the capitals, I thought it was a woman's hand. As I walked down the hallway to the kitchen, I unpeeled the envelope. Inside was a blank A4 sheet of paper folded precisely in three. Opening it, in black ink and in the same careful hand, I read the words, 'Dawn is having an affair with Philip Rennie at work. They have sex in the dinner hour. We thought you should know.'

I sat down on a kitchen chair and struggled to regain my composure.

I felt a sense of shock initially. Disbelief that this was happening.

Angry too, that I had been cheated on, cuckolded, made a fool of. A laughing stock.

I looked over the letter for hidden clues. I checked the spellings, although there were no mistakes. I examined the hand – the block capitals were quite small and written carefully. I even lifted the paper up to my nose to smell it. Nothing.

I thought – although it was no more than an educated guess – that it was more likely to be a woman who had written this rather than a man. A man would not have written so carefully. And they would not have used the coy phrase 'have sex'. They would have used the f word. Despite the 'we', she had probably acted alone. It would not have been this man's wife; too dispassionate. A co-worker most likely. Someone who did not like him. Or her. Both, possibly.

Easy to check, though. Out and about, investigating, I could take my lunch hour at the same time as hers.

Park up a little way from the school, tucked in at the top of a side road, unnoticed among a row of cars.

Watch and wait and follow them. See for myself.

There is a sudden clatter of the letter box being opened and something being pushed through and falling to the floor. A letter or two maybe.

I go and check what it is. A colour pamphlet for a new supermarket opening soon, with some vouchers inside. A leaflet about gardening services. Something to do with satellite TV. Another about stair-lifts for the elderly and infirm. All junk. I put it to one side. I have other matters to think about right now.

I did follow them. Him and her. The next day. A minute or two past 12.30, I saw her come out of the school building first, walking through the gates and turning right, away from me. She strolled along as if she were making her way to the nearby convenience store.

I stayed put.

I'd been there five, ten minutes.

Knew he had not yet left.

A few minutes later, no more than two or three, I saw a car pulling out of the school car park. A blue car, a Honda Civic. I was too far away to read the plate. The car turned right, as if following her.

Stop. She gets in. I know what happens next.

They drive off together. To a quiet lane, a field, somewhere over by the marshes. Where they do it.

Come back. She gets out up the road and walks the last ten yards, no one any the wiser.

I drove after them, keeping my distance, suppressing the urge to drive up hard, ramming them, forcing them off the road. I had a wheel brace in the boot and I would gladly have beaten him with it. And then her. But I knew I had to be careful. Not give into instinct, that I had to plan and plot and work out how I was going to get my revenge.

They did not go to a field as I expected. Instead, they just went to a pub, turning into the car park as I drove by quickly before they got out and might see me. I looked straight ahead just in case she spotted me – so she'd think I was just out and about 'on duty', visiting a taxpayer.

I parked further up, pulled into a side road, watched and waited.

An agony of time passed as I sat, waiting to see them come out again.

They did, some 40 minutes later. They walked back to his car, to return to school.

As they approached the car, she was slightly out of sight to me. But I saw him stop and put his arms around her, pulling her towards him. I could just see her head resting on his shoulder. They stood like that for what must have been two or three minutes and then he seemed to start rocking her gently from side to side. As if cradling a baby!

As he released her, he went to kiss her.

She moved her head and was slightly obscured from my view and I could not tell if he kissed her cheek or her lips.

But their heads were together, close and touching, for a further minute or more until they turned to get inside the car.

Before the car could reverse out and pull away, I started my car and drove off at speed back towards the office in Ipswich. I had seen all that I needed to see. Love. Affection. Physical closeness. I knew our marriage, such as it was, was in its final days.

WEDNESDAY 26 JULY, 3.43PM

I do not think anyone has ever come for afternoon tea at my little bungalow. Not with me anyway. And not for many years with anyone else. I have never encouraged visitors. They are more trouble than they are worth. I cannot say that this is something I really want to do now, what with one thing and another.

While Adrian went into town on the bus to fetch her and bring her back, and after my diary and trip to the shops, I have been preparing an afternoon tea as best I can in the living room. I should perhaps say here that Adrian does not drive. He is not allowed to. He has this thing where, now and then, he 'freezes' for a moment or two; what's known as an absence seizure, where he just stares into space. He 'wakes up' a second or two later and carries on with what he was doing, almost as if he is not aware he has temporarily 'switched off'. He is therefore not permitted to drive a car.

This switching off is not an issue in itself.

Unless, of course, he was doing something potentially dangerous at the time. Like standing on top of a ladder to clear the gutters. Or crossing the railway track to retrieve a blown-away scarf.

Then he could, quite possibly, be killed.

"What happened?" someone might say.

"He must have had one of his absence seizures," I would reply, ever so sadly.

I tidy the living room as best I can, jabbing at the cobwebs in the corners of the ceiling with a rolled-up old newspaper. Dusting and polishing the surfaces with some lemon polish spray, which leaves a nice scent. Vacuuming the carpet and dabbing at the stain on the arm of the sofa, before plumping and rearranging the cushions to cover it. It is an unsightly dark stain, almost black, but it does not smell of anything.

It is a dated room dominated by a rather bulky television. It is an old one and I do not have satellite television nor a DVD player. The VHS recorder sits there, largely unused now, although I have a small number of tapes in the sideboard; a few Agatha Christie

Poirots mostly that I taped and watch occasionally when there is nothing else on 'live'.

I have seen some of them so many times that I remember not only what happens but sometimes the words spoken by Poirot in his denouement. On one or two occasions, I have spoken along in a cod Belgian accent (for my own amusement).

I also have a few tapes of *The Two Ronnies*, who were rather funny fellows. I remember, at one Inland Revenue Christmas event, doing a skit from one of the shows and everyone found it most amusing. One colleague, who I have never really liked, laughed so hard that he had to leave the room.

There is a knock at the door.

I stop what I am doing, hold my breath. Wait a minute. Two. Three. It is not Adrian, he has a key.

I will not answer it. Hope they – whoever they are – will go away.

After a few minutes have passed, I slip along the hallway into the front room, peering out through the blinds. No one about. That blue car is still parked there, though. I ignore it, go back to what I was doing.

The coffee table has seen better days but I cover it as best I can with a folded-over wipe-clean tablecloth from the local Co-op. On this, I arrange various plates of differing sizes with assorted sandwiches, again from the Co-op. These save me the time and trouble of making them myself, a chore I have never enjoyed and, truth be told, I have never advanced much beyond cheese or ham with pickle.

I have tried tomatoes on occasions, but I do not like to use the ends, which seems wasteful, and what I call 'a bulging tomato' can create a soggy sandwich. I do not use eggs either. I do not like the smell. When I was at school, I was bullied rather badly and the big boys would hold me down while Chatfield would sit on my face and break wind. Boiled eggs remind me of that and I do not wish to recall it.

But I digress. One of the Co-op sandwiches has salmon in it. It was 20 per cent off and a little stale but warming it through for ten seconds in the microwave has revived it. Two packets of Mr Kipling cakes, Viennese Whirls and some angel slices, and a jug of orange squash with some slightly faded but perfectly serviceable beakers from the back of the cupboard, complete my display. And very nice it is too. If I do say so myself. A lovely spread for our guests, not too fancy, not too plain.

I hear noises at the front door again, rustling sounds.

I put the knife in my hand down, then pick it up again.

Sounds of movement. Someone coming in. Adrian's voice.

I am not happy about this, to be caught 'on the hop'. They are here a little sooner than expected. I had hoped to watch them arriving from the bedroom window. To see how they were together, acting naturally rather than as they will be; presenting themselves as they want me to see them, a happy and perfect couple. As a tax inspector – yes, former tax inspector – I know there can be a huge difference between the two.

They stand there, the three of them, waiting for me as I get up and walk to meet them. She is tall and lean, her dark hair tied back. She wears a white T-shirt, quite loose over her slight breasts, and dark-blue jeans cut off below the knee with a simple pair of white sandals. She has an oversized denim handbag over her shoulder. Despite the heat, she is clean and tidy and she has a pretty face and smiles warmly at me and makes eye contact. What this strong, fit beauty sees in big, gawky Adrian, I do not know.

She looks down as if to introduce her daughter, the girl of Adrian's drawing. She has a mass of dark brown, fluffy-looking hair and a wide, smiley face, which she half-hides, peeking out from behind her mother. I think she is playing a game with me already but cannot be sure. I smile at her. And then chuckle to show I am a friendly sort of fellow. A kindly uncle bouncing a little girl on his knee. She does not respond though, ducking her head behind her mother's back.

Adrian stands there quietly, almost proudly, as if he has been abroad for years, is visiting and is now introducing me to his never-met-before wife and daughter. "There," he seems to be saying, "see what I've gone out and got for myself, I've won first prize and you thought I was a big useless loser."

I can see what he sees in them – the woman's strength and beauty and the girl's sweet mischievousness. But I don't know what they want from him. This awkward-looking, self-conscious man-child. I simply say a neutral hello as I have been trained to do when meeting people for the first time and they say the same back and I beckon them through into the living room.

I reflect, just for a moment, whether I should have shaken hands, maybe ruffled the child's hair.

These days, people hug when they meet each other. I cannot bear to hug people, let alone strangers.

The touch of breasts and stomachs, the close proximity of genitalia. The smell of people's bodies and their hot breath on my cheek.

There is a moment's hesitation in the living room as to who will go where and then the little girl struts across to the sofa, sits in the middle of it and lifts her feet and puts them on the edge of the coffee table. She folds her arms, cocks her head to one side and smiles at us. I think this is a child who knows how to play cute. I also think her Little Orphan Annie act will become wearing rather quickly.

Josie, who I expect to correct the girl, just laughs and sweeps her up onto her lap as she takes her place on the sofa. Adrian sits next to her. I take my seat in one of the armchairs opposite. Adrian leans forward and straightens plates and moves beakers into neater lines. I can't help but wonder if she has spotted his OCD behaviour yet.

He asks her, Josie, if she'd like a coffee and she nods her agreement. Adrian smiles tightly at me, as if to indicate I have overlooked something – the offer of coffee or tea – and have somehow let him down. Embarrassed him. Made him look foolish. One final move of the jug, so its handle is facing towards Josie, and he is up and has gone into the kitchen. He will have to work hard to disguise his OCD from her.

I observe as she pours a beaker half-full with orange squash and passes it to Lily with a stage-whispered, "Hold it carefully."

Lily takes it and holds it carelessly – almost provocatively – at an angle so the squash sloshes over the rim of the beaker and onto the carpet.

Josie does what looks like a mock glare at the child – as if she feels this sort of behaviour is perfectly acceptable – and gets up to go into the kitchen.

Lily and I sit and look at each other.

I am not sure if she is going to smile or look away.

I smile. She looks away.

Adrian and Josie come back in. He is holding two mugs of hot black coffee, which he places carefully on the table in front of them. They are both matching, but chipped, mugs from the back of the cupboard. From when Prince Andrew married Sarah Ferguson. I would not have used them. I do not why he is drinking his coffee black. He never has before. She has what looks like six or seven sheets of kitchen roll, far more than she needs, wrapped around her hand and she uses these to mop at the wet carpet.

Eventually, and there is a lot of what I'd call 'a performance' from them (acting up the cuteness for my benefit), everyone is settled and so I spread my right arm above and across the food and drink on the table and invite them to "tuck in".

And they do so with various comments about the "nice choice" and "tastiness" of the spread. I look on, smiling.

Even so, Josie pulls apart two sandwiches, picking bits out, placing them on the side and passing what's left to the child. Feeding time at the zoo, this is.

Adrian sits there as if it's perfectly normal. But it is tactless, rude even, to play with food like this especially when you are a guest. I do not comment. I do not reveal my thoughts.

There is a knock at the door again. "Leave it," I say, "Jehovah's Witnesses. They've been up and down the road all morning."

Adrian looks flustered. I can see he wants to go and answer the door. The beauty just smiles. Lily looks from one to the other of us. She makes a bbbrrr-innnggg, bbbrrr-innnggg noise as if imitating a door bell.

I sit here, my skin crawling, waiting for a louder, more insistent knock. I know I would have to answer it – otherwise, it would seem peculiar. "Ssshhh," I whisper to the little girl who is looking at me, "they'll go away." And after a long, tense minute, maybe two, they do, whoever they are, and we resume our tea.

We chat generally, Josie and I, about the weather and other inanities, with Adrian looking on and the child picking and fiddling with cakes and her nose and then the cakes again. One way or the other, the child touches every single cake – after poking her fingers in her nostrils – so that no one else would want to eat them. I keep quiet but she really needs admonishing. No one does though. Both Adrian and the child eat the cakes. I do not.

As a (former) tax investigator, I always have clear in my mind, when meeting someone, exactly what it is I want to know, to uncover, to find out. The truth. With this young woman, I want to know what she sees in Adrian and, more importantly, what she wants from him. Clearly, these are not questions you can ask directly but I want to get the answers nonetheless. Fortunately, I have been trained in such matters. And I am something of an expert.

I start by asking if she comes from Ipswich. She replies, with only the slightest encouragement from me, that she had been brought up on one of the nearby council estates by her mother.

She goes on, without prompting, that her father died when she was little. She talks a little of "mum and me" with an almost wistful tone to her voice. I think, but do not press, that the mother has died, but again, quite voluntarily, as if she wants to tell me everything, she adds that the mother had remarried a few years ago and moved to Cardiff for the stepfather's job.

"So did you not fancy going to Wales with them?" I ask gently. A pause, a shake of the head. A comment about being pregnant at the time with the child. The admittance, in the way she speaks, her manner, that parting from her mother was a tough moment in her life.

And the suggestion, a half-started answer, tailing off, in response to a nod and an encouraging smile from me that the stepfather was a difficult man, unpleasant for sure, perhaps even more. I do not press her.

There is no talk of sisters or brothers or wider family.

I assume that she is, to all intents and purposes, other than the child, alone here.

Just the two of them. Lovely mummy. Naughty daughter.

And then, as the tea eventually draws to a close and Adrian starts his twitching and fiddling again and suggests that it's time to go and get the bus "before it gets busy", I ask the question that I know will give me the answer I am looking for. "And, uh." I pause to show concern. "Do you still see her – a quick look at the child – father?"

A brief silence. And then I have my answer – what she wants from Adrian. He goes to speak, hesitating as he tries to pick his words carefully in front of the child, staring up at him with her big moon eyes.

"He's not kind or gentle," the young woman interrupts, smiling and putting her hand on Adrian's knee. "Not like Adey." He looks at her – Adey! – and smiles shyly, before glancing at me.

I tut, loudly enough for her to hear, as if to say, "Oh dear, there there."

As Adrian gets to his feet, signalling that it's time for them to go, she says, in something of a rush as Adrian shepherds the girl away, "He won't leave us alone, he's forever coming round, making trouble, wanting to see Lily… he won't let me get on with my life."

And she looks at me, with what I am sure are tears in her eyes as she turns to go.

And for a moment, I almost feel sorry for her.

She tries to smile as she reaches for my outstretched hand but then goes to hug me. Her great big bag swings in the way and so I just pat her arm instead.

Then, just as soon as they had arrived, they have gone. And I am not sure how I feel. Part of me is excited. She is an attractive lady, for sure. Another part of me is anxious. My mind dwells on the child. And things generally. I am not sure what to think.

WEDNESDAY 26 JULY, 7.46PM

It has been two and a half to three hours since they left and I am still thinking about them. In fact, after I had cleared everything away and washed up and had a tidy round and a hoover, I have been sitting here, before resuming my diary, just reworking their visit in my head over and again.

Big, stupid Adrian. That lovely, troubled woman. And the annoying little child. I go over what was said and when, and how and what I said to get them talking and by way of reply. It all unsettles me and I cannot quite work out why.

The truth is, I do not know what I think or how I feel about them. Something worries me, but I cannot think what. So I will, for now, return to my diary and the moment I found out the reality about her and him. It is scratched and torn into my memory.

As a tax inspector – ex-tax inspector, I must remember – I am well aware that many people, both honest and dishonest, are creatures of habit. They are, for the most part, also lazy. When it comes to passwords, for example, people use the same ones time and again – most often, the names of their children or pets or dates of birth, or variations thereof.

Uncover one – and with some online accounts you can simply enter variations endlessly without being blocked – and the chances are that you can then go into most or even all of their other password-protected accounts to see what they've been getting up to. With her suddenly going out for a walk one Sunday morning – at least, at the time I thought she was walking – I knew as I slipped into the bathroom and saw her mobile phone she'd inadvertently left on the side that it would have the passcode of 1210. Her birthday, 12 October.

I thought, as I went and sat down with the phone at the kitchen table, holding my breath for a moment, that I had at least the best part of an hour before she returned. Adrian was in his room listening to his music, which he did most Sunday mornings. Clicking 'phone' and 'recents' I could see the calls made and received. I was able to scroll slowly through them one by one for the past two months.

I saw, among the everyday calls to the bank and to the library and the chemists for her repeat prescriptions, a pattern emerging of calls between her and him before work, 8.30am to 8.45am, typically, and after, 4.15pm to 4.30pm usually. Most of these calls were of about 10 to 15 minutes' duration.

They got more frequent over the weeks.

Longer too.

I imagined the words and phrases that passed between them.

I then clicked back and forth to find 'gallery' and looked through the pictures one by one. I dreaded what I might see. But they were almost all dreary. Endless shots of a black cat that sometimes came into the back garden. A pigeon sitting on a bench by the library, a car number plate that ended 54NTA and what, at first, seemed to be a lumpy smear of sick but, on zooming in, was a home-made pizza. I do not know who made it nor for whom. I imagine it must have had some significance. It is not something I would have photographed, let alone kept. I doubt I would have eaten it, truth be told.

I found only one photograph of him – and her – and that was early on before the phone calls increased in their intensity. It was a photograph that must have been taken of her and her colleagues, including him, at their Christmas party. I remember her saying it was held in a pub over Felixstowe way, in Trimley St Martin or Trimley St Mary, I forget which. No matter, they are both equally ghastly places: two big housing estates of little identical boxes full of dim-witted dockers.

There were about 10 or 11 people in all. Some seated to one side of the table, others, presumably those who had been sitting on this side, crouching and smiling and pulling faces and doing thumbs-up signs in between. She, next to him, was to the left of the picture, sitting there all shiny-faced, with him to her right with a paper hat at a jaunty angle on his head and his arm draped casually around her shoulder. I could tell from her face that she was aroused.

I do not know why.

Short with sandy hair, and pink and fleshy.

He'd win no prizes for his looks.

I turned at last to the messages, where I knew I would find the truth of their relationship, which lay hidden behind the list of phone conversations and that single photograph. The messages stretched back some two months again and I dipped into one or two early ones where my wife wrote a series of, to me, bewildering texts in an unexpectedly girlish manner for a woman of her age. 'Camembert. Pooh whiff' was one. 'Mrs Angle is the angle/angel of death!!!' was another. These infantile remarks made no sense to me. His responses, 'Danish blue for me please' and 'She's no angel that's for sure' were at least a little more grown up.

I had the sense that she was flirting, chasing him.

That made me so angry.

The thought of her, the local whore.

I scrolled through and noted that, as with the phone calls, these messages became more frequent and longer over the two months. They were, from what I could make out, sent and received in the evenings while my wife was, so she said, having a bath. I could see, going through one text after another, a growing relationship between them as banter turned into warmth and then more besides as smiley-face emojis were replaced by xxx kisses and, finally, hearts.

There were one or two, more recently, that tore at my heart; I cannot write them out because they upset me so much but they were messages of love and of promises about the future. And messages galore on Saturdays and Sundays, which she must have sent while I was close by. And there was one, the final exchange, from moments before she dashed out of the door.

Him to her. 'I'm free, sweetheart. I can meet you now, usual place. Are you free too? Please come now.'

Her to him. 'I'm on my way, darling. As quick as I can.'
Him to her. 'Hurry! Hurry! Hurry! I don't have long.'
I wondered if they were doing it right then.

I must stop there. Writing this down is not easy; in fact, even now, it is incredibly painful. The GP said that by writing things out time and again, it would be easier to come to terms with it all. I don't know that I ever will.

At the moment, it almost reduces me to angry tears. That she could do this. Lie. Cheat. Whore herself around. I can tell you this – it took all of my powers of calm and control not to turn on her as she came back from that so-called 'walk'.

I was in the kitchen and washing a wok that I had in my hand. She came in quite cheerfully, like some giddy teenager, her face beaming. She was almost jigging from side to side. Literally, beside herself with joy. How I stopped myself turning and hitting her full in her stupid fat face with that wok again and again and again and again and again and again and again, I do not know. But I know that from that moment, as she waltzed back to the bathroom to find the mobile phone that I'd put back carefully on the side, that I hated her fat guts.

THURSDAY 27 JULY, 11.26AM

It is another swelteringly hot day today; the barometer in my room suggests it is close to 90. It may have broken. It does not seem to have moved for some days now. Or perhaps I have just not noticed, what with everything. The heat seems relentless, only easing a little at night and then starting up again the next day before breakfast. It is endless. Draining. Exhausting.

Bang. (Ignore it.)

I had a bath before breakfast – I ate alone as Adrian stayed out again last night – and then had another bath a while afterwards. I have since been lying on my bed trying not to sweat and stain the sheet.

Thump.

I have been thinking – trying very, very hard to think – about things; Adrian, Josie and the child mostly. I have concluded that all of this may actually work in my favour. Something's going to go my way for once. He is out so much that I think Adrian will soon leave and stay at hers, perhaps permanently.

I will not have to deal with Adrian after all. He will not bring the police to my door.

Whatever he does, he will do it there. I will not have to get involved. I will not know.

And I can see out my days here, quietly and anonymously.

There are still things that trouble me. I need to earn some money. My earnings from HMRC are coming to an end. My pension, such as it is, will be inadequate. I can barely afford to live on it. My savings will not last long. I need to find some sort of job somewhere, to keep me ticking over.

Thump again. (I take no notice.)

I do not know where to look for a part-time job. Much of what is out there – working a till at a supermarket, stacking shelves, watering plants in a garden centre, standing among teenagers with a baseball cap on back to front at McDonalds – is beneath me. And I do not want to leave my bungalow, at least not for very long.

I tense, knowing there will be another loud noise any moment.

And there's that DNA sample the police took when I had my run-in with that girl's stepfather at the delicatessen. I wonder what they have done with that. I do not like the idea of the police holding the DNA of millions of citizens. Checking. Comparing.

Matching. It is like Orwell's *Nineteen Eighty-Four*. A police state.

Bang. (Ignore it.)

And now the noise that's been all around me these past few hours starts to crank up. I can hear the shouts of neighbouring children, the banging of a ball against the wall of the garage that separates the top of my garden from next door. Then the thump as the ball hits the fence, my fence, over and over again.

I keep myself to myself, me. Don't want to talk to next door. Have the young woman or her latest boyfriend popping round to borrow milk for the children's breakfast, asking me questions about her, wanting to know what's what. Having to know my business.

Bang. (Fucking bang.)

But the banging, the sheer, mindless, thoughtlessness of it, drives me mad. It is all I can do to stay here.

Thump.

I want to go into the back garden, take my broom and bang it in time against the fence, echoing the ball so they get the message. Shut up. Shut up. Shut up. Stop it. Stop it. Stop it. Take the ball and play somewhere else. Leave me alone. For Christ's sake, give it a rest.

Bang. (Fucking bang again.)

I am up and at my kitchen window. I open it and slam it loudly, hoping they will hear. I do it again, crashing it shut. Got that? Hear it? Do you fucking hear me?

Bang.

They take no notice, just keep going, a ragged assortment of bangs and thumps as the ball hits the garage wall, then the fence, and the garage wall again.

As I stand there, looking out and listening, the ball comes over.

A perfect arc.

It lands in my back garden, in the middle, in front of the air-raid shelter.

There is silence, blessed silence for a moment. I stand and think, calming now. I do not want to throw the ball back. If I do, the bang-thump-bang-thump-bang-thump-bang will start up again, driving me mad. If I do not, they will be at my door, knocking, ringing, wanting the ball back. If I ignore the door, they will be at the side gate, pushing and pulling to open it. The woman's boyfriend, the stupid, mindless yob, may even kick it down.

The doorbell goes. They have come straight round, the children, or perhaps the mother or the boyfriend.

I think suddenly of the Honda Civic.

It worries me.

More than I can say.

Do I want to answer the door, do I want to deal with that? If I ignore it, will it all just go away?

I open the back door of the kitchen slowly, step out and take the three or four paces to get the ball. I throw it back over.

And I sit and wait.

Knock, knock, knock.

For whoever it is at the door to go away and leave me alone.

Knock, knock, knock.

They will go.

Knock, knock, knock.

For now anyway.

But I know that one day – one day soon – they will not.

THURSDAY 27 JULY, 12.30PM

I have decided to write more of my diary.

About her. And him.

And how it all ended.

She told me, a morning or two later as I was leaving for a walk to the shops, that she was going to see a show with friends, at short notice, at the seafront theatre in Felixstowe that evening, a Tuesday. Last-minute tickets, given away for free.

I did not believe her. Not for one second. I knew straightaway what she was going to do.

See him.

Have sex with him.

The two of them laughing and joking about me behind my back. Humiliating me.

I simply looked up from polishing my shoes and nodded casually and then smiled and feigned a cursory interest. I had a hot soup spoon in my hand at the time – it helps add that extra shine to black leather – and I needed all my powers of self-control not to jab it into her stupid cow face. But I did not at this stage want her to know that I was aware of what was going on. I wanted her to think I was still a happy, loving – cuckolded – husband. I wanted to be sure, see for myself, be certain of what she was doing, before I decided precisely what to do.

There was the bungalow, mortgage paid off. Relatively meagre savings. HMRC does not pay well. Divorced and shared between the two of us, it would not amount to much; to anything really.

The rest of my life on or close to the poverty line. Benefits. I could not face that shame. To have fallen so far. From what I had been. Respected. Master of my own little kingdom. Feared by tax dodgers and cheats.

And she had a life policy worth a tidy six-figure sum. When she died, that is. Enough for someone to live the rest of their days in relative comfort. Should he get this? No. Never.

As I tied my shoelaces and got to my feet, I glanced in her general direction rather than meet her eye. My gaze, bland though it would have been, might have alerted her to my knowledge of her behaviour.

I do not know if she would have held my gaze, defiant, or whether she would have looked away, ashamed. I did not want either response. I wanted to retain the element of surprise for what I would do once I knew the truth for certain.

If she left me, I would lose my home, the savings, everything, including my reputation. That was not going to happen. As I turned to go, I just asked her the usual questions that any loving husband would do.

Did she want a lift?

What would she do about eating?

What time would she be back?

For some extraordinary reason my innocuous questions made her snigger – more of a derisive laugh, really – and I have to say I came close to addressing the matter of her lies and cheating there and then.

But I contained myself, as I have been trained to do in the face of the most extreme provocation. I pretended not to notice as she stifled the laughter and turned away to continue washing up the breakfast things in the sink.

I waited for a moment as she composed herself and then thanked me but advised that she was getting a lift to the theatre with friends.

As I picked up my reusable shopping bag and took the few short steps out of the front door and into the porch, I stopped and turned and looked back at her. I watched as she switched on her radio on the windowsill and started humming to herself. Perhaps thinking I had gone, she then began jigging about in a lumpen, ungainly fashion.

I do not know why, but I had, at that instant, an almost overwhelming urge to do her some great harm. If I had had anything more substantial in my hand than my soft shopping bag, I think I might well have done. I may have bashed her stupid brains out. As it was, I restrained myself and stepped out of the porch and closed the door quietly behind me.

I hear, from the bottom of the garden, the sound of a train, a freight train carrying containers to or from the nearby port, braking slowly. The squeal. The screech. The eventual grinding to a halt. The long and endless silence that plays havoc with my mind, triggering my imagination.

The driver, waiting for the red light to change, is sitting there, looking down into my garden. I can imagine him. Checking the garden bit by bit. Watching until something catches his eye. It does. He opens the door of his compartment. Dropping down from the train. He takes a closer look. He reaches for his phone in his pocket, making a 999 call as he moves from the track into the garden.

Only the sound of the train suddenly lurching into life and pulling away breaks my thoughts. I find that I have been holding my breath. I gulp in air greedily. Reach for a sip of water from the glass by my bedside. Pause. Think. Relax. Continue my writing.

She spent ages getting ready to go out that evening. She was in the bathroom for 25, close to 30 minutes. I listened at the door, heard her using the toilet, moving to the basin, cleaning her teeth, getting into the bath, lying there for what seemed forever, moving, noises, the splash of more hot water from the tap. A long silence. A final noise. A minute or two's silence. Then the rush of water as the bath drained away and she stepped out, busy now, drying herself, coming out of the bathroom wrapped in a huge towel.

I pretended to tidy around and dust and polish and move things about, coming in and out of the bedroom to see everything she did. She ssshhh'd and shooed me away in increasing irritation. She had in recent years become somewhat coy, going into the bathroom to change her bra and pants, even to put on or take off her dress.

And so she did this evening, going back and forth each time as she tried on this and then that, making sure she was just so for him. I noted, from the waste-paper basket to the side of the dressing table, cut-off labels from underwear from Marks & Spencer. Even when we were intimate, and it had been so long, I never recall her wearing matching, let alone new, items for me.

I felt myself rising. Against my will. I did not want this.

The desire, at least for physical release, still there after all this time.

But other feelings too, of disgust and loathing and anger. Fear as well, that I might lose everything to her; and to him. The courts always favour women. Every time.

And then her final touches at the dressing table and mirror. Pampering. Preening herself. Wrapping a new red and white silky scarf around her neck. Brushing down her new dress. Stepping into new red shoes. Checking she looked nice. She'd never spent so long – taken so much care – before, not for an ordinary night out.

She was doing it for him, of course. I could see it all in her face. The flush of excitement. Worry too. Doing her best to disguise her lined face and flabby figure.

I saw no sense of shame, no feeling of respect towards me. I was of little concern to her. I studied her, flicking her hair, looking at herself from side to side, changing earrings, pursing her lips, smoothing her clothes.

I felt the anger surging in me.

The thought of her with him.

Him inside her. Her face in ecstasy.

I had to walk out of the bedroom, the bungalow too, and went to the car and then to the garage. Raising the up-and-over door, moving inside. To potter about, distract myself, let my emotions subside. My body as well. To stand in the shadows. To see but not be seen. I wanted to watch what happened next.

She had said, when I had pressed her for an answer, that there was no need for a lift. That she was being picked up. Just after seven. I wanted to see who was in the car that would pull up outside of the bungalow. Him. Alone? Or with others? Maybe just others? Surely she would not be so brazen as to be picked up by him on his own?

After a few minutes, standing there, out of sight, I heard the front door being opened and then closed, the sounds of her clickety-clack heels on the path and the gate screeching open and shut; and the sight of her moving along the pavement to the left and away. She did not turn or call back at me, although she must have known I was there in the garage. I waited. In agony. Not sure what to do. If I moved out of the garage, down the driveway, to the edge of the pavement, I would see her, what she did, who came to fetch her – but she would then see me watching her.

So I waited. Two minutes, three – maybe four. To the moment when I came close to walking to the road to see where she was anyway. And then I heard, but could not see, a car pull up a little way along to the left. A door opening, slamming shut. The car pulling away.

I saw the car, a Honda Civic, with him closest to me and her next to him, moving across the road at the top of our driveway, gathering speed. They were already in an animated conversation, both laughing. I could not remember when I had last laughed with her. Not like that anyway. Not loving. Comfortable. At ease with each other.

I could not know for sure that they were going to the seaside theatre.

They could have been going anywhere. A pub, maybe. Or fields or woods. A country lane.

But I got in my car, and I followed and saw the car in the distance as it turned onto the by-pass and down towards the seaside town of Felixstowe.

I hear, from somewhere at the front of the bungalow, the sound of a heavy vehicle slowing and pulling up outside. It sounds like the lorry that comes for the bins. But that is not today. And it is not the bin van.

I know what it is. I do not need to go and look.

It will be a pick-up truck. It has come to collect and take away that blue Honda Civic that sits over the road in the cul-de sac. It has come to remove it and I suspect that it will be preceded or followed by the next knock on my front door. I think it has to be soon.

Eventually, I sat and waited on a bench in the clifftop gardens, as dusk fell and turned into night and the theatre down below me was lit up both inside and out.

There were sparkly lights along the front. People came and went, couples arm-in-arm, old men walking their dogs, a group of teenagers taking photos of themselves with mobiles. All happy, having fun in their own little ways.

I could have gone into the theatre, bought a ticket, slipped in and sat at the back as the lights dimmed; watched them, as my eyes got used to the dark, sitting next to each other.

I did not need to. I could imagine them there together, her head on his shoulder. And they might have seen me. And then what would I have said or done, the element of surprise gone?

I could see the entrance of the theatre – entrance and exit being one and the same – and simply sat and waited, obscured by ornate railings and bushes, until, at some time close to 10.30, she emerged with him, arm-in-arm, in the crowd after the show.

I followed them – easy in the dark and at a distance – to see what they did next.

They walked further than I expected, to his car, tucked away quiet and dark in a wooded area.

I stood there, some distance off, to the side, not sure what to do. Waiting for something to happen. For me to decide what to do.

As the minutes passed, the car seemed to move slightly, so imperceptibly at first that I was not sure it was happening. But, soon enough, it was clearly rocking from side to side. Not much, not so you'd really notice if you were passing by, but enough for me, watching closely, to know what they were doing.

Her passenger seat laid flat back. Knickers on the floor, shoes kicked off. Him on top of her, trousers loosened and half pulled down. Riding her back and forth. His head up above the top of the seat so he could see out, would know if anyone were approaching.

I could have run forward at that point and confronted them. Hard to deny what was going on with her legs spread wide and his backside bobbing back and forth in front of me.

But I did not. I stood, half out of sight, half watching, imagining his grunting pig face as he brought my wife, her back arching and making little whimpering noises, to the brink of ecstasy. The thought of this angered me more than I can say.

I must stop here, pause a moment, for it still upsets me greatly. Regain my composure. Gather my thoughts.

I will stop there. It is a suitable moment to do so.

Let me just say though that I knew, as his car came to a sudden juddering halt, that I could rush them, wrench the door open suddenly, surprising them. I had a knife in my pocket. I could have used it. First on one, then the other. Stabbing and slashing and cutting away at them one by one. Over and over.

Yes, I could have slain them there and then and no one in their right mind could have blamed me. But I did not. For I am a smart and clever man. I did not – do not – want to go to prison. And I had a plan forming in my mind. I held myself together as best I could. And so I went home. To have a cup of tea and a custard cream biscuit (slightly stale) and to wait and watch for their return.

THURSDAY 27 JULY, 3.20PM

I would never, in a million years, have ever expected to be doing what I am doing now. I am babysitting, if that is the correct word, the little girl while Adrian and the beauty have gone to the pictures.

Babysitting is not something I wish to do!

(I have, in my head, amused myself by now thinking of them as 'Beauty and the Beast', given Adrian's stooping gait and general ugly awkwardness. Not that I would refer to them as such out loud. Not in front of her anyway.)

By the by, I have not become a children's entertainer!

The three of them turned up, out of the blue, just after I finished my last diary entry. Their arrival, unexpected as it was, made me jump. It was only when I recognised their voices as they entered the hallway that I realised I had been holding my breath for what must have been half a minute.

I mopped the sweat from my face and under my arms, tidied myself, made myself decent, as it were, by changing into a fresh, dry shirt, and went to see them. They were carrying bags from Greggs the bakers and bottles of water. She invited me to join them for lunch. They went into the kitchen. I sat in the living room, waiting.

Have lunch with us, she said. (Have lunch in my own home!)

They busied themselves in the kitchen, Adrian coming back and forth to set up and arrange the table in the living room in his usual obsessive, stop-check-repeat, stop-check-repeat way.

Madness, utter madness.

I do not understand how she has not recognised this yet. Perhaps she has and just ignores it. Because she loves Adey as she calls him. Aaah! Not for long, though. It will drive her mad eventually, as it does me.

We sat down to eat the assorted rolls, crisps and pastries and what I call 'vegetable things'. They are vegetarians apparently – no doubt 'Adey' will become one too. The meal was something of a free-for-all. The child reached greedily for whatever it wanted and pushed food into its mouth like a fat little pig. While I was distracted, watching the girl, Josie asked me if I were doing anything that afternoon.

I had noticed already that she has this habit of looking down while glancing up at you in a disconcerting manner; as if she were rather shy. It is, in its way, rather endearing.

I answered cautiously, "No, not especially" but immediately wished I had said the opposite; that I was very busy indeed. (But then Adrian would have given me one of his sly, sidelong looks and maybe said something to make me look foolish and I do not like to be made to look stupid, not least because I am a highly intelligent man.)

I expected her to want to play happy families in some way.

A walk in the park. A go on the swings. A tea-time picnic on the beach.

Not my thing. No, not my thing at all. I would have said so, politely.

But she talked in a rather forlorn little Minnie Mouse voice, quite at odds with her strong, firm body, about not having been out with Adrian on "a proper date", never really having had "quality time" together, a cinema trip and a meal out and all of that.

(Although, I thought to myself at this point, they had got to know each other well enough to have, I assumed, been 'going to bed' with each other.)

Then she asked if I'd babysit the little girl that afternoon.

A "play date" she called it, laughing suddenly and putting her hand to her open mouth as if it were the funniest thing in the world.

I saw Adrian give her a warning look and an over-emphasised shake of the head. I did not know what that was about.

I queried the phrase 'play date'. I had never heard it before. I thought it sounded strange. She explained that it simply meant two children getting together to play.

I am not sure whether she was suggesting that, being together, the little girl was one child and I was the other; or if she just meant generally. But I smiled at her as if I found this amusing too and so, two hours or so on, here we are now, Beauty and the Beast at the cinema and me and the little girl – little madam – in the living room.

The child sits in front of me on the carpet on the other side of the coffee table. She has taken off a pink rucksack with a cartoon pig on it and has unzipped it, taking one item out at a time and placing them neatly in a row on the coffee table.

A handful of sheets of white drawing paper, A5 sized, some used, others unused. All rather soiled and scruffy.

(She looks up solemnly at me watching her.)

Next, she brings out a pencil case, which she empties with a clatter as crayons and felt-tipped pens tumble across the table.

("Oops," she goes, putting her hand to her mouth – just like mummy – and giggling at me; even though she must have been aware that would happen.)

Then, knowing I am watching her, she makes a show of searching at the bottom of the rucksack, before taking out three small tubes; one looks to be full of small golden stars. The other two contain red and silver pieces of glitter respectively.

(She puts the tubes neatly on the table and looks at me with her hands on her hips. She sighs. I sigh too, knowing she is playing a game with me. I spread my arms out as if in amazement at what I am seeing. She does the same.)

One last dig about in her rucksack and we have a pot of glue with a brush on the table along with a small carton of drink and something wrapped in foil, presumably a snack.

Josie had said something about this being her calm time.

Then a drink and a snack. And a nap, but not for too long. More of a snooze while I get on with finishing my diary.

Somehow, I doubt any of this will happen just like that.

I watch as she starts to use various felt-tipped pens to draw a picture on a sheet of paper. I notice she is left-handed, like me. It is hard to tell what the picture is meant to be. But she uses one felt-tipped pen confidently after another, going back and forth between them, until, eventually, it is one big mess of colourful squiggles.

I had, to be frank, lost interest some time ago, and was just sitting thinking about this and that. The garden. The heat. The overflowing bins. The terrible smell of rotting meat. Maggots. You get maggots in this heat. Lots of them. And I don't have any bleach. But then she stops drawing and holds the picture up to me and smiles. Beams, more like.

Christ, what do you say?

It's hard to make sense of it. That's definitely a castle, I think.

And a dragon? With three wings?

I smile at her and she smiles back mischievously. "Very nice," I say, resisting the urge to ask her what it is or even which way up it is meant to be.

She unscrews the pot of glue. The lid has a big brush attached to it. She dips the brush into the glue and smears a great lumpy glob of it on the paper; it's meant to be over the castle I think, but it spreads right across the edges.

"Here," I say, taking the brush from her, "give it to me." (Otherwise it will be all over everywhere and trodden into the carpet.) She lets go after a moment's resistance and I push the blob of glue into place on the castle. I smile at her. "Do you want me to put some glue on... the dragon?" I add, pointing to the dragon.

She laughs, and says it's a dinosaur, and then calls me "silly!".

If I am honest, I was surprised that the little girl agreed to be looked after by me when Beauty and the Beast went out. I had thought, from what had been said, that it was pretty much the two of them on their own without anyone else.

But the little girl, who I would have expected to have been shy and nervous with what is after all a near stranger, seems remarkably at ease. Self-possessed, even. A less tolerant man than I might even say she is full of herself. *Just William*'s Violet-Elizabeth Bott.

I put a smear of glue on the dinosaur, not that it looks like any dinosaur I have ever seen. I push the glue out along the edges and make a neat-enough job of it.

She cocks her head to one side and looks at it as if in a thoughtful fashion. I again get the impression that she is much older than she looks and is almost acting the part of a cute child. There is a knowingness about her. I am not sure that I like it. In fact, I don't think I do.

She reaches for the three tubes of glitter. Although I know what will happen the instant before it does, I am not quick enough to stop her opening the tube of silver glitter and knocking it over the table.

She laughs in delight and claps her hands. "No harm done," I say, using the side of my smallest finger to gather up and tip the bits into the palm of my left hand.

"On the dinosaur?" I ask and she nods agreement and so I carefully shake the contents of my palm onto her drawing. I use a finger to shape the glitter on the dinosaur itself. To be honest, it's a mess really. It looks like a halfwit has done it. But she seems to like it and it keeps her quiet, which is good. I rather think she could be a noisy little so-and-so if I set her off.

Again, before I can stop her, she enthusiastically pulls the lid off the tube of red glitter and shakes it everywhere, literally everywhere, while making a stupid and irritating 'err, err' noise. The glitter is on the drawing, the table and the carpet. I am sure there is, err, err, something wrong with her.

Masking my (natural) irritation, I say "There, there, never mind" as if she might be upset by losing half of the glitter, but, glancing into her wide, vacuous face, she just seems to think it is the funniest thing ever.

I manage to get most of it back into the tube and give it to her, putting my hand over hers and guiding it over the paper. "Where do you want it?" I ask, "The glitter?" She makes a noise, a kind of growl, at the back of her throat and I can feel her little hand resisting. I let go and she shakes the tube, rather less wildly, but still too messily, over the castle. Again, I tidy the glitter with the edge of a finger.

We look at each other.

She reaches for the last tube of glitter. Too late, I have it in my hand.

She looks at me, a flash of anger.

"Do you want it?" I ask, holding the last tube of golden glitter towards her. She looks back, her arms crossed. She is defiant. She wants it all right. But she will not say. I look at her, holding her gaze. And I will do it until she looks away.

She does and, as I go to give her the tube, she reaches instead for the red one again and, before I can stop her, she shakes the glitter all over the drawing. Some of it goes on the table. Most of it is on the floor. Then she stands up as if satisfied with what she's done and, in doing so, knocks the open tub of glue over. I see a small, snotty blob fall onto the carpet.

She goes very still. Will not look at me at all.

It is all I can do not to slap her stupid little hand. But I will not. Nor will I speak sharply to her. For I am a calm man.

I leave the room to get some kitchen roll.

When I return, she is still standing there, almost motionless, looking down at the table and her drawing. I pick it up and shake the glitter off carefully and hand it to her. She will not raise her hand to take it. I push it into her hand but she will not open her fingers.

I place her drawing carefully on the edge of the table as I start to clear up the mess as best I can, putting the paper to one side with the glitter and glue on top, and wiping and mopping and folding the scattered glue and glitter from one piece of kitchen roll to the other. I walk back to the kitchen and put it in the bin.

When I get back, she is sitting quietly on an armchair, having unwrapped some raisins and is eating them one by one. She looks at me as if she is close to crying – it may, I think, be an act – and holds the carton of drink up towards me. I take it, pull off the straw on the side, put it in the hole and give it back to her.

"Do you have anything to say to me?"

I expect her to say sorry. She does not. She asks for her drawing.

I hand it to her without a word.

We sit there opposite each other for a few minutes as she looks at the picture while she drinks from the carton and picks at the raisins. When she is finished, she slips off the armchair and takes a step to the coffee table and places the carton and the foil carefully next to each other on the edge. She looks at me.

"Time for a nap?" I ask.

"Peppa," she answers. I echo her word in reply, as if asking a question.

She reaches for her pink rucksack, pulls at the zip and takes out a little pink pig.

At that, she seems docile, even tired, and, to my surprise, she reaches for my hand as I walk her towards Adrian's room. I expect her to be fractious and awkward, not wanting to lie down, or sleep, but she climbs readily enough onto his duvet, arranges the pink pig next to her face and seems to be asleep almost as soon as her head touches the pillow.

I sit quietly in the living room for a minute or two, to get my breath, deciding what to do next. I cannot remember how long the child is expected to sleep for. Not long, I think. Not enough time to do anything properly. I will, I think, just take a few minutes to complete my diary about her and him. And how it all ended.

THURSDAY 27 JULY, 4.00PM

I will write about the pivotal moment in what will be my decline and fall.

The end of the marriage.

This came no more than one hour after what I call the seafront incident.

Returning to the bungalow, I drove the car onto the drive and up to the garage. I sat there, the headlights on the faded brown door, thinking what to do. Subduing my anger and fury. Going over my plan. Working it all through logically, the pros and cons of each option. Step by step. Confirming my plan of action is correct. The only way. No other choice. After a few minutes, having decided, and with things clear in my head, I got out of the car and walked to the front of the bungalow.

She had cuckolded me. Would leave me, start divorce proceedings. To be with him.

I would lose the bungalow, the life savings, my pride, my standing, everything that was important to me.

I'd be finished. My share of the money would amount to no more than a caravan on some ghastly site, drip-feeding the little money that was left until I ended up on benefits to the day I died. I cannot have that. That is not right and proper. Not for me. A (former) officer of Her Majesty.

The outside light cast a dim glow over the porch. Adrian must have turned it on when he came in from his evening work and went to bed. He had left a paper bag containing food and drink from McDonalds on the doorstep, which annoyed me. He should have taken it round to the bins and put it in there, but, I assume, could not be bothered to do it in the dark and had left it there until the morning. Or maybe he'd put it down to let himself into the bungalow and had then forgotten about it. Either way, a cat had got to it. There was half-eaten food and wrappers everywhere and a stream of Coca-Cola had zig-zagged its way down the drive. I pushed the food and wrappers to one side with my foot and entered the bungalow.

Listening quietly.

I walked slowly to Adrian's room. Put my ear to his door. I could hear, I think, the faint sound of his steady breathing. Asleep but a light sleeper. He would wake up to any noise, loud voices, shouting, maybe even a sudden cry or scream.

I went to the kitchen.

It was a full moon that night. I remember it well as the light shone through the window and I could see how smeared the pane was; the wipe marks, spreading the grime back and forth in a rainbow-shaped arc. I looked around the kitchen and found what I was looking for. What I needed. Holding it, I turned and went out of the bungalow, pulling the front door and then the porch door gently to behind me.

Moved to the car, got in, reversed it out of the driveway and then back in so the front faced out towards the road. I left the headlights on, blinding anyone looking in.

Out and to the garage, door up and in, pulling it half-closed behind me.

I stood by the shelves at the back of the garage. Looked at what was there. A pot of acid for tree stumps. An axe. Hammers. A spanner. Saws. Old rope.

I waited there for her to arrive back.

Minutes passed.

Five? Ten? It seemed so long.

I came close to losing my nerve, leaving the garage, turning off the car lights, going back indoors, getting ready for bed. So near to changing my mind, giving in, accepting the outcome, and all that would happen to me if I did not act now.

As I hesitated, a car – his car – pulled up, drove a little way along. Stopped, just out of sight. When she got out, I was not sure, seeing my car headlights on, what she would do next. I held my breath.

I thought – I assumed – she would say goodbye to him, then walk up the path and see the car lights on and the garage door open and walk in to check what was happening. I would be here, waiting for her. Could pull the garage door down behind her.

That was what I expected and I was ready for that moment.

Or she might ignore the car, the lights, the half-open garage and simply go into the bungalow. But the rubbish, Adrian's leftovers kicked to one side, would stop her in her tracks. She would clear them up, bring the bits and pieces round to the bins by the gate by the garage as he should have done. I would open the garage side door and, as she put the rubbish into the blue bin, she would look up and see me standing there, smiling benignly at her.

I was ready for that possibility too.

Either way, I was prepared.

For what I was going to do.

What I did not anticipate was what actually happened. I heard voices on the driveway, soft and talkative, and then a sudden silence, followed by brisk footsteps, and the sound of the porch door being opened. Her. Going in. I turned and moved to the side door of the garage, unlocking it, opening it a little so that I could see the three bins, grey, blue and green. Waited for her to appear, carrying the rubbish over from the front doorstep.

I stood there, tense, on edge, ready.

The garage door behind me was pulled right up above head height.

A voice. His. "Hello, everything alright?"

I stumbled forward, dropping what was in my hand on the ground outside the garage side door. I stepped back, turned, looked at him in the dim twilight. Did not know, for a moment, what to say.

"Has your car got a flat?" he asked, moving forward to see me more clearly. My face could be seen, I think, from the moonlight through the side door.

"I'm a friend of your wife, Philip, from school. We went and saw a variety show over at the Spa, several of us from work. Very good it was too." He stepped further forward.

I smiled at him. My mind racing. Not sure what to say.

Or do. I had not expected this. Was not ready. The bare-faced cheek of it. The lies. The sheer brass neck of the man.

I shook my head. Cleared my throat. Answered him.

"All is well, thank you," I said carefully. "I've just been looking for..." I tailed off, could not think of what to say.

We both stood there for a moment looking at each other.

He has the nerve of the devil. Coming in like this. Pretending he's just a friend. I know better. I read your texts. Not one hour ago, I stood near your car, watching it rock from side to side. When you were deep inside her.

I gestured towards the front of the garage, indicating we should both leave.

We walked together to the driveway. I opened my car door and leaned in to turn off the lights. He took a few more paces and stopped and turned.

Too late now.

A chance missed.

He spoke.

"Well," he said, neutrally, "nice to meet you. I'll be seeing you." He then paused and, although I could not see his face clearly, I could swear that he smiled a not-very-nice smile, a sneer, as he added the words that changed everything. "And do say goodbye and give my love to Dawn."

I simply turned and walked back into the garage.

Pulled the door down behind me.

Moved to the side door. Saw her at the bins, just as I had thought she would be.

I bent over and picked up what I had dropped.

She looked at me. I smiled at her.

And she looked down at the heavy, copper-bottomed saucepan I was holding.

Our eyes met and I could not help but giggle just a little bit.

I will pause here. I am writing about it as best I can, as well as I can remember it.

I will then, once I have made sense of it all in my mind, tear out and burn the pages.

I do not want anyone else to read them. Ever.

THURSDAY 27 JULY, 4.42PM

It's really just too hot to do anything other than sit here writing my diary nice and slowly. I should move, maybe tidy up the lunch things. I said to leave them, that I would do them. They hurried off to the cinema fast enough. Left everything to me. But it is all too exhausting.

Thirty minutes, was it? To leave the child asleep? That's not long. Is an hour too much? Do I leave her until she wakes? I cannot remember what Josie actually said. I think I may just sit here and listen. Wait until I hear her stirring. Then go and wake her up.

If I am honest, I could do with shutting my eyes too. Just for a moment – 10, 15 minutes at most. To recuperate. To recharge the batteries. To rejuvenate myself, refreshed and ready for the child waking and getting up. The heat makes me sleepy at times.

I awake suddenly, disorientated for a moment, not sure what it is that has woken me. I must have nodded off. I sit here, drenched in sweat, listening. Frightened of what is coming. I turn towards the door, assuming I have been woken by the sound of someone racing into the bungalow, coming straight for me. I struggle to my feet, as if to defend myself.

I wait here, in not much more than a crouch, but there is nothing but silence. Just my imagination. And then I remember the girl, asleep in Adrian's room. I get fully to my feet, but slowly, finding that somehow my lower back has stiffened up on me.

I walk, plod really, towards the bedroom, to wake the child. I did not check the clock in the living room, and have no watch on my wrist, but it feels as though I, and she, have been asleep for some time, an hour, possibly two.

I remember now that she was not meant to sleep for more than 30 or 40 minutes, that a longer one would make it harder to get her settled tonight. I need to wake her so they will not know how long she has been asleep when they return from the cinema. I will simply say "not too long" when asked.

I push open Adrian's door.

She is not on the bed. Nowhere to be seen.

The duvet is as it was.

I panic for a moment, then check myself. I am all jittery, my nerves on edge. Assuming the worst. She will be in the bathroom, going to the toilet. I walk to the door, stop and listen, knock on it. There is no response. I wait a moment. Open the door. She is not in there.

I pause, thinking.

Is she hiding from me?

Gone off to explore?

I go back into the bedroom. Look around. Nowhere to hide here. Except? I go down onto my knees, slowly, move the edge of the duvet back, looking beneath the bed. No, not there. The wardrobe? The only place – but the doors are pulled to. She could not have got in it and shut them behind her. Could she? No, but I check anyway. To be sure. No, not there.

I move quickly from room to room. Resisting the urge to panic.

The kitchen. Opening and shutting cupboards, the larder. Checking everything carefully, step by step.

The other bedroom. Under the beds. In wardrobes. She is not here. She is not in the bungalow. Not anywhere.

I move to the front door as quickly as I can, straining to stand fully upright to loosen my back. Could she have opened it, moved into the porch as I am now doing, opened the porch door and gone up the drive into the road? I move to the pavement. Look up and down. No sign.

Back to the bungalow.

The garden is the only place she can be. The garage is shut. Too hard to open it out and up and over her head at that age. The side door is locked. She cannot be inside. She must have gone out of the kitchen door and down into the garden.

I open the kitchen door and look down the full length of the garden. The railway line at the end. She is not there.

The trees, the stumps that I cut down and dug over. Not there either.

I look at the old air-raid shelter, its domed roof above ground, maybe two-thirds of the way to the railway line. There are three steps down, old broken, concrete steps to the entrance, which is boarded up.

I see her there, just the top of her head. I move quickly towards her.

She is bent forward, peering in through the tiniest of cracks. As I get closer, I can hear her talking, saying something into the crack. "Hello," she says. "Hello?"

She turns as I start running towards her and says, "Look!" and then turns back and points towards the crack in the door. "Scarecrows!"

Part Three

THE AIR-RAID SHELTER

THURSDAY 27 JULY, 4.59PM

As I rush to grab the little girl there is – at the instant my hand closes around her arm – a terrible commotion at the front door. Shouts. Ferocious banging. Yells.

I am undone.

I let go of the girl's arm, deciding to run. Down the stretch of the garden. Up and across the railway line. To the fields and river on the other side. And away. But where? A head start, no more than that. Not enough. But what else can I do?

I have not prepared for this moment. Not like this. That I might flee. I should have done.

A debit card. Cash. A change of clothes would give me a chance.

But I have nothing. Nowhere to run, nor hide. I am ruined.

I stop, turning back, stepping beyond the bewildered child. I hear screaming. A woman's screams. The sound of the front door being broken down. A loud, splintering, cracking noise that ricochets through the air.

Then silence.

I am confused.

I do not know how to react.

Adrian, flustered and twitching, and the young woman, behind him and reaching for his arm, race out of the back door towards me. The young woman sees the child and sweeps by me to lift her up in her arms. She stops and turns, with Adrian, towards the bungalow, as if waiting for something awful to appear. Before I can speak, to ask, to demand to know what is going on, Adrian is talking all of a gabble at me.

"It's him, Leon. He was upstairs on the bus. Saw us get off. He's after us," he shouts, looking straight at me as if I am going to do something about it. "Leon, Josie's ex," he adds angrily as he sees my blank expression; like I'm supposed to know who 'Leon' is.

"We need to hide," the young woman cries. "In case he finds us here. He won't give up and he'll have a knife on him."

I look at them both.

They are clearly terrified.

Of this horrific man, this Leon.

I usher the three of them quickly across the garden. Away from the out-in-the-open air-raid shelter. To the patch of scrub tucked behind the garage. We stand there, huddled together for a minute, maybe two. Adrian and the young woman look tense, frightened, waiting for their world to cave in. And mine too if they did but know it. She pulls the child – who looks wholly unconcerned by it all – next to her.

Adrian explains, in a series of stage whispers, "Leon was on the top of the bus… We were on the bottom deck… he saw us get off… Josie had her arm round me… he banged on the window… jumped up, to come downstairs… we ran… He must have got off at the next stop… he's coming back after us."

She then adds, "He won't stop until he finds us, not now he's seen me with Adey. Lily's not safe either – he might snatch her from me… He's on methadone," she adds.

I nod, a sign of understanding, and then it occurs to me, but I do not immediately say it, that breaking down the front door was not only unnecessary (given it needs to be repaired) but also unwise. If this Leon is steaming down the road looking for them, he's sure to come up the path when he sees the broken door inside the front porch, smashed in and swinging on its hinges.

He will barge into the bungalow.

Searching from room to room.

Charging out the back door into the garden.

Thoughts rush through my mind. I try to make sense of them. If he appears, right now, this next moment, this drug-crazed fury of a man, he will see us crouching here, half-hidden, half-watching.

What will he do? Cut Josie's face? Stab Adrian in the stomach over and over again? Would he do that in front of the child?

Will he punch Josie, then Adrian, and grab the child? Run off with her?

Or just stand there and shout and swear and bluster like so many of these low-life bullies do?

Whichever way, the police will come to my door.

Even if he stands there, threatening Adrian, the neighbours might hear him and make the call, pressing 999.

I cannot have the police here, looking around, asking questions.

I have to do something. Slow things down from this overwhelming sense of panic into some sort of calm. Walk steadily to the front door before this Leon gets to it. I have to stand there, in this never-ending heat, pretending to be tidying round, doing the flower beds. Doing nothing much at all.

Me? Seen anyone?

No, no one here, mate. (That's what these morons call each other, 'ma-aa-aa-t-e'.)

I saw a couple running that way, though, a few minutes back.

Then I'd point him far, far away, send him on his search somewhere else. Maybe I'd add a clever comment: "I saw them flagging down a cab." That would fool him, that's for sure.

"You wait here," I say to the young woman, "I'll go and see what's happening."

She looks at me, scared but grateful, the handbag over her shoulder now clutched defensively to her chest, as if to protect her. Adrian pulls a face. He has this nervous twitch, a tic, I think they call it, where he moves his jaw to the left and then the right and back again. I don't know if he knows he does it. It's to do with stress. He repeats it endlessly when he's under pressure. I've seen it before when he had his troubles with the police. The little girl just looks at me, her face a blank canvas.

I move out and up the garden.

Eight, nine, ten steps take me to the back door.

I stand there, listening, trying to hear if this Leon is inside, thrashing about.

All I hear are noises from the road to the front of the bungalow. Cars. A motorbike. A lorry pulling away up the hill. Louder than they should be. The noises. The front door must be wide open, the outer porch door too. So loud that I cannot hear if anyone is moving about the rooms, from one to the other, a knife in his hand, ready to slash and stab anyone he comes across.

I have to step inside the back door. Appear calm, as if I am going about my everyday business. Pottering in the garden. So hot, I have come in for a glass of water. If he's there, what do I do? Feign surprise for sure. Act angry, what the hell are you doing in my bungalow? What have you done to my front door? Dare I do that if he's off his head on drugs?

But he'll realise, won't he?

If he sees the front door caved in – he'll realise that someone has knocked it down and come through at speed; and it can only be them. Who else would it be? He'll push past me, shove me to the floor and head for the back garden where Christ knows what will happen.

Ambulances. Police. Forensics.

They'll all be at my door. And in the garden.

And it will all be over for me. Today. This evening at the latest.

I have to get to the front door and out into the porch before this Leon appears by the bungalow. Tug the front door to behind me as best I can. Pull the porch door closed as well. Stand in front of it, obscuring the view, pretending I have been tidying around and weeding, am standing there just taking a breather.

I take steps, four, five, six. Stand in the middle of the hallway, listening.

No noise from the rooms to either side. Adrian's bedroom. Mine. The bathroom. All the doors are ajar, no one inside.

I take the final steps to the front door, 10, 11, 12. Into the porch, look out, no one in sight.

I steel myself to walk, as nonchalantly as I can, down the path, to the gate and beyond. I stop and turn, as if I am fiddling to fix a broken hinge, while looking around me. Up the hill, I can see what looks like a couple of young girls walking away, almost out of sight. On the other side of the road, near the top, and going the same way, is a man, in what looks like a black T-shirt and jogging bottoms.

I think that must be him, disappearing into the distance.

There are cars coming up and down either side of the road and, as I turn and look the other way to where they would have got off the bus, there is only a short, stumpy-legged woman walking towards me with three gormless-looking children in tow. Two boys and a girl, who is shouting at the top of her voice. I pity the poor father of that little lot.

He has gone.

Leon.

All is well.

I sigh, step back and walk into the bungalow. The front door is not as bad as it sounded. There is some damaged wood on the frame and some twisting of the metal by the latch, but it seems to close well enough with a little pushing and shoving from me.

As it jams into place, I hear the creak of a floorboard behind me.

I jump, my nerves in tatters.

And then I turn and face down the hallway.

THURSDAY 27 JULY, 9.57PM

Six hours on from their return – Beauty, the Beast, the little girl – we are all now finally settled into place. I have agreed that Josie and Lily can stay, at least for tonight, until the danger from this Leon has passed.

As Adrian said – as he sidled up behind me in the hallway – this Leon will never let it go. He will not leave them with Adrian. He will go back to where they live and will lie in wait there for their return. "They are only safe here," said Adrian, surprisingly firmly. "This is the one and only place he can't find them." He then added, "We don't want to call the police." And I agreed with that. Not here anyway. I don't want them at the bungalow.

So we all had tea together and smiled and nodded as Adrian jerked and fiddled his way through that and the washing-up and the sitting around and playing with the little girl afterwards. They then went to bed in Adrian's room while he "kipped down," as he put it, in the living room. I have retreated to my room where, finally, with the sweat of the day drying on my back at last, I write in my diary one more time. About her. And how it ended.

As she stood by the bins, tipping in the rubbish, she looked across at me as if she wasn't surprised to see me there at all. She did not look ashamed or guilty about what she had been doing – nor was she worried or concerned about me in any way. She did not even smile. She simply raised her eyebrows, pulled a face (as if to sneer 'oh, it's only you') and kind of sniggered to herself. I swear she sniggered. I know she did. I saw her. I heard her too.

It was the snigger that made me so angry, if I am honest.

If she had not sniggered, I would have thought better of what I was going to do and walked away. For sure, I would have. Yes.

But she did. And so I had to do it. The fact is, she made me.

I smiled back at her when she sniggered. And then I hit her in the face with the heavy saucepan as hard as I possibly could. The first blow seemed to stun her into silence. Before she could regain her senses and scream, I hit her as hard as I could again. And Again. Again. Again. Again. Again. Again. Again. Again. She was not able to scream after that. No, not at all.

If I am frank, I did lose my temper somewhat – my little 'moment of madness' as it were – and I hit her more times than I care to remember. In fact, I cannot recall just how many times I actually hit her.

I do know that I hit her quite hard each time and, towards the end, I found myself grunting out loud in time with the blows. It was only when I became aware of the grunts – quite out of character, I must say – that I realised exactly what I was doing.

Strangely, for you would think she would fall backwards and lie on the path on her back, she did not. She sort of crumpled in on herself – it is the only way I can describe it – and fell straight down onto her knees. She then slumped forward onto me, her bloodied, snotty face landing on my thigh, leaving a nasty smear, before I stepped back and she fell flat on her face by my feet.

My first instinct, and it was not easy to do with all the spluttering and sighing sounds she was making, was to try and listen to hear if anyone from either side or Adrian inside the bungalow might have heard anything. I could not see any lights going on nor hear any sounds of movement or noise of any kind. I had, with more than a little luck, 'got away with it'.

(Do you know, I can hear, quite clearly, singing from Adrian's room? Clear as a bell. The young woman. She has a sweet and melodious voice. Quite sure and steady. I know the song – 'Annie's Song' by John Denver, from years and years ago. From when I was young. Mother had the record and used to play it for a while before father broke it. It is soft and gentle. Sad and even a little melancholy the way the woman sings it. She is singing the child to sleep.)

It is not an easy thing to do, to end a life. Especially with a grown adult. It is not like drowning a stupid puppy that's outstayed its welcome after Christmas. I went, many years ago, to an Agatha Christie play, I think it was, at a local theatre. Some amateur nonsense. With dimmed lights, a man, in silhouette, strangled a woman – 10, 20 seconds and the deed was done. It is not like that. No. Nor is it like a TV show or a film where someone is shot or stabbed and goes "ooh, argh" and falls down dead on the spot. No, it is not like that at all. People don't like to die. She didn't, that's for sure.

As I stood over her, waiting ages for her huffing and puffing to come to an end, she finally stopped and fell silent for a moment.

And then – and I cannot explain it properly – she started groaning to herself while dragging her knees forward as if she were going to struggle up and onto her knees and then somehow stand on her feet.

(The young woman's singing is calm and soothing. I do not mind it. I do not mind it at all. But it does not last. I hear the child thump-thump-thumping her feet against the wall. She does not want to go to sleep, the child. No. No. No. The woman stops her singing. There is a moment's silence. Then she starts singing again, soft and plaintive. The thump-thump-thumping begins again too.)

I dragged her body – not yet a corpse – through the side door and into the quietness of the garage. There was blood on the path and I moved a bin to cover it, making a mental note to clean it up in the morning. I would burn it away with some acid I had left from removing the tree stumps. I kept the side door half-open, both for the moonlight, so that I could see what I was doing, and to hear if anyone was moving about outside.

I am going to be quite honest here, although it reflects no credit on me at all. I will be matter of fact about it. As I rolled my wife over, her décolletage somewhat spilled out and over her low-cut dress and I was aroused by this, notwithstanding her general battered appearance and the less-than-pleasant surroundings.

My wife had not allowed me to have sex with her for several years at this point – talk of the menopause and the permanent wearing of sanitary appliances and all of that had, I felt, been exaggerated and so I took the opportunity to check 'what was what' down there. It was more than a moment of curiosity. I wanted to get to the truth of the matter. She was, after all, hardly in a position to discourage me.

I discovered, and I must say I was not the least bit surprised, that there were no signs of anything untoward. No blood and guts, shall we say. Anyway, let me just add that, what with one thing leading to another, and, as I stated, she had denied me for some years, I satisfied myself with her. It does me no credit.

(Josie has stopped singing once more and I can hear her trying to reason with the child. There was another series of thumps against the wall – the child's feet, I assume – followed by one or two words in a raised voice from Josie and then a high-pitched whine from the child. On and on it goes. For God's sake, why won't the stupid child shut up?)

I had assumed that hitting her with a rather heavy, copper-bottomed saucepan both in the face and around the head so many times would have dealt with her. But no, it was not enough. I hesitated for a moment, wondering if I might let her live – if I might, somehow, reverse what I had done. I admit I had second thoughts. Regrets even – for I am at heart a decent sort of chap. As I say, this sort of thing is out of character.

I pondered for a while as I looked down at her still-gurgling body, her face little more than pulp. It was her face that decided things for me. If she were to survive, she might be in a vegetative state and would be a silent, but reproachful, burden on me for the rest of my days. I did not wish to have to feed her nor wash her dirty parts or push her around in a wheelchair for years on end while she blubbered nonsensical words about what I had done to her. If she recovered enough to function, to speak, to converse properly, then she would no doubt say something to someone and I, one way or the other, would eventually go to prison. I could not have that.

I had no choice and so I finished the job. I had, on the garage shelves, an array of tools and equipment – saws, rope, acid and so forth. Enough, more than enough, to attend to matters properly. I have to be honest and say that I have always had something of a squeamish nature when it comes to bones and offal and the like, so I did not use the saws or acid on her body. I did not wish to see 20-odd feet of her innards spread out across the garage floor. I simply strangled her with her scarf and for quite some time to make sure, until I could not feel a heartbeat nor hear bubbling breath from her mouth. And so it was done.

(Now Adrian is up. I hear the living room door open carefully, clicking shut behind him. Two or three footsteps in the hall. The door of the bedroom opening, going straight in, no knocking, no forewarning. The girl stops her wailing. There is the sound of low voices talking, then silence. Long may it last.)

Putting my head outside the side door of the garage, all was peaceful in the moonlight. I walked slowly across to the air-raid shelter, pulling open the door at the bottom of the steps. The lower part of the door had largely rotted away and the rest was going that way. I looked down at the two benches on the floor to either side. I had not been in here for years and the smell of dirt and decay was strong.

We used the shelter for storage when we first moved into the bungalow but the damp soon got into everything and covered all of the items with mould. The shelter had been unused for more than a decade, maybe closer to two, and should have been filled in, flattened and have disappeared into the ground a long time ago. But it all cost money we could not afford and so it stayed there year after year untouched. Now I knew that it was the perfect resting place for her.

I pulled her dead weight from the garage across the garden and down the steps and onto the floor of the shelter. My goodness, she was a great big lump. As I closed the door behind me and followed my path back to the garage, I saw that one of her new red shoes had come off, so I picked it up and tucked it down inside of a bin. The floor of the garage, clicking on the light, had some smears and stains.

I made a mental note of what I would have to do the next morning when Adrian was out. I would need to clean thoroughly beneath the bin. And scrub the garage floor too. Most important of all, I must secure the shelter door with wood and nails so that Adrian would not accidentally stumble into it. And that would then be that.

This is how I did it.

Writing it down like this, in my matter-of-fact manner, makes it seem not so bad really.

I did what I did and that is all there is to it.

I hear noises from Adrian's room. It is the child, who obviously has no idea of the concept of peace and quiet, silence and sleep.

She is talking at the top of her voice as if no one else but her matters. The mother answers in a quieter voice. Then Adrian's deeper rumble. I cannot make out the words. I hope they will go to sleep, giving me some peace in this endless hothouse.

Adrian's door opens and closes. Footsteps to the bathroom. Opening the door. Closing the door. Clatterings. Other noises. The sound of the toilet roll spinning. Everything then repeated in reverse, doors opening and closing, voices and so on, until there is silence again. For the moment, at least.

As I lie here, with the sounds of the road and the rail line somehow sounding louder at the moment and all of these other bangs and unexpected noises so much closer, I consider how much longer I can stand all of this. Everything is closing in and suffocating me.

And I worry about Josie and the child being here. I think about what might happen. Adrian has never shown any inclination to sunbathe or potter about in the back garden. I rather fear this woman and child, in the ever-present heat, will spend all of their time there. If they do, it will not be long before the child mentions what she has seen in the air-raid shelter and they will then both go up to it and peer in through a crack in the shelter door. And what will happen then?

FRIDAY 28 JULY, 9.17AM

The banging on the front door begins again; it's just after 9.15am. The four of us are in the living room, sitting here after breakfast, talking about what they will do next.

Knock.

Knock.

Knock.

We all fall silent except for the little girl, who looks at the young woman and makes another nonsensical "bbbrrring bbbrrring" noise like she did before. The woman hushes her and we sit here without speaking, hoping whoever it is will go away.

Knock.

Knock.

It goes again. A little louder but still respectful. Not a furious knocking, not an 'answer-the-door-or-else' sound. But someone is out there. And they want someone in here to respond, to come to the door. Now. Those of us in the bungalow are trapped, cannot do anything, dare not take a chance. Of answering the door. Even of being heard, if it's this Leon.

Adrian has his head down, his back arched with tension. Not looking at anyone, just doing the left-right, right-left thing with his jaw. Josie has a calming hand on the little girl's shoulder, close enough, I notice, to clamp over her mouth if she makes a noise, if she yells or shouts out. The woman's head is down too, and she seems to be biting her lip.

Knock.

Knock.

Knock.

I sit there impassively. If it is this Leon, if I know for sure it is him, I will go to the door. No, I'll say, no one of that description here. I'm a widower, I'll add, recently bereaved. Still grieving. Now, if you'll excuse me, I must get back to what I was doing. Remembering and reflecting. He'll shuffle away, shame-faced, never to return.

But it might not be. It could be something to do with him and his car, which is still there, parked over the way. I thought it was being taken away but it hasn't. It might be someone who wants to come into the garden to look at the train tracks, to check if they are buckling and twisting in the sun, asking questions, being a nuisance, noticing the air-raid shelter and more, sticking their nose in where it is not wanted.

Now there is silence.

There are no sounds of voices or notes being put through.

It's all quiet and I assume they have gone away.

I am the first to get to my feet now I am sure whoever it was has left. I say to leave it 10 to 15 minutes and then it will be time to go home. For them to go home, I repeat. To their own home, to make myself absolutely clear. They just sit there, the young woman getting her phone out of her bag and giving it to the child to play with, Adrian looking up at me. I can see the fury in his face. He speaks, his voice cracking with emotion, on the brink of tears.

"If Josie and Lily go back… he'll be waiting there… or he'll break in when it's dark…"

I soothe things, suggesting Adrian can go back with them, take his things, stay for a while, until everything has settled down, blown over. But this seems to anger Adrian even more. He shakes his head and pulls gurning faces as I speak my measured and calming words. And then he answers defiantly as he stands up.

"He's too strong… (he lowers his voice suddenly as if mindful of the child)… he's violent… on drugs… he could do anything… absolutely anything to any one of us."

The young woman, who has been staring into space, speaks, looking across at me as she does so. "He forced himself on me… several times…" She nods towards the child, "… in front of…"

"Well," I reply, taken aback by what she said but pressing on. "Anyway, I think the three of you should go back there, to your home, with Adrian and his things… I will call you a taxi and pay for it… and then you must call the police when you get there.

Someone will soon come round, a policeman, two of them probably, one will be a policewoman, and they will take a statement and
have a word with him… he won't bother you if the police have had
a quiet word, warn him off."

At this, Adrian steps forward and laughs in my face. His breath
smells of onions.

I think for a second that he is going to raise his hands and strike
me in anger. His impotent rage.

I step back, arms down and at my side to calm the situation as I
have been trained to do.

"Don't you understand? Did you hear what Josie said?" (Josie
gets to her feet and lifts up the child and moves towards the door.)
"He could… kill me and (as they leave the room)… rape Josie…
murder Lily."

In spite of everything, it is hard not to laugh at him as he stands
there, twitching and shaking, red-faced and tearful, full of indignation and self-righteous fury. Adey. The saviour of Josie and Lily!
Mr Bloody Superman!

He follows them out of the living room – regardless of whether
anyone might still be standing in the porch, looking through the
little piece of glass in the front door and seeing him, all of them
together, in the hallway.

I brace myself for the sound of shouts and kicks at the front
door as it caves in and this Leon attacks them, pushing and punch-
ing, and slashing at Adrian with a knife. But there is silence except
for the door of Adrian's room clicking closed followed by the low
murmur of their voices, talking quietly.

I sit here, dripping in sweat from the heat and feeling agitated,
partly because they clearly do not want to take my advice and go
but also because of the fear that if they don't, this Leon will come
back. He might break in when I am asleep.

I look out down the garden and notice, by the top of the steps by the air-raid shelter, a cat, a sleek black cat, that is looking towards the door of the shelter. After a few minutes, it moves down the steps out of sight and I wonder what has attracted its attention and what it will do next.

The smells from the pig farm and the fields full of cabbages and cauliflowers are so strong in this heat, especially when the wind is blowing this way. But beneath those, from the shelter, there are other smells too. Strong and awful smells that attract a hungry cat. Maybe rats have got in by now, made themselves a nest there; next to their source of rotting food.

I am scared of rats and cannot face having to deal with them. But it is something I will need to check. I will have to take a spade, just in case. I will sort it if I have to. I cannot have the neighbours calling the council about it, having those snooping busy-bodies round with their clipboards.

There is someone at the door again. I have been distracted by the heat and smells. It makes me jump.

Knock. Knock. Knock.

I sit here, my nerves stretching close to snapping, waiting for them to go away.

Knock. Knock. Knock. Knock.

All is quiet in Adrian's room, both of them holding their breath, Josie with her hand over the child's mouth. I imagine the child struggling if she holds it there too long. Will this Leon go before the child cries out? Touch and go, I think.

Knock. Knock.

It must be him, this Leon. I ask myself if, with the three of them shut in Adrian's bedroom, I can answer the door, bluff my way through, get him to go quietly, convinced they are not here. If not, if no one ever answers, he will keep coming back. By a process of elimination, other householders having answered the door, he will focus finally on this bungalow and, stepping inside the porch, he will see the splintered lock by the door and maybe put two and two together. I know I would. But then, perhaps I am so much cleverer than most people.

Knock. Knock.

One more time, if it goes just once more, I will get up and walk to the door. I cannot hide here, away and out of sight, like some cowering, beaten animal until he bursts in. I will open the door and I will say to him, this Leon, quite brusquely, "Hello, yes, what do you want?"… "No, no one here by that name."… "No, no little girl."… "Now, please… excuse me… I'm very busy."

Knock.

I have to get up. Make him go away. Leave me alone. Let me be in peace here. On my own.

Knock, knock.

That's it. I am up, wiping my face and hair and my glasses and pulling free the shirt that's sticking to the small of my back, and I am out of the living room and into the hall. To sort this. To get him gone. Away from here, far away from the bungalow. So I can stay here in peace and quiet, to mind my own business, to see out my days without all this anger and fury at my doorstep.

I look up, tense and expecting to see this thuggish Leon.

But it is a young policewoman standing there.

Before I can turn, retrace my steps and duck out of sight, she sees me.

FRIDAY 28 JULY, 10.06AM

I make eye contact with the policewoman, keep a steady gaze and smile as I have been trained to do in stressful situations when I need to look calm and at ease. I open the door.

Nothing to see here.

All very ordinary.

Move along please.

Act relaxed, speak a little louder than necessary so that Adrian hears me, so they know it is not this Leon. That it's the police. Stay put. They'll be on their way in a moment.

"Morning, constable," I say, cheerfully enough to seem natural. "What can I do for you?"

She half-smiles back, busy, professional, perhaps irritated by my failure to answer the door before or quickly enough for her this time. Then turns away from me as she speaks.

"We're making house-to-house enquiries about a car over the way." She points at it and then, as if I am slow-witted, tells me the make and model of the car and its number plate. "And the owner, who has been reported as a missing person."

"Yes," I reply conversationally. "I had noticed it has been parked over there for a while now… I had not seen it before… I assumed someone had moved into the road."

I stop speaking, knowing I am saying too much – the more you say, the more you give away, as any tax investigator will tell you. Keep quiet. Let them do the work. What I need to do is get her to the point where I can close the conversation down and see her on her way as quickly as I can.

"What can I do for you?" I add. "How can I help?"

She gives me, frankly, a slightly odd look before she speaks.

"We're just asking everyone, door-to-door, if they have seen this man." She shows me an A4 photo of him. The fancy man. "Or anything out of the ordinary over the past few days. Since Tuesday."

I shake my head, as she carries on speaking her well-rehearsed words, repeated endlessly up and down the road at each door.

"He was reported missing on the 25th by his family, who say he'd driven off in his car at about midday to buy some cigarettes and hasn't been seen since. One of my colleagues spotted the car late last night. We're making enquiries."

"Well," I say, as confidently as I can, "I have seen the car but not the man." Then, to distract her and send her away, I add, "Perhaps his car broke down or ran out of petrol and he walked into town? Maybe he was taken ill somewhere in the heat?"

Again, she gives me another odd look as she continues speaking without actually answering my question.

"You have the railway line running across the end of your garden, I believe? Can it be accessed easily from your garden?"

I see where she is going with this… the unspoken query… the suspicion of suicide. A body somewhere on the track.

"Yes, easily enough… a wire fence, that's all… but he wouldn't have come through here. I have the gate locked… bolted at the top… and I am here at home all day. He'd have had to get to the line further down, towards the roundabout. He could then have walked to Felixstowe along the track… or back into Ipswich."

"Do you live here on your own?"

"Yes, pretty much. I have a son, Adrian, but he's out and about most of the time. Adrian…"

She interrupts. "I… if I might have a…"

Before she can complete the sentence, "have a… word with him", Adrian, who must have been listening intently, comes out of his room, shutting the door carefully behind him. She'd have been gone in a minute or two at most without a second thought or look back. If only he had stayed put.

And here he is, standing in front of her.

With his great gormless face and staring, vacant eyes, eager to please.

The stupid bastard.

Now we're going to have to repeat the process with him gulping and twitching and rolling his eyes as he stutters his way through the same answers again. And I am going to have to stand next to him, and make sure he doesn't say anything that might keep her here any longer than necessary. That he doesn't, in his own igno-rant, blundering way, drop me in it.

He looks awkward, sheepish even, as he smiles at the police-woman. I can't help but think he seems shifty. Adrian stares, with his boggly eyes, down at the A4 paper that the policewoman still has in her hand. With a picture of him. And then Adrian looks back up at her.

He points at the paper and speaks.

With something close to excitement.

"That's Mum's friend…" he says louder than he needs to, as if this is the most wonderful moment of his wretched life. "That's Philip Rennie!"

FRIDAY 28 JULY, 10.14AM

The policewoman sits in an armchair in the living room, opposite Adrian and me on the sofa. I sit quietly, calmly, in a relaxed, mat-ter-of-fact kind of way. I saw her glancing round the living room, taking it all in, its run-down grubbiness, as she sat down. She then asked for our names and noted them carefully in a little notepad. She is now looking at the picture of him, composing herself and thinking what to say.

She'd radioed up to a colleague – telling him where she was and what she was doing.

Then invited herself in, near enough, to talk to Adrian.

And, I know it's coming, to ask me why I did not say I recognised the man in the picture.

I think for a moment, looking at her, that she might not be a proper policewoman, but one of these volunteer specials. This matter, a missing middle-aged man, is a little practice for her. She looks young – younger than Adrian – and nervous, uncertain even. We need to get her up and out, satisfied with what's been said, before one of her regular and more experienced colleagues up the road joins her and asks some awkward questions.

"Adrian," she says, looking at him and smiling in an encouraging, well-practised manner, "how do you know Mr Rennie?"

I sit there impassively, my hands resting gently on my thighs, with a pleasant smile on my face as I look at Adrian as he answers. I am calm. I pick a small thread of cotton off my trousers and put it in my pocket.

He leans forward, keen to help. "I don't kn… know him really. He's a friend of my mum's. They work together at the school." He then pauses and looks across at me with a half-smile. I am not sure what to make of it.

The policewoman looks briefly at me too before she continues to talk to Adrian, "When you say your mum's friend…" She looks at and then addresses me, "Are you and Adrian's mother married?"

I clear my throat, "Oh yes," I answer. "Dawn and I… my wife and I, have been married… very happily… for, oh let me think, almost 30 years."

Adrian looks at me, but I ignore him. "And is Mrs… Todd in at the moment?" the policewoman asks. I am not sure if she is asking Adrian or me.

I pause, waiting.

Adrian breathes in sharply, making something close to a snorting noise.

Almost derisive, it is.

"… Dawn…" I answer mildly, ignoring Adrian, "… is away at present, her father's been ill. Seriously ill." I look at the policewoman, with my steady gaze.

She looks back at me and then turns to Adrian. "Do you know when Mum will be back, Adrian?"

"I don't know." He shrugs and turns to me as if I am expected to answer both questions for him.

"Where is she at the moment?" The policewoman presses.

I clear my throat again. "I seem to have a frog in my throat." I try to smile but my lips are sticking to my teeth. I clear my throat once more as she waits patiently, looking steadily at me all the time. Two or three more goes and I can speak.

"She's up north… with her father. She should be back soon. Her father's been ill. Very ill. She should be back when he's better."

The policewoman nods, taking it all in, processing things, working it all through, creating a list of questions in her mind. Answers she expects to hear. I could do with a glass of water right now, to be honest.

"When did she leave?" she asks.

"Sunday night, three weeks ago. The… um… ninth, I think."

"Have you heard from her since?"

"She calls once a week, Sunday nights."

I know, as the words leave my mouth, that I've made a mistake. But what else could I say? No, she's never been in touch? That would be odder, surely. The policewoman would dig deeper if I said that, wanting a phone number, an address, so much more than I can provide without giving myself away as soon as she makes that call or an officer goes to the address.

Adrian looks at me. He knows it's not true. The Sunday night calls anyway. I ignore him. Have to hope for the best. Hope that she does not now turn to him and ask if he has spoken to her. I can hardly breathe as the interrogation, for that is what it now is, goes on between the policewoman and me.

"Is it possible Mrs Todd and Mr Rennie could be in touch with each other?"

"I wouldn't have thought so… they were just work colleagues, that's all."

"You know Mr Rennie well then?"

"I don't… No, I don't know him at all."

"So, they could be in contact with each other?"

I don't want to look at Adrian, don't want to turn to him for help, but I don't know what else to say or do.

"I assumed… from what Adrian said…" I turn towards him.

"Adrian?" she says, looking at him.

He's not sure what to say; his early enthusiasm has ebbed away and I can see he's sitting there tense and nervous. His eyes flicker this way and that; another of his tics, no more, but one that makes him look dishonest. He shrugs and says he doesn't know. She turns back to me.

"Mr Todd, if you know Mr Rennie… your wife's friend… well enough to say you don't think they'd be in touch… why did you say you did not know who he was…?" She holds the picture of him up in front of me.

"I know the name… a little about him… passing conversations… but I do not know him personally… have never seen him… or a picture… I've not met him."

Adrian speaks up. "Mum showed me a photo of herself at a works do and pointed everyone out to me. She said he was nice to her, a good friend. I wouldn't remember all of them but I remember him because he has a 'tache."

"And yet, of all the places Mr Rennie could go," says the policewoman, looking from Adrian to me and back again, "his car is parked over the road from you, just 30 or so metres away from where his good friend… your wife… your mother… lives. He's driven here from across the other side of town. Quite a coincidence, wouldn't you say?"

She looks at me. I shrug and pull a slight face, expressing surprise, a little bewilderment.

She looks at Adrian. He doesn't answer; doesn't know what to say. His eyes, those empty, mad eyes, steady for a moment; as if he's trying his hardest to disguise something.

She reaches for her radio, to call her superiors, to get them to come and speak to us. To dig deeper. To finish me off. To end it all here and now. As she goes to speak, there is a high-pitched, ear-piercing scream from Adrian's bedroom.

FRIDAY 28 JULY, 10.20AM

The policewoman is up and out of her chair, radioing "Back up, back up" as she moves quickly towards the door.

Adrian is slow to react.

Two steps behind her.

I follow him into the hallway.

The policewoman has already pushed open Adrian's bedroom door. She stands there looking in as Adrian and I come up behind her.

The little girl stops screaming, surprise on her face as she looks up at the policewoman. She is standing and her finger is caught in the side of one of the drawers of Adrian's chest. It cannot be as painful as the scream suggested as she is silent now, awkward even, cowed by the uniform as she silently takes her finger out. I could swear she mouths the word, "oops".

Josie, sitting on the bed with her handbag on her lap, looks over at Adrian and whispers "sorry" at him before speaking, adding that the child was looking for a towel. It is unbearably hot in here. There is a strong smell of sweat, of musk, of the woman's body. She has not opened the window, for fear of the policewoman hearing, I suppose. Her face looks flustered, her brow and hair damp with sweat. The girl looks wet, the edges of her hair all frizzy.

I worry, as we stand there and the seconds pass, why this Josie has hidden herself away with the little girl. Why she did not follow Adrian out when he heard me talking to the policewoman on the doorstep. Why she did not sit next to him, holding his hand, the child at her feet, everything normal, as the policewoman asked her questions she could not answer. Why did she stay in the bedroom, keeping as quiet as she could?

There is a sudden, loud banging on the door, "Open up, open up!"

I look towards it, a policeman's face at the pane of glass, contorted with anger.

"You," he bellows, seeing me, "open it now." I run towards the door before he breaks it in.

He pushes – shoves – me to one side as he moves towards the policewoman. There is a moment's confusion as the two of them touch each other's arms and hands and the policewoman speaks, "It's okay." He relays that into his radio to call off more back-up. And then the policewoman explains to the policeman that she was speaking to us and heard a scream. "Just the child… caught her finger."

A moment's silence as we all compose ourselves. I stay standing rather than inviting everyone out of the hallway to the living room, to indicate to the police that they've done all they need to do here. That they need to go.

Josie puts her handbag by her feet and pulls the girl onto the bed and hugs her. Adrian squeezes by the policewoman and sits next to them on the bed and turns and smiles at the policewoman. "My girlfriend... come to visit," he says proudly, "Josie... Josie Wilson."

I can't help but notice the glance – slightly longer than a glance actually – between the policewoman and the policeman when they hear the name. Or is that my imagination? There was no obvious look of recognition from either of them when they saw her. Josie smiles slightly in their direction but does not, as I would expect her to have done, say something like, "And this is Lily." I find that peculiar. Most peculiar.

The policewoman then steps forward and shows Josie the photograph of him.

Josie shakes her head, "No, I've never seen him before."

"Have you heard the name Philip Rennie?" presses the policewoman.

Josie shakes her head again as the small child holds her finger up towards the policewoman. There is, I think, a tiny smear of blood on it, where the nail has been nipped. The policewoman, too young to be motherly, ignores the outstretched hand and continues speaking.

"The car over the way, a blue Honda, have you seen that?"

Josie shrugs and then shakes her head as the policewoman tells her the number plate.

There is a pause. It's hard to see where the policewoman's going with this.

I reflect, for a brief moment, as the policewoman tucks the photo away, whether I should ask Josie if there is anything she wants to mention to the police. "Leon," I would mouth. But I hesitate. I can't help thinking – sensing really – that this would not be well received by her or Adrian. I don't know why. And I do not want the police – any of them – here any longer than necessary.

I turn towards the policewoman and see her looking at me, watching me. I smile at her but it does not come easy. There is something about her that unsettles me. She goes to speak – to damn me, I think – when the policeman's radio goes, a sudden blur of words, something's "been found", somewhere "near the top", I think it was, whatever that means, and he signals that they need to go. Now. Quickly. As if it's something important. Very urgent.

I know, as they walk quickly along the hallway to the door, that they will be back. Once the policewoman gets a chance, a quiet moment, to speak to her colleague in more detail. Him being known here. The friendship with her. The fact that they are both unaccounted for. That they have both disappeared. A routine matter becomes something more serious.

It won't be long before they return.

Wanting an address for her. And a telephone number.

And then, I think, God help me, my time will almost be up.

FRIDAY 28 JULY, 12.31PM

I am unnerved by the morning's events but will, as Adrian and his 'little family' sit and eat their lunch, keep to my plans. For now anyway. The worry, the fear, the dread of the police's return needs to be suppressed while I think over what to do. I must not panic, acting out of the ordinary, giving myself away.

I have time. Not much, but a little. It will only be when they have come back and I give them various details – the phone that's never answered, the address that does not exist – that I need to act decisively. Until then, I will hold my nerve and act as normal. If they come back – if. It is by no means 100 per cent certain. If I were to panic, to run now, for example, I would give myself away. And, anyway, where would I go?

So, while I get a moment to myself, I am going to write one last diary entry. The final diary entry before I tear out these few pages and burn them. Away to nothing. So no one ever sees them. Nobody will ever know anything by my hand. This last entry will help me to think things over, get my mind straight and move on from all of this. If I can. I am going to write about him. Everything was done and dusted. Neat and tidy. Then he turned up, banging on the door. Near enough accusing me of murder.

"Where's Dawn? Where is she? What have you done to your wife?" That's exactly what he said. Word-for-word. Shouted more like. On my doorstep for everyone to hear. Neighbours to either side. What would they think hearing that? They'd be puzzled, concerned. They'd turn to each other and one would say, "Thinking about it, I've not seen her for a while." "No," the other would reply. "She just vanished." Then they'd look at each other and one of them would reach for the phone, calling the police.

I opened my front door wide. Bluffed him. Good and proper.

"Come in," I said as casually as I could, making eye contact and gesturing him inside with as warm a smile as I could muster. I stepped back. He stepped in. I turned and he followed me down the hallway to the kitchen.

Thinking on my feet, constructing a plan on the spot. I'd got him, for sure.

In the kitchen, I stopped by the rack of knives, then turned and faced him, my hands behind my back. He stood towards me, tense and nervous, fiddling with a little brooch, a gold-coloured train, on the lapel of his jacket. The doorstep bravado was gone all of a sudden. Scared he was. I think he'd plucked up the courage to come to my front door, the sad little nobody, and had said what he'd said on the doorstep to shock and maybe frighten me. Now he was inside – following me automatically without thinking what might happen and now realising – and his nerve was failing him.

"So, have you told anyone?" I said, looking into his eyes.

"Told them what?" he answered, glancing away.

"That I murdered her. Who have you told?" (I needed to know, didn't I?)

"Oh, well, I never said that exactly." he replied, with a nervous flutter in his voice. He then went on. "No one, I was… just joking really, being a bit daft… I just thought… I wanted to know where she's gone… why she just took off like she did. I don't understand. It's… so out of character."

He stopped, paused for breath.

"One minute she was there, then she was gone." He went on, "She just disappeared. I called her mobile, left messages… texted here once or two… several times as a matter of fact… and she's never replied. We're friends…" he paused for a moment, before adding "… just friends… pals."

As I reached for the kettle, I gestured to him to sit down at the kitchen table, at one of the two chairs to either side. He did so, and sat there, half-turned away from me, while he wittered on with his nonsense.

"Yes," he said, gathering a little confidence. "I know Sally and Cathy from work had called round to see why she'd not been in and *you said her father had fallen ill unexpectedly and she had gone up to Scotland and that she wasn't responding because she must have left her phone behind but... this is what I don't understand... well, several things really... I thought her father lived in Canada?"* He turned and looked at me.

I gave my well-rehearsed answer casually, as I busied myself in the kitchen, getting out mugs and teabags and milk and sugar. "He'd moved back last year but never told us. Then his wife called and said he'd been given days to live. She went up straightaway."

"But... I mean, they hadn't spoken for years, had they?... how would he... his wife... know how to contact her... Your phone number? That's puzzling me. And... you see, the thing is... she's never been in touch... with anyone... with me... I would have expected..." He stopped – I think he thought he had said more than he should have.

I put the mugs side by side, noticing one had a crack in it and the other a tiny black speck on the rim. I picked it off with my nail. I'd have that one. I put in the tea bags. Added boiling water. Stirred one after the other with a teaspoon from the drawer and then, the words clear in my head, I replied, sighing as if I had explained this so many times before.

"... She went up by train the moment she heard. I dropped her at the station. She's been there since. He's hanging on in there," I added cheerfully. "Still with us. I expect he'll... well, one way or the other... soon enough."

I handed him a mug of tea and noticed that, as he took it, he did not look at me, nor say any word of thanks. He seemed distracted, puzzled. I turned back to pick up my mug and then stood looking at him as he went on.

"But, you see, the thing is this. As I say, she hasn't contacted anyone... not her work... friends... any of us. Leaving as she did *before the end of term, well, it caused some staffing issues. For someone as… well, as reliable as she is… well, that's very unusual… don't you think? It's rather troubling, I'd have expected her to have contacted… someone… by now."*

Then he looked at me.

And did not stop looking.

Not for a moment.

I laughed, rather jovially, and replied, "I suppose she's been busy, what with her father dying, contacting you would be the last thing on her mind at a time like this, I'd have thought." I stared back at him, but he did not blink or turn away. His thoughts then came thick and fast.

"The first few days, yes, maybe even a week or so… that's understandable I suppose… possibly… but, by now, she'd have been in touch for sure. She would have had a moment or two to herself. Her father would have a landline or his own mobile… or she could have written, sent a card, anything. But no one has heard anything. And that worries me… more than I can say."

He paused, wiping his nose with the back of his hand. He then asked, "Do you have her phone here?"

"Oh," I said, thinking quickly. "No, no, I don't."

"Did she take it with her then, lose it somewhere?"

"No, as I said, she left it here. My son Adrian would have had it, put it somewhere safe."

"You don't know where that would be? I'd like to see it… if I may. Would it be in his bedroom?"

"Why do you want to see her phone?" I said, with a note of incredulity in my voice.

"I just would," he answered, looking back at me. "Just to check out… any clues… Has she been in touch with you at all?"

"… Yes… well, when she got there – on the phone – just to let me *know she arrived safely, nothing since."*

"Do you have her phone number there... the landline... or the address, somewhere to write to? The school sent a letter here, I believe. Do you have that? Or did you send it on?"

I shook my head. Not sure what to say to any of that. He pressed further.

"Have you got your landline to hand?" he said, looking around and seeing it on the side by the fridge. "If we click back through the calls received up to the day she... disappeared, there should be a number we can call back."

"No," I replied, "there isn't, I'm afraid."

He stood up to walk over to the telephone. "No, no," he said, "there will be a number."

"No, no," I echoed, and then added quickly, "do you know... I remember thinking at the time... it was a number withheld... or unavailable... one or the other."

"That's very strange," he said as he reached for the phone. "Why would she withhold the number?"

He stopped for a moment, his hand on the phone, thinking what to say or do. Then he spoke, "I'm really worried. Vanishing into thin air like this. It's not like Dawnie. Anything could have happened to her. I think we need to call the..."

I stabbed him. With my biggest kitchen knife.

Just as his mouth framed the word 'police'.

In his back, as hard as I could. I twisted it too.

He did not die instantly. In fact, he turned right round, the knife still stuck in his back, and looked at me with such an expression of utter shock on his face. It was all I could do not to laugh. Oops! Butterfingers! I stood there for a moment, looking back, waiting for him to fall down. Instead, he spoke, almost as if he were talking normally, "You... killed... her," he said. "My God... you..."

I reached for another knife and stabbed him again, twisting the blade once more. "And you fucked her," I said. I don't normally swear but my anger was rising as he seemed to half-smile back at me. A dirty little smirk. The third time, his eyes rolled upwards. I stabbed him again, four, five, six times, perhaps many more, pulling a third knife in and out, plunging it in and out – like he fucked her – over and over again. It was quite satisfying in a way.

He fell eventually, but it took some time until I was sure he was dead. I will not dwell on the struggle I had getting him down to the air-raid shelter, where, in a sudden fit of silly humour, I put him in a very 'compromising position' with her. I checked his pockets, which contained nothing but a credit card and two ten-pound notes and some keys. No phone, though. I then had enough time to clean up the kitchen floor with my trusty Vileda mop and bucket before Adrian arrived home. We had tea together – I boiled some fish with mashed potatoes and peas (a personal favourite of mine) and went to bed as normal as if nothing untoward had happened at all.

I sit back and am rather pleased with what I have written. I have explained it very nicely. In a pleasant, story-book kind of way. And I feel I have exonerated myself. He came to the door, banging on it. He shouted the accusation. He strode into my bungalow. He did not accept my explanations. He was going to call the police. So there you have it. I had no choice.

I did – 'enjoy' is not quite the right word – feel quite pleased about killing him. 'Pleased' is not the most appropriate word either, but it will do. 'Satisfied' is closer but sounds rather smug. Anyway, no matter. He took a slight intake of breath, he almost squealed each time I turned the knife in him. And he looked at me as I stabbed him again and again. I rather think that I may have shouted "fuck... fuck... fuck" each time I stabbed in and out. I did, I have to say, rather lose myself in the moment.

Although I have ended lives, I do not see myself as a bad sort of chap. I am not what mother would have called a 'beast in the field'; like father was. I have not indulged. I did only what was necessary with her, with her silly smirk, and him, who was going to bring the police in. They were not easy endings. I did not particularly relish them.

I would not do it again.

I have no reason to.

I just want to see out my days in peace and contentment. That is all.

FRIDAY 28 JULY, 1.23PM

I have, for a little while now, been worrying about the police having my DNA and what they might do with it. When I last went to the library I used the computer to look up various matters and then printed off some notes. I am reading these now while I have a quiet moment. I cannot quite make sense of them.

They, the police, have the right to take a DNA sample from you if you have been arrested. This can then be checked against the Police National Computer – to see if it matches DNA found at earlier crime scenes and so on.

I am not sure if this – the checking, the comparing – always takes place, though. The law gives the chief officers of each constabulary 'the right to add a person's DNA to the database but does not oblige them to do so'. It is the 'do they or don't they?' that concerns me. The uncertainty of it. I…

There is a knock, more a gentle, hesitant tap, at my bedroom door. Even so, it makes me jump.

"Come in," I say.

It is Adrian standing there, pulling a face as if there is a bad smell in the room. Maybe there is.

The heat.

Sweat.

Body odour.

He twitches and gurns and then speaks without looking at me, almost shame-faced, "Where's Mum?"

I push the notes under my pillow and then sigh and answer, "How many times! I told you, didn't I? Before. Same as I told that policewoman. I've told you this more than once. Several times, in fact."

His eyes flicker towards me then away, not wanting to meet my gaze. A moment's silence, maybe more. He watches his foot as it moves back and forth, as if stubbing out a cigarette on the floor.

"But... Grandad," he says eventually, "it's been... They've not... Mum... she did not even... she said..." His nonsensical, muddled words tail off as he sees me looking at him struggling to say what he means. What he thinks. What he knows. Or at least guesses.

I shrug, closing my diary, signalling that this is the end of the matter. I get up. Hoping that we can move on and talk about the young woman and the child leaving. Him going with them. Leaving me alone. In peace.

"What are you writing about now? In your notebook?"

"Just stuff," I answer slowly, reluctantly. "I told you, notes. I might write a book."

He looks at me and laughs. There's no two ways about it. He laughs out loud. A spluttering, mocking laugh. It angers me but I do not react.

"You? What sort of book?" he says. "Is it poetry?"

I move away from him to put my diary in a cabinet. With my

back to him, I lock it and then reply.

"About tax matters. For the Revenue. Guidance notes. For new employees. Procedures and regulations."

"But I thought…" he says, then stops and nods, as if he is thinking carefully about what to say next. About my departure from the Revenue. I turn towards him, indicating our conversation is over, that I want to get by him. Go to the kitchen. A cold drink. Ice cubes from the fridge.

He does not move.

There is the longest pause. I gesture to him to move out of the way.

Then he gets to the point.

"Do you think Philip Rennie and Mum…?"

I do not answer. My head down.

"They might… you know?"

I look up at him but do not reply, my mind whirring. Realising suddenly that I might turn this to my advantage.

"Mum used to… talk to me. Sometimes. About, you know… things." He swallows hard and his frog-eyes are here, there and everywhere. Anywhere but on me.

I shrug, not sure what to say.

Another long pause.

An awkward moment, both of us full of embarrassment.

He talks on, ever so cautiously, word-by-word, almost whispering conspiratorially, "I know Mum hasn't been in touch, has she?"

I shake my head to confirm.

"And I know she and this Philip Rennie were… more than friends."

I nod, just once, curtly, in agreement.

"They've gone off together, do you think?"

"Yes," I say, thinking quickly. "But I don't want… the police… the world... to know my... our... business. Do you understand me?"

He nods, pleased with himself that he has uncovered the truth, as he believes it.

He moves to one side. I step by him, going towards the kitchen. As I do, I know that this – this revelation – will only be the beginning of it. The start of Adrian gnawing and chewing and tearing at things.

Where is she, do you think?

What's she doing!

Why hasn't she been in touch with me?

He's put two and two together, so he thinks, and understands why she's not been in contact just yet. But his birthday is not far off, in early September, and he will expect a card and a present or something then. If – when – he doesn't, he'll start asking more questions. He'll dig. And dig. Deeper and deeper.

She must be ill, surely?

Something wrong.

She wouldn't forget my birthday!

He'll sit there, worrying about her and him running away together, working things through, weighing every thought, the ifs and buts and maybes, wanting to know, needing to know, on and on, until he gets what happened clear in his head. At some point, he will work out the truth. He will see it staring him in the face as clear and as bright as a sunny summer's day.

She vanished on Sunday 9 July. Rennie's car appeared on the 25th. Sixteen days later.

They vanished separately. Independent of the other.

So where are they if they did not disappear together?

FRIDAY 28 JULY, 2.24PM

We are sitting on two old bed sheets, me on one, them on the other, in the garden, the four of us. They are eating and drinking, a makeshift picnic of sorts. I am sweating. We are ignoring the smell of the pig farm and the fields. The air-raid shelter is just ten yards away. "Scarecrows," the girl is going to say at any moment. Then she will raise her finger towards the shelter. Adrian will amuse her, pretend there are scarecrows there, taking the girl down to the door, pulling and pushing until it cracks and opens. And they then will see everything inside.

I am leaning forward. My back strained and tense. I can hardly breathe.

I feel my heart pounding. More than it has ever done.

I am acting normally, as best I can. But I feel my heart may stop at any second, that I might fall forward and die.

It was Adrian's idea – coming outside – as we all sat in the living room talking about what to do. About Leon. About them leaving. Or staying here. Hiding away. Close to arguing, really. They are not going to go. Not now. Not for a while yet.

I said to call the police, claim harassment.

This would anger Leon, they replied. Make him even more dangerous. "Madden him," she stated. We had to wait, until he calmed down.

How long would that take, I asked? They could not say. Days, I questioned, weeks… forever? They did not know.

Adrian broke the moment by saying we should sit in the garden, that the girl could run around, let off steam. I did not want to go outside. Not at all. But I could not explain why. Josie smiled her agreement and the child stood up ready to go. I suddenly said we could not.

No rugs.

No garden chairs.

No toys.

But they were already up and going. Adrian said we had some old sheets in the airing cupboard and we could take some tumblers of squash and some crisps and biscuits from the kitchen. It would be nice to sit in the sun and sunbathe for a bit. So we sit here, all rather awkwardly, on and on, doing nothing. None of us is sunbathing.

I can hear noise from the road in front of the bungalow, that ever-steady flow of stop-start traffic, revving and braking. I let it wash over me. It is of no importance. At the bottom of the garden, a freight train moves ever so slowly by. They seem to almost crawl along in this baking-hot weather, these trains. So agonisingly slow that, at times, I swear you could walk, even stroll, alongside them and move more quickly.

Adrian says he guesses there will be 30 containers. Josie says 10. I go in the middle, 20. They turn to the little girl and ask her, but she does not seem to understand how to play this guessing game so Josie says she will guess for her and chooses 15. As she says it, the girl yells "one million" at the top of her voice and waves her arms about.

I do not know how long it will take for the rumbling and squeaking and grinding to fade into the distance and disappear but it seems to go on for ages. I could almost scream as they count the number of containers one by one to 10, through to 15 and then to 20 and we, I am expected to join in cheerfully, then count the final few through 22 and 23 and on up to 26, 27 and 28, the last one.

"I win," says Adrian.

"Winner, winner, chicken dinner," laughs Josie, the little girl echoing the last two words.

It is all I can do to sit here quietly.

The gardens to both sides are silent for once; I assume no one is there. But it could be that they are indoors, sitting in front of fans, cooling themselves. The heat out here is tremendous. Too hot to do anything. Too stifling to relax. We all sit, dripping in sweat and melting away, on and on, just doing nothing at all but smelling smells and pretending we're not.

"I know," says Adrian suddenly. "Wait here."

He dashes back into the bungalow. Out again with the key to the garage. I stiffen. I don't want him digging about in there either. What with one thing and another.

Too late. Before I can say anything he has opened the door and is inside.

Josie looks at me and smiles. She is sitting there leaning back slightly, her hands keeping her upright. Her bag between her legs. The child to one side. She is very pretty, prettier even than I had at first thought. Her features are really quite exquisite. I notice that her top is damp from sweat and clings to her breasts. I look away, imagining for a moment what she would look like with her top off. I think she would be truly beautiful. I feel myself reddening and, despite the heat, and the horror and the fear of what happens next, I feel movement down there.

This is not what I want. Not now. Not ever.

Not really. But it is hard not to imagine what it would be like if it were just the two of us here together. I think we'd get along just fine. Her and me.

She seems to me to be a warm and caring person at heart.

The child distracts me, us both, as she suddenly walks around in a circle as if she is marching. I have no idea what makes her do this but am pleased that she is. Josie laughs and claps her hands.

The child joins in, clapping clumsily and almost in time with each step. She looks at me and smiles again, encouragingly this time. I clap along too, although part of me is sick with worry.

And then Adrian is out, saying he cannot find the hose. But he has an old tin watering can in his right hand.

He goes towards the outside tap to fill it noisily. Then turns towards the little girl who is watching him closely.

He mock-snarls, waving the can full of water towards her. She squeals delightedly and runs off towards the air-raid shelter.

I sit, barely able to watch, expecting her to go down the steps, trying to pull the door open to hide inside. I fear the door is so rotten, not just at the bottom, that one strong tug might open it. There, it's all laid bare for everyone to see. But, as she approaches the steps, she swerves to one side, almost losing her balance, and is then away and down the garden towards the tree stumps and railway line.

Adrian follows her, waving the can and splashing the water just behind her, a thin spray catching her as she screams happily. She turns, just beyond the shelter, and comes back in a wide arc of a circle towards Josie.

He is closer to her now, swinging the can back and forth with splashes of water hitting her repeatedly. He could catch her easily but keeps far enough back to get her wet but not so close that she over-reaches herself and falls over. She runs into her mother's open arms and they fall back onto the bedsheet laughing.

Adrian slides onto his knees as he catches up and falls theatrically on top, grabbing them in his arms and rolling back and forth. I look away, feeling awkward and embarrassed to be sitting here watching this show-off behaviour with its laughter and breathlessness and grunts. But I am relieved that they did not go down the steps. All I have to do now is to get up and suggest we all go indoors to lie down and cool off.

I am about to speak, to mention, ooh la la, a siesta, when the little girl wriggles free from Josie and Adrian.

She sits up and speaks. "Why," she asks, quite curiously, "are there scarecrows in that house?"

And, just as I feared, she points at the air-raid shelter.

FRIDAY 28 JULY, 2.43PM

There is, for a moment, complete and utter silence.

I hear nothing from the road or railway line, nor from the neighbours to either side.

Neither Adrian nor Josie speak. The child's hand remains out-stretched.

I am thinking fast, the thoughts and idea tumbling through my head. I can laugh, deriding the child's nonsense. But she might break free, running forward, insisting they all look through the crack in the door. And they might follow, humouring her by peering in. "Oh My God," Josie would cry out, scream even, "Adrian, look!"

But instead, "Ssshhh," the young woman says quietly to the child, "… don't be silly."

I could pretend 'scarecrows' was a game we played when I babysat the girl. That these magic scarecrows were there but now they are hiding somewhere else. We'd look in the bungalow, turning the game into hide-and-seek. But what if the little girl tried to hide in the air-raid shelter? Started screaming for help when she realised what the scarecrows really were.

Adrian glances at me and away. I don't know what he's thinking.

And then it comes to me. A story. I'd pretend I'd been telling her a story about scarecrows. But I can imagine the little girl standing there, hands on hips, "No!" she'd shout. "No, no, no! That never happened!" And, to placate her, they'd go down to the shelter. Adrian would wrench open the door, "Look, see..." he'd say smiling, before stepping inside.

What else can I do?

I smile, followed by a warm, friendly laugh.

And I start my story.

"Once upon a time," I say, "there were two scarecrows standing in a field at Mr McDonald's farm. Can you remember what they were called, Lily? When I told you the story?"

I look at her with a patient expression on my face. She shakes her head, puzzled.

"The scarecrows were called Tommy and Tina. And their job was to keep the crows... all the birds... away from Mr McDonald's... flowers... and corn... and... strawberries. You remember the story I told you, don't you Lily?"

She shakes her head again but relaxes now, expecting a story, and leaning back into her mother, who moves a little from one side to the other to get them both comfortable. I go on.

"One day, Mr McDonald came out of the farmhouse and walked into the field where Tommy and Tina were standing."

(So far so good, she's paying attention.)

"'Where,' asked Mr McDonald, looking around, 'are all my lovely flowers? My beautiful roses and my sweet tulips and my big yellow daffodils?'"

"Tommy and Tina stood very still."

"'And where,' asked Mr McDonald, going very red in the face, 'is all the corn that I was going to gather in with my tractor this afternoon?'"

"Tommy and Tina did not move at all."

(She's following the story. She's forgotten all about the shelter. She has her thumb in her mouth now.)

"'And where are all the strawberries for my tea?' shouted Mr McDonald, jumping up and down."

(I move the top half of my body up and down as if I am jumping and the little girl laughs and turns her face into Josie's stomach, all of a sudden tired now.)

"Tommy and Tina were as still as they could be."

"'The rabbits have eaten all the flowers,' said Mr McDonald. 'The squirrels have eaten the corn. And I just don't know who's eaten all of my lovely strawberries! Was it you?'"

"Tommy and Tina just stood there ever so quietly."

"'Wait there,' shouted Mr McDonald. 'I'm going to get my axe from the shed and chop you into a thousand tiny pieces to put on my fire!' And he hurried away towards the shed."

(The little girl laughs and looks at Josie, who smiles back at her and then at me. Adrian has his head down. I know he is embarrassed by me and the story I am telling and the lively way I am telling it. I have to, of course, to distract the child.)

"Tommy looked at Tina. Tina looked at Tommy."

"They both turned slowly, as scarecrows do, towards the shed and saw Mr McDonald coming out with his big red axe."

"'Run!' they shouted to each other at the same time. And run they did!"

(I lean forward towards the child.)

"They ran across the field."

(I squiggle two fingers across the girl's knees.)

"They ran up the hill."

(I run my fingers a little way up the top of the girl's left thigh.)

"They ran down the hill."

(I run my fingers back down the girl's left thigh.)

"They swam across a river."

(I paddle my two fingers between the girl's knees.)

"And reached the other side."

(I move my two fingers onto her right knee.)

"They ran down the train tracks."

(I run my fingers down her right ankle.)

"And jumped down off the tracks."

(I put my fingers between her feet, flicking them back and forth.)

"And hid. And kept very, very still and really, really quiet."

(I keep my fingers unmoving by her feet and look at her. She looks back, hanging on my every word.)

I think, for a second or two, that I have made a fatal mistake. That I have drawn everyone's attention back to the air-raid shelter. Where the scarecrows in my story have been hiding. Josie looks across at me, an encouraging 'go on' expression on her face. The little girl waits patiently. Adrian still has his head bowed in embarrassment. And then I suddenly see my way out.

"As Tommy and Tina sat there, as quiet as they could be, they heard big heavy footsteps."

(I bang my fists on the ground.)

"Boom, boom, boom!"

(I bang my fists again, harder, one, two, three times.)

"Boom! Boom! Boom!"

(The little girl stares across at me, an excited-to-be-scared look on her face.)

"'Where are you?' shouted Mr McDonald. 'Come out, come out, wherever you are!'"

"Tommy and Tina did not move. They were very, very scared. Of Mr McDonald. And of Mr McDonald's big sharp axe."

(I pretend to swing an axe around and above my head. The young woman squeals and pulls the little girl tighter. Adrian sits there furious, wishing I would stop.)

"'Where are you?' shouted Mr McDonald again. 'I'm going to chop you up with my axe into a hundred pieces... a thousand pieces... a million pieces... a billion, trillion pieces.'"

"Tommy and Tina held their breath as the farmer was very, very close."

(I look at the little girl, suck in my breath and hold it, moment after moment, for as long as I can. I can see her tense, holding her breath too. I let mine out in a long spluttery shudder and then draw it back in as noisily as I can. I wait, sensing Adrian's shame-faced tension, and then continue.)

"Boom! Boom! Boom!"

"Tommy and Tina sat there shivering with fear."

"Boom, boom, boom."

"They could hear Mr McDonald moving away, further and further from their hiding place."

"Boom, boom, boom."

"They could hear his footsteps moving into the distance."

"Boom... boom... boom."

"Tommy and Tina breathed a sigh of relief... He'd gone!"

(The little girl breathes out and relaxes, cuddling into Josie. Adrian looks at me at last. It is a steady, sour look that unsettles me. I have not seen such a look before. I try to ignore it as I go on.)

"Tommy and Tina looked at each other. They both knew the farmer would come back on his way home to the farm. 'Run!' they shouted to each other. 'Run! Run! Run!' And they got up and ran and ran and ran just as fast as they could and ran and ran and ran and ran and ran and ran one more time and they were never ever, ever seen again... they lived happily ever after in a field on another farm far, far away for ever and ever."

I sit back, satisfied with my story. No more talk of scarecrows in the air-raid shelter now, that's for sure! I smile at Josie and Lily and they smile back all big and warm and friendly. I ignore sour-faced Adrian. There is another silence, but a more companionable one this time; my story has broken the ice with Josie and Lily.

"Josie? Lily?"

A loud, angry, bellowing voice. We all jump.

Leon is here.

FRIDAY 28 JULY, 2.54PM

Josie is up, grabbing her bag, pulling the girl into her arms, and running towards the air-raid shelter.

Adrian is slow to react, knocking over a beaker and then treading on it as he stands up.

I am quicker, surprising myself, running after the young woman and reaching her as she puts her left foot on the first step down.

I tug her back by the shoulder, and she turns and looks at me as she steadies herself, mistaking the expression on my face as the same fear as hers.

"Not here," I gabble, "… no exit… the garage is… safer."

She follows me as I hurry back to the garage, open the side door and the four of us, Adrian a few steps behind, stumble inside.

I push the door to, just slightly ajar so I can hear outside.

We stand there breathing heavily.

Trying to listen, to hear this Leon.

He is out in the road as far as I can tell, walking up and down, to and fro, shouting out their names one after the other again and again. Off his head, I assume. Drugged up, a mix of rage and insanity. He knows they are here, somewhere. His woman. His child. His wounded, bestial pride. This side of the road, maybe. Inside one of six, eight, possibly ten houses. Yelling their names, to scare them, to try to get them to come out.

How long will it be?

Before his drug-raddled fury drives him to force his way into each house in turn.

And when will he get to this bungalow?

I move to the garage door, can hear him now further up the road to the left, up the hill. Not so far away that I cannot hear his cries of "Josie" and "Bitch" and "Whore" and "Slut" as he stands there demanding she comes out.

"We should phone the police," says Adrian quietly to Josie. "Anonymously," he adds.

She shakes her head. "He'll go," she answers, "when he doesn't get a response. He'll go and cool off somewhere. We just have to wait."

Josie bends to cuddle and say a few quiet words to the child. She looks up at Josie with her big eyes and nods her head.

"If you call the police," I say quietly, more of a whisper, "he'll tell them Josie's name and that policewoman or that policeman will put two and two together and come here."

"And you wouldn't want that, would you?" says Adrian, who glares at me with what looks like anger. "Would you?" he repeats, louder.

I hold his gaze, defy him, go to answer calmly and reasonably, but this Leon calls out again and this time, this time, it sounds as though he is directly outside, by the edge of the driveway.

"Lil… y," he calls out this time in a sing-song voice. "Lil… y."

A pause.

"Daddy's here. With a birthday present for you. Come and see."

"Birthday?" I ask.

"Last month, six weeks ago," the young woman replies.

I nod, looking at the little girl, who seems excited but confused.

There is a silence outside as if this Leon is listening, waiting for something to happen.

I am hot, have been so hot in this weather. But I feel a trickle of sweat running down my back. A sense of fear. The breaking of the front door at any moment.

I cannot bear it much longer.

The sense of dread.

That everything is circling around me.

And then, as suddenly as he came, he is gone, at least for now, further down the hill to the right where I hear him repeating his plaintive cries of "Lil… y… Lil…y."

"What will he do next?" I ask Josie.

She stands up, releasing the child, and answers with a shrug, "He'll hang around for a while, I guess, see if any of us come out. Then he'll pass out on a bench or in a park. He'll be back round at my place this evening, forcing his way in."

I nod, thinking, working through the options. She and the child and Adrian won't go back there. No chance of that now. I can't have a fuss made, though, calling the police, anything like that.

And if her place is left untouched, this Leon will simply keep roaming back and forth between here and there until he sees one of them. God alone knows what might happen then.

But if her place is emptied – stripped bare of her belongings – he may just think she's moved away. Been rehoused. He may then not come here again. And it will give them – the three of them – time to find somewhere else.

"While he's here, round here, go and get their belongings," I say to Adrian. "Cut along the train track to the top and then come out and get yourself a taxi. Bring the stuff back here later. Get the taxi driver to come up on the drive and into here and through this way so you won't be seen."

He stares at me with such a look. I thought he would be grateful, appreciative. I don't know what he's thinking, nor what to say. He has always been a thoughtless, worthless boy.

She answers, saying she has her keys in her bag and a ten-pound note for the taxi. Before she opens it, she leans forward and puts her hands on the top of my arms, one to the left, one to the right, and holds me tight. I don't know what to do.

She kisses me, missing my cheek as I move my head slightly and her lips touch the side of my mouth.

She whispers, "Thank you." I imagine her, suddenly, saying, "I love you" in the same, slightly husky voice.

And I do not know what to say for the moment as I am moved by her words and actions.

The little girl smiles up at me as if she knows I have done a truly wonderful thing and she reaches out her hand. We turn and walk, hand-in-hand, out of the garage and towards the bungalow. Josie follows, arm-in-arm, with Adrian. It is a marvellous, magical moment.

If only Adrian wasn't so sour-faced and sulky, we would be the perfect happy family.

The four of us.

Maybe just three.

FRIDAY 28 JULY, 3.08PM

Inside the bungalow, I let go of Lily's hand and she and Josie lead the way into Adrian's bedroom. Adrian follows them as I move down the hallway to the front door to look out for Leon. I stand there, sweating away and watching the road.

All clear. To the left and to the right.

But he is there somewhere, nearby.

And Adrian needs to get out and away without being seen by him.

I step back, out of sight, as I see the two fat slobs who live next door coming along the pavement, carrying stretched and sagging plastic supermarket bags full of cheese quavers and orange fizzy drinks and God-knows-what junk foods. I notice, and I have seen this often when I have investigated husbands and wives, that they are remarkably similar in appearance.

They are both dark and intense-looking and short and stocky, maybe 5 foot 2 or 3. I would guess that both would tip the scales in excess of 16 or 17 stones. They are husband and wife but could, to be frank, be brother and sister, if not twins. They are both from Norwich originally, I believe, and that sort of thing is quite common there, of course.

I see, as her breasts swing slowly back and forth, that she is not wearing a bra under her dark blue T-shirt. I imagine, for a moment, what she would look like topless and whether, when they are shouting and singing loudly in their back garden, she is half-naked at these times. I contemplate this as the slobs turn into their driveway and out of sight.

"I'm going now," says Adrian, walking up behind me.

He is so close that, if I turn, I will collide with him.

I stand there, my back to him, not wanting him to see my arousal.

Adrian takes another step towards me; we are almost touching. He drops his voice, so that Josie and Lily cannot hear, and says, "I want you to wait here." He says forcefully, "By the front door. For 15 minutes. Can you do that, wait here?"

Taken aback by his sudden show of authority, his big-man approach for Josie, I nod my reply. His proximity, and I can feel him brushing against my back, makes me feel uncomfortable.

"I am going out the back way. I have my mobile phone. I want you to wait here for 15 minutes. Check your watch."

I do, making a show of it.

"Yes," I reply, "15 minutes."

The boy is scared, expecting this Leon to reappear at any moment.

He has 15 minutes to get away.

I need to be careful that this Leon does not see me, my presence, my watching, giving the game away.

I turn, to say something, to ask Adrian what he wants me to do if I see Leon. But he is already walking down the hallway. He stops, puts his head inside the bedroom door to say something, goodbye I assume, to Josie and Lily. I turn away, watching the road again.

A steady flow of traffic up and down.

One or two people passing by, a boy on a bike. A group of stupid, giggling girls. An old woman with her shopping trolley. Mrs Gibbs, I believe. Her son was a tax dodger; taken to court and fined. I'd have sent him to prison. Teach him and the other cheats a lesson.

No sign of Leon, though.

I stand here, waiting, and it strikes me suddenly that this is the worst thing I could do. Leon knows they are here somewhere. But he does not know where for sure. If he comes back down the road, he will shout and curse and call out, but, in broad daylight, with people coming and going, I do not think he will do more than that. If the bungalow appears locked and empty, he will simply pass on by.

Unless he sees me standing guard.

Then he will come striding up the path, shouting in my face, jabbing his finger in my chest. "Where the fuck is Josie?"

They might make a noise inside and then we are all done for.

I turn and walk back down the hallway. I stop and look into Adrian's bedroom. Josie is stretched out on the bed, her head on Adrian's pillow, the child's head resting on her bare stomach, her knees raised and her legs slightly apart. I cannot help but look and imagine. I am not sure whether to speak as they look as though they are both asleep or close to it. I think Josie is trying to act calm to soothe the child; not that she seems all that aware of what's going on.

I imagine Josie lying there naked.

And what I would like to do.

If the little girl was not there.

I decide to get a glass of cold water from the kitchen and to spend some time in my room, with the fan on, thinking about things. Josie, maybe. I may, in fact, have a little rest for an hour or two, as I think Josie and Lily are doing, until Adrian returns with their clothes and belongings and we can regroup.

Or perhaps I might wake Josie early.

See if the little girl wants to sleep on.

Josie and I can spend some time together.

As I move into the kitchen, I reach for a tumbler from inside a cupboard and go to the sink to run cold water from the tap. I have to run it a while for it to go really cold. Next to the sink, I have a row of squashes: orange, summer fruits (for Adrian) and Ribena. They do the Ribena in a sugar-free version these days – for fatty diabetics – but I much prefer the original. It has a nicer taste. I pour a thick inch of Ribena into the glass and, having run the tap for another minute or two, I top it up with cold water. Lovely.

As I lift it to my lips, I look out of the window.

I see Adrian, his back to me.

He has forced open the air-raid shelter door and now, as I watch, he steps inside.

FRIDAY 28 JULY, 10.12AM

I sit on my bed in my room, as hot as ever, still sweating, even though the temperature drops a few degrees at night. The heat still torments me. But the bungalow is quiet and peaceful; they are asleep in the bedroom. All I can hear is the slow screeching and squealing of a train and its containers edging their way slowly along the track at the bottom of the garden. On and on it goes, as it seems to do all night, every night.

I did not expect to write another diary entry; not now, not ever, not having covered everything and come to terms with it all. Every last thing. I have absolved myself. But I will now write one more, final time and then, instead of tearing out various pages here and there, I will destroy the whole diary and move on with my life once and for all. There are better times ahead for me now.

I cannot keep looking back, dwelling on matters. It is not good for me. What is done is done. I have things straight in my mind. I have accepted and made sense of it all. I did what I had to do and that's that. I had no choice. I had to kill Adrian.

I picked up the hand-held fire extinguisher, the heaviest thing to hand, from beside the kitchen bin. I opened the back door, closed it behind me – so that Josie and Lily would not hear – and ran down the garden towards the air-raid shelter as fast as I could.

As I got to the steps, Adrian had turned and was standing inside the doorway. He had his hands to his face and his mouth hung open and his eyes stared straight forward into space. It was hard not to think of Edvard Munch's 'The Scream' (a picture I have always rather liked) at that instant.

I believe, writing now, that talk of scarecrows and the air-raid shelter had raised his suspicions and, hardly being able to believe it, he thought he'd put his mind to rest by checking before he set off down the track to Josie's.

He did not seem able to focus even as I moved into the doorway, put my hand on his chest and pushed him back just as hard as I could down the stairs inside the shelter. He stumbled, took two steps backwards, then seemed to lose his feet from underneath him and tumbled back and fell heavily to the floor, already dazed.

I hit him with the fire extinguisher. About the head. Many times. I do not know how many. Very many is all I would say. Too many.

He was dead at the end of it. And I found myself crying, sobbing even. As I am doing now.

I must stop writing for a moment, gather myself together. I am not a bad man. I am not cruel or nasty or violent or evil. I am a calm and rational man. I do only what has to be done. What I have to do. No more than that.

I do not doubt Adrian would have called the police once he had pulled himself together. I had only seconds to spare. There would have been no reasoning with him, no chance of explanation. No way of getting him to see sense. To explain the reasons why. He was always his mother's son, not mine, not really. He was what they call a mummy's boy.

I contemplate whether his instruction for me to wait by the front door was nothing to do with Leon and all to do with giving him time to check and then dial 999. I would, if I had stood at the front door for much longer, have seen the police cars racing to my driveway. I would have been arrested. Charged. Put on trial. Sentenced, no doubt, to life, perhaps many times over. The rest of my days would be completely ruined. I might even die in prison. So, the fact of the matter is, I had to do it.

I knew, when I had finished, that he was dead. I had, to use a rather childlike expression, 'bashed his brains out'. There was surprisingly little blood and mess all things considered. If I had had some of those cleaning wipes that people use in kitchens these days, I could have wiped and tidied things and, sitting him up with his head at a slight angle, it would have looked as though he were simply sleeping. I have never used wipes, though, preferring a proper cloth you can wring out and use time and again. I had nothing like that to hand either, though.

I pulled Adrian past her and him and pushed him flat across the back of the shelter. I then took his phone to stamp on and to throw the bits on the railway line. It occurred to me at this point that if I were to move her and him too, to a similar position at the back, they would not be readily visible unless you came most of the way down the stairs, and actually into the shelter.

I did this as best I could and I will not dwell on the matter other than to say that, given the intense heat of late, the bodies were in a state of considerable decay. The heat, the smell and the flies, big fat bloated flies buzzing in and out, combined to make me physically sick more than once. It was not until after I had left and secured the door and walked down towards the train track to stand and breathe that I regained my composure and was not physically sick again. It took a good while.

I am now what the television and newspapers would call a serial killer. I have taken three lives. Her. Him. Adrian. I do not deny those. But I do not count anything else; dirty puppies or cats who soil my flower beds. I am not Jack the Ripper. I am not a proper, nasty murderer.

I do not know how I would describe myself actually. It is something of a conundrum. The fact is that I had thought about killing her, but that is all. She was having an affair and would have left me and taken half of everything, leaving me destitute! I do not think I would have done anything, though. Not really. Not me. But then she smirked and laughed at me – quite openly – as I debated what to do when she was standing by the bin; it was that sniggering – her laughing at me – that caused me to momentarily lose my calm. When I had recovered myself, I did only what I had to do.

Him? I did not ask him to come round! But I had to get him to come into my bungalow when he did. I could not have him on the doorstep hollering and then, if I shut the door in his stupid face, going away and calling the police with his wretched suspicions. Even when he was in the bungalow, I would not have done anything. But he insisted – he was adamant – that he was going to call the police. So that was that.

Adrian – the thought of that upsets me, actually. But I now have to be strong and not let it get to me too much. I have much to look forward to. Me and Josie and the girl. We are, in our own funny little way, something of a family.

Several minutes later, after I had checked myself over, for signs of blood or mess on my hands or clothes or shoes, I turned away from the railway track to go back indoors. Looking up, I saw, framed in the doorway, the little girl watching me.

I did not know how long she had been there.

Nor what she had seen.

I beckoned her forward urgently – be quick!

She came down the garden and stopped just in front of me. She looked up, with her mock innocent face. I thought quickly, remembering she was asleep when I went into the kitchen and saw Adrian on the steps.

How long was I in the shelter?

Five, six minutes?

And out of it, by the railway line?

Five, six minutes more?

I thought, at worst, she might have seen me coming out of the shelter and being sick by the railway line. I grasped her arm, leaned forward and spoke quietly and forcefully.

"Keep away from the shelter, do you hear me? Keep away."

(She did not respond until I repeated myself and she then gave what seemed to be a quick nod of agreement.)

"The scarecrows are back and they are hiding in the shelter from Mr McDonald."

(She looked up at me with her big brown eyes, ever so serious.)

"Keep away from the shelter. Otherwise Mr McDonald will kill you. He. Will. Kill. You."

(She looked frightened and went to pull herself away from me to run back into the bungalow.)

I grabbed her, going down on my knees to hug her and hold her. "Don't say anything. Please don't frighten Mummy," I whispered into her ear. She struggled a little, perhaps more than a little, but I held her even tighter and kept whispering sweet things to her until she seemed to relax into my arms. "It's our secret, Lily. Just you and me. Please don't scare Mummy." And so, with me holding her arm, we went back into the bungalow to see 'Mummy'.

I was worried, had expected even, that the girl might say something to Josie about the scarecrows, Mr McDonald, the air-raid shelter – what I said, how I said it – the moment she saw her. I stood close by, ready to do something, I was not sure what, if she did.

But the little girl simply reached out her hand, as Josie awoke, and sat up on the bed, and stroked Josie's arm over and over again, as you might do with a purring cat. After a moment or two, Josie was up and moving into the kitchen to get the girl some squash and a piece of fruit.

I followed and we pottered around like a happy little family. By the time we sat down in the living room, I knew all was well and, if I might be forgiven for a moment of jollity at this point, I couldn't help but think that we might live happily ever after.

SATURDAY 29 JULY, 3.13AM

I awake suddenly, not sure what it is that has disturbed me. I sit up in bed, listening. My first thoughts are that this Leon has broken in, either through the front door or the side gate, the noise alerting my subconscious mind to imminent danger. I reach for the kitchen knife I keep tucked behind the clock on the bedside cabinet. Hold it ready.

But all is quiet.

No noise from inside the bungalow.

Nothing outside either.

I wait, knowing that something is wrong, amiss in some way and that whatever it is will become apparent at any moment. I cannot relax until I know what it is. I wonder, for a second, whether Josie has upped and gone and taken the little girl with her, the sound of the door shutting behind her waking me.

"Where's Adrian?" she had started asking from early evening onwards. "He should be back by now." Over and over again, she said it, getting on my nerves (not that I showed it).

I said, so many times through the evening, one way and another, that it would have taken a while for him to get to her place, gather her things, wait until dark and all was clear before getting a taxi back. It all takes time, I emphasised. Nothing to worry about, I said, repeating myself time and again.

"He's not answering his phone," she said, echoing herself, in various ways, as the evening progressed. "Leon… Leon might have… What if Leon…" She would begin to say, as if thinking out loud before checking herself and falling silent.

I told her to wait, until morning, before deciding what to do. That Adrian may have seen Leon outside her home and that he was keeping his head down until he'd gone. "But he's not answering his phone," she'd reply every time and I had no real answer to this other than to say he might have dropped it somewhere, climbing over a gate along the railway line on his way out. She shook her head, unconvinced. And so we moved towards bedtime in an uneasy silence.

I realise suddenly what has woken me. A flash of lightning lights up the sky outside my window.

One-Mississippi, two-Mississippi, three-Missis…

The loudest clap of thunder I've ever heard. The heatwave, thank God, is ending. And we are about to get rain. Lots of it, I suspect.

When Josie and Lily went to bed in Adrian's room, with Josie still going on and on about his phone and him not answering it, I decided I had to do something; otherwise, by morning, she would be in such a state that she would insist on going to the police. I cannot have the police back here. Her. Him. Adrian. Piecing it all together. I simply cannot, no matter what I had to do.

What I did was very simple. I took the landline phone from its base in the kitchen and put it on my bedside cabinet. I dug out her old mobile phone from her handbag at the back of my wardrobe. I charged it a little. A fiddly affair, but no matter. Enough of a charge to make a call anyway. I then thought for a few minutes before pressing the numbers of the landline phone carefully on the buttons of the mobile phone. A pause. Clicking. The landline phone started ringing. I put the mobile phone behind me, under the pillow, out of sight.

I let the landline phone ring on until I heard Adrian's door being opened carefully. Imagined Josie tip-toing across to my door and standing there, waiting and listening for news of Adrian. And then I spoke my quickly made-up and rehearsed lines as I answered the phone.

"Hello?... Dawn!... How are you?... How's your dad?"

(A pause for the answer. I could imagine Josie at the door, listening intently. I made various commiserating noises before I spoke again.)

"Oh no... I'm so sorry to hear that... do you want me to come up?"

(I'm a clever man, I am, I really am.)

"Adrian's with you?... Well, I was puzzled where he'd got to!... It's good to know he's safe. He left so quickly. You must have called him."

(Another pause, a long-ish one, as if I were listening to her endless woes and misfortunes. Again I made various comments, "yes", "oh dear", "lost his phone", and so on until I thought it was time to end the conversation.)

"Well, look, Dawn, don't worry. And tell Adrian not to worry about his phone either. All is well here... Yes... well, I'll wait to hear from you again soon... Once you've heard from the coroner... next week? Yes... lots of love to you and Adrian, Dawn. Speak soon... Love you too... Bye... bye."

(I could not help but smile to myself as I clicked the phone off and I could hear the floorboards in the hall creaking as Josie crept away back to the bedroom. I will tell her the 'news', as if I don't know she heard my one-sided 'conversation', in the morning.)

And now, with peace and happiness in the bungalow at last, at long, long last, the rain starts to fall. It is as if the heavens themselves have opened.

Torrential, I hear it on the roof and on the windows.

On and on it goes, 40 days and 40 nights worth all in one go.

I pull the half-open window to. Lie back on my bed, satisfied. Josie and Lily are here. They will not leave because this Leon is out there somewhere. They are safe in the bungalow.

They will be happy too without Adrian, at least for a while. I will, in a week or so, tell them that Adrian has stayed on to help with clearing up and selling her father's house. Then, later, that he has met and fallen in love with someone else and won't be coming back.

Josie will be upset, of course she will, poor thing. There will be tears and sadness. She will sob and cry and throw herself dramatically on the bed, kicking her legs up and down, close to hysterics. I will be there, naturally. Sitting and waiting. Until she is ready.

She will sit up, her shoulders slumped, and I will take my place next to her on the bed. "There, there," I will murmur gently as she leans against me and rests her head on my shoulder. I will put my arm around her and pull her close. And she will look up at me with tears in her eyes. And I will kiss them dry for her.

For the first time in weeks, I pull the duvet up and over me and snuggle down.

Josie and me. And Lily. An odd little family perhaps, but a family nonetheless.

Happy days lie ahead.

Happy days.

Happy, happy days.

Part Four

THE RAINS

SATURDAY 29 JULY 7.51AM

Today is, as people say, the first day of the rest of my life.

And very good it is too.

It is one of many perfect days that lie ahead.

Josie and Lily are in the living room, sitting at the table, waiting patiently to begin their breakfast. I am preparing this in the kitchen, going back and forth, wanting to get it all just so on this wonderful day. I am not – usually – a fussy sort of chap but I am this morning and I feel rather embarrassed, bashful really, about this, but in a nice, excited kind of way.

I do not think I have ever felt so happy.

We are a family. We really are.

And I know, yes, I am certain, we will all live happily ever after.

I am putting together a breakfast you'd have in a four-star hotel. A bit of a treat really for the girls. (I won't say "my girls", not yet anyway!) It is a continental breakfast as Josie and Lily are both vegetarians, of course; something I have thought about but will now consider fully, talking to Josie about it at length at some point today before converting. I think she would like that.

I tick off, mentally, what is on the table so far. After the plates and bowls and knives and forks and such like, I put some yoghurts down. One is just outside of its sell-by date but is far too good to waste (it is not one of the usual Co-op own brands). I have taken off the lid to indicate that one is for me. I added a jar of honey. Another of lemon curd (which I rather like). But no marmalade.

(I opened a jar of marmalade recently with Adrian and it had a little growth of green mould in the middle and he made his usual gagging and retching noises. "There," I said, scooping off the mould with a teaspoon, "the rest of it is fine." But it seemed to make things worse, what with his wide-eyed, gulping noises and all, and so I ended up throwing it away.)

I have just done some toast, white and brown, cut into triangles and looking rather nice in their own little toast racks. I have put these on the tray with a tub of fancy margarine. Not a Co-op own brand or anything like that. I then add a box of cornflakes and another of shredded wheat, both Kelloggs, along with a cup full of sugar and a small jug of milk, and there we are, 'good to go'.

I smile at Josie as I sit down at the table and she smiles back.

Lily does not look at me but turns away. Sulky little madam!

I do not say anything, not today. Another time, yes. I will start correcting her behaviour soon enough. It is important she learns her table manners. For now, I will let it pass.

"It's still raining," I say conversationally, looking out across the garden. "All night long."

Josie twists to look out of the window too and smiles at me as she turns back to the table. "It will be good for the garden and the flowers. It will save you watering everything."

I smile and nod my reply as if agreeing, although I have never really watered anything much out the back. I have always near enough left the garden to its own devices.

I am curious how long this rain will last and what will happen if the air-raid shelter floods. I have a terrible image, all of a sudden, of three bloated corpses full of wriggling maggots floating about inside the flooded shelter. I dismiss it. I cannot think of such things any more. Maggots. And eye sockets. And rats nesting in chest cavities. I must put them all behind me.

"Would you…" I go to say.

"Have you…" she says at the same moment.

We both laugh together, happily, and I gesture for her to go first.

"Do you have some water, tap water, for us, for Lily?"

I suddenly realise that, among all the goodies on display, I have not put out anything to drink. Not even glasses. Silly me!

"Yes, yes, of course," I say, feeling myself redden. I get up to go to the kitchen as Josie leans towards Lily and says something. I don't catch what it is but assume it must be something like "Cheer up" or "Sit up straight" or words to that effect. Naughty little girl.

I return with a jug of tap water and three glasses and put these on the table. I then go back into the kitchen as I remember I have two half-full cartons of juice inside the fridge door, one apple, one orange, which they might like.

"What's the matter?" I ask as I go back in and see Josie picking at the rim of the glass while the child sits back in her chair, kicking her legs to and fro against the table leg.

Josie looks up, a little surprised. I came back in quicker than expected. She mumbles something about thinking there was a hair-line crack in the glass. I take it from her and hold it to the light. The glass is a little smudged and dusty as it has been at the back of the cupboard for a while and I forgot to give them all a wipe over in my haste.

"Here," I say, pushing my glass towards her and hoping it is cleaner, "have mine."

She takes it and, without looking, pours herself and then Lily some water.

"Come on," I add. "Eat up, lots to choose from!"

I observe Josie as she carefully takes a piece of brown toast and runs the edge of her knife along the top of the margarine in its tub. She looks at but does not take any honey or lemon curd. She then bites carefully into the toast.

Adrian used to make a gagging noise if he saw a smidgen of butter or a crumb of toast – "stuff" as he called it – in any of the jars. "It makes me think of bogeys," he once said when he was younger.

But Josie did not open either of the jars to look inside so I think she simply does not like them.

I make a mental note to get some marmalade or maybe some Marmite when I go to the shops. Anything for 'our Josie' as I have taken to thinking of her.

She is a precise eater, and rather nice to watch. I notice she is wearing the same clothes as yesterday and wonder whether this might become an issue soon. The girl too is wearing the same clothes and hers look crumpled and creased as if she has slept in them. I don't think Josie slept in her clothes. She would have taken them off. Slept in her underwear or possibly even naked. I do not want to think about that. Not now, anyway. Not yet. Maybe later when I am on my own.

I reach for the radio, which I have on the side of the table, and turn on Radio 4, just in time to hear the eight o'clock pips.

Adrian and I had hardly any conversation about the news. He just listened to my comments with little more than a nod or a grunt. I might as well have been talking to a brick wall.

I think Josie and I, once we get to know each other better, will talk freely and openly about all sorts of matters. Politics, the economy and so on, enjoying our time together at the start to the day. I will enjoy teaching her the ways of the world. She will be an apt pupil.

I go to say something, to comment, to ask what she wants to

do today, when the little girl, whose legs have been swinging back and forth, kicks me. It seems to me that she did it deliberately. For attention. To get between Josie and me.

I look at her sternly but do not say anything.

"Lily," says Josie in a slightly raised voice.

And to me, "She doesn't usually have a proper breakfast like this."

I smile, not sure what to say.

Josie goes on, "She usually has Coco Pops watching cartoons on the telly."

I nod, "Well, I can get some of those from the shops later this morning. I think the Co-op has them. She can do that tomorrow. Watch television." (I'm not sure I agree with this, but still. We'll see.)

The girl seems to perk up a little at my words and, with some gentle cajoling from Josie, she eats one piece of brown toast followed, slowly and almost reluctantly, by another.

"She likes Nutella," says Josie, as if that explains the child's reluctance to eat. I must have looked uncertain as she adds, "It's a chocolate spread." I go to say, "For breakfast?" but manage to stop myself and smile instead.

For a few minutes, we are all quiet, each of us drinking and eating happily enough. I note they eat only the toast, the brown toast, as I eat the white, and Josie politely declines another round.

I eat a yoghurt and then a bowl of cornflakes, crunching my way through the silence as quietly and as slowly as I can. They sit waiting for me to finish. I feel a little awkward.

I notice the little girl glaring theatrically at Josie whenever she thinks I am not looking. I ignore it, as does Josie.

Today's weather report is on the radio and I lean forward to listen, to see how long it will rain for and whether it has broken for good the endless, day-after-day, week-after-week, heat. It will give us something to talk about, to chew over, to debate. To enjoy each other's thoughts.

As I do, the girl makes a noise, halfway between a gurgling and blowing a raspberry, so that I cannot hear properly. On purpose, for sure.

I go to turn up the sound and then, astonishingly, the little girl sits up and reaches, almost sprawls, across the table, knocking over the box of cornflakes.

As her hand touches the radio, to turn the sound down or change the station, I'm not sure which, I grab it and hold it firmly. Both to stop her and, yes, to punish her. She falls silent in surprise that someone might actually prevent her from doing what she wants whenever she wants to do it.

It is all I can do not to squeeze her hand so tightly that she squeals – a well-deserved punishment for her bad behaviour.

But I let her hand go and she pulls back, knocking the jug of milk over her top. She sits there in sullen silence. I smile at Josie as if to say, there, no harm done.

The moment passes as Josie gets to her feet, picking up the glass and the box of cornflakes, and heads for the kitchen to find something to mop up the spilt milk. Reams of kitchen roll, no doubt.

As she leaves the room, I tut quietly and slowly, two or three times, to express my disapproval. The girl looks at me. She pulls a sort of smarmy, mock-sorry face. She does not mean it.

I look at her, staring her down.

And I think at this moment that, actually, I really don't like her much at all and wish she wasn't here, spoiling everything for Josie and me.

SATURDAY 29 JULY 9.23AM

I have been lying here on my bed, thinking about things, since breakfast. I am waiting for the rain to stop so that I can, assuming there is no sign of this Leon anywhere, go to the shops to get my daily milk and bread and other groceries. It is my habit. My routine. I enjoy it. The simplicity of my life.

I listen to the rain on the roof and at my window.

And think about things. Her. Him. Adrian.

And other things before that. Many years ago. The babies, mostly.

Josie, after breakfast, took herself and the child off to Adrian's room and then the bathroom. The door shut. Bath running. Taps turned on. I slowed as I walked by, on the way to the kitchen for a glass of water, and could hear them talking quietly. Their words obscured by the sound of running water. Josie telling the child to behave better? I could only hope. I think I could possibly live with a well-behaved child.

I stopped and listened again on the way back. All I could hear was splashing water. The two of them in the bath together. I could imagine that very easily. But do not want to. Not yet. Not until we are closer. Friends. Perhaps more. Time will tell.

Truth be told, I never really wanted children. The babies. Nor Adrian.

When there is a child, the mother puts them first, before anyone else. Every time. Nothing else matters.

The husband, the father, is there to do little more than provide. Money. Food. His wants and needs, his feelings, his heart and soul, do not matter. He becomes nothing.

I hear the bathroom door being opened and the soft footsteps of Josie and the child walking back to Adrian's room. I imagine

Josie wrapped in the bath towel, her hair wet and tied back, her skin still glistening with specks of water. The hand towel wrapped around the child's waist.

I must tell Josie that there are other towels in the airing cupboard. I should also, some time soon, buy some more. I cannot remember when new ones were last purchased. The ones I have are scratchy and threadbare in places. Our Josie deserves better!

I think, aimlessly, about what Josie and the child will do. What they will wear.

If they will simply put back on the clothes they have been wearing.

Or whether Josie will come, wrapped in the towel, asking me to go to her house to fetch some clothes.

The rain seems to be starting to ease, ever so slightly. I think that it will soon clear and a soft hazy sun will appear and the air will feel fresh and clean after the long stifling heat we have endured. It will be as if the rain has washed away the heatwave and all that came with it and the summer can begin again, warm and gentle this time. As it should be.

I sit up. Josie is tapping gently at my door. "Come in," I call out.

She stands there, in one of Adrian's old T-shirts, black with a skull logo on it. She is wearing it as a dress, her legs long and bare, and I wonder if she is wearing underwear or not. I feel myself moving and flush with embarrassment. She does not seem to notice as she starts talking conversationally.

"I'm wearing this, this morning, if that's okay, and Lily's in her underwear... in the bedroom... as I've just rinsed her things through and hung them up. The milk would start to smell if it gets hot again later... I seem to have been wearing the same things for ages... I just fancy a change." She looks at me and smiles, as if waiting for my approval to wear Adrian's clothes.

"Hang them over the radiator in the bathroom," I reply. "I'll get up in a minute or two and turn the heating on and the radiators in the other rooms off so we don't get too hot... what will you do for clothes?"

She looks so beautiful that I catch my breath as I finish my question. Her hair pulled back from her almond-shaped face. She is sleek and willowy, all legs and arms and dainty, bare feet. I can almost smell her freshness and want to reach out to touch her, pull her into me, hold her tight. I'd never let her go.

She shrugs as if it is of no importance and replies, "We'll be okay for today. Lily's clothes will dry quite quickly as they're only thin and she can put those back on for today. Adey's got a pile of T-shirts I can wear and I can rinse out my things to dry overnight... maybe in a day or two, one evening, you could drive me back home to get some more?"

"Did you want to go back home to stay?" I find myself holding my breath as I wait for her answer. Fact is, at this moment, I don't want her to go.

She pulls a face. "I think... at the moment, with Leon as he is... out there somewhere waiting... I won't be safe. When Adey is back... I think we'd be looking to get our own place somewhere... and... I could work and maybe Lily could go to a nursery... but not round here. Leon won't stop if he thinks I'm with another man. I don't know. I... we feel safe here... if we could stay until Adey gets back?"

I nod and smile. "You call him Adey."

"Yes," she laughs. "And he calls me Pops."

"Pops?" I ask.

"After Popeye, the cartoon character." She flexes her muscles. "I used to do weights... and kick-boxing."

I smile at her. "You are safe here. No one knows where you are.

You could vanish in a puff of smoke as if you'd never been here. No one will find you. It would be as if you never existed."

She smiles at me, reassured, and then adds, "Do you think Adey will ring tonight? From his mum's?"

"Would he know your mobile number off by heart?"

She shakes her head, "No, I changed it not so long ago because Leon got hold of it... but Adey would have it on his mobile phone."

"His mum said he'd lost it, when she called... but he might call... in a night or two maybe... it all sounds rather traumatic up there right now... what with the old fellow dying."

She looks disappointed, so I continue talking, "Give him time, I'm sure he'll be back soon. A week or two, no more. And then you can pick up where you left off. You can stay here until then... for as long as you like really, you're no trouble."

She thinks for a bit and then smiles at me at last, looking a little happier, and adds, "Lily likes you."

"And I like her," I respond. (I don't, but what else can I say?)

"She can be mischievous at times. It's always just been her and me on our own... since I broke up with Leon... she runs rings round me sometimes. She can be wilful. I think she needs a father figure... and some friends to play with."

I nod, not sure what to say to that. What she needs, the madam, is a bloody good wallop and an evening shut in her room with the lights off and nothing to eat. That would teach her to behave, but I don't think this is something I should say to Josie. Instead, I nod and smile as if in agreement.

"Anyway, I'll let you get on," she says, turning to go back to Adrian's room. "You're going to the shops when it stops raining?"

I nod.

"If you get something nice, I could make us a lunch... it will give me something to do... I could be your housekeeper for you while we're here." She laughs and then goes on, looking around the room, "Just do some cooking and tidying around? A bit of cleaning. I'd not want paying… just to earn our keep."

I nod again in agreement and get up off my bed to follow her out of the bedroom. Josie turns into Adrian's room and I see the child lying on the floor scribbling inside a book. One of Adrian's. I also see some red and yellow scribbles on one of the walls. This angers me. The child is little more than a savage.

I am about to suggest to Josie that the child sits and watches the television in the living room for a while. Where she can do no harm or damage. It might also give Josie and me the time to talk, to chat and to get to know each other better.

As I start my words, I look out of the window. From where I am standing, I can see out into the road. It seems to have stopped raining, although I hardly notice that.

His car, over the way, has gone. Vanished. Disappeared. I don't know when.

I feel an unexpected surge of relief and can barely contain my joy.

The police have moved on with their enquiries and I am free. At last.

SATURDAY 29 JULY 9.57AM

It is raining slightly and I am sitting quietly in my bedroom again waiting for it to stop. Josie's words – "tidying around, a bit of cleaning" – are on my mind. I look at my room thinking how she must see it; the ancient flock wallpaper, the single beds with flowery duvets, the walnut-coloured wardrobe 'too good to throw away' when mother died, the ill-matching chest of drawers and bedside cabinets from when pine was fashionable and the peach-coloured carpet, which, I suspect, never really was.

It is old and faded as is everything in the bungalow. It all looks shabby and soiled, although I clean round regularly enough.

I feel ashamed and think it is time I bought a bucket and a sponge and a scraper and some paints, to freshen up the walls and the door frames and skirting boards. Give them a good going-over.

Josie will think better of me and will want to stay here, I think, if I can make the place look nicer. It will be something of a new start for us all.

She is a sweet-natured girl, is Josie. There is a lightness about her, a jolliness, that I find so appealing, and her looks are very attractive to me. She is beautiful, inside and out. I want to be with her as much as I can, but the child is always there, in the way, being a wretched nuisance. I had sat in the living room with them for a while after breakfast, watching inane cartoons, but with increasing irritation and then anger.

It's Josie I feel sorry for. She deserves better.

The child never sits still. She fidgets. She twitches. She sings and then stops. She leans on Josie. She sits up. She pinches Josie's arm for attention. She gets up. Does a little dance around the room. Changes television channels. Sits down. Gets up again. Moves an ornament. Plays with it. Puts it back in the wrong place. Always something or other. On and on.

It is all I can do not to reach out and slap her.

So I am back here in my room and I can still hear the endless cacophony of the child. So loud. So random. So intrusive. I am distracted. I cannot think. I cannot relax. I have always been aware of noise, from the road, the railway, the neighbours, but this endless, jarring bedlam – stop... start... long silence... start again...

stop… a sudden noise – drives me to the brink. It is all I can do stop myself screaming out loud.

It is easy to stop a child's noise, you know.

You pinch their nose and hold their mouth shut.

That's all you have to do. That, and wait a while.

It sounds to me as though the child is now marching up and down. I hear her footsteps on the creaking floorboards. Then there is silence. The TV channel is changed again as the child searches for new and different cartoons to watch. I hear snatches of TV programmes before she settles on one. The sound gets turned up. Then down again, so low that I can barely now hear it. I count the seconds of peace and quiet. I do not think it will get above ten.

…25.

26…

…27.

Now the child is singing again. I do not recognise the tune. It is a not a nursery rhyme I had sung to me by mother when I was a little boy. It will be a song by some crass American pop star or other. It sets my nerves on edge. Then Josie starts singing, a sweet melody I do not know either but it is gentle and haunting and sounds to me like an Irish ballad. I suspect she might have made it up, and is musical. It seems to soothe the child, who falls quiet. And it eases my nerves too.

Another sudden noise, a bang as if the child has run against the living room door.

The door is pulled open, a sense of urgency. I sit up.

The child runs along the hallway. I do not know what's next. I am on edge again.

I can hear the child in the bathroom. She has not shut the door. I hear the toilet seat crash down. A silence. I then hear the child urinating, a strong and steady flow splashing into the water. She has not even shut the door. I sit here tense and waiting for what will inevitably come next. This is not right and proper. I should not have to listen to this.

I hear Josie in the hallway, saying something, closing the door, showing decorum. Some respect for me.

I do not know how long I can put up with this nonsense.

This utterly ghastly child.

Now they are back in the living room and there is quiet for a while. At least there are no sudden shouts and bangs and noises from the child. Just the gentle murmur of Josie speaking softly and slowly in careful, measured tones. As though she is telling a story. I listen, the words little more than a soothing sound, so soft I think I could fall asleep. But then, as I listen on, starting to relax slowly, there are sudden, ever-rising querulous noises from the child, asking questions about Josie's story, wanting this to happen, and that, something else, a different ending. The child is never happy, never satisfied.

I look out of the window, distracted.

The rain has finally stopped. A watery sun is breaking through.

It is time to go to the shops. I will be pleased to get some peace.

And then it hits me. My trip to the shops. I usually go alone, of course, but today is different. As I think it will always be, one way or the other, from now on. Josie cannot come with me, to choose whatever she wants for lunch, in case this Leon is out there somewhere. He would attack her, me, and the police would be called by a passer-by. That would bring the police back to my door.

But the child could come, a little later when her clothes are dry. I could say to Josie it would be an opportunity for her to stretch her legs, let off steam, tire herself out. Of course, we would have to be careful not to be seen but we could cut along the railway line and out the back way and I could tell her to wait quietly in the copse of trees while I went into the Co-op for the shopping.

That would also give me the chance to talk to her on her own. To sort her out. To tell her a few home truths. To ask her nicely to behave. Tell her what's what, what's right and what's wrong. She would look up at me, remorseful and grateful, and say she was sorry and that she would behave better from now on. Then, when we got back home, with armfuls of goodies, Mr Kipling's cakes and more, and the child having chosen a few penny chews and what have you, we would have a nice, peaceful lunch.

Without any stupid behaviour or noise from the child. Nonsense that I would have to deal with.

As I say, it is easy to stop a child's noise for good by pinching their nose and holding their mouth shut.

I know how to do it. I've done it before. More than once, actually. But I don't want to do it again. Not unless I have to. Unless I am forced to do it for Josie and me.

SATURDAY 29 JULY, 11.42AM

I have been to the shops alone and have come back and am now sitting waiting patiently, reading today's *Daily Mail*, in the living room on my own while Josie makes lunch 'helped' by the child. As if. Making a bloody nuisance of herself, more like. I asked Josie if the child would like to come with me to the shops to "get some sweeties" and even stood up and held out my hand. The child backed off – she actually moved away from me – and stood behind Josie.

I thought the child was very rude but said nothing.

Josie seemed embarrassed, even ashamed of the child.

She gave me a rueful smile and mouthed, "sorry".

I had asked Josie if she wanted to come too, regretting the words as they left my lips. She shook her head and mouthed "Leon" and then shrugged. She suggested what I should buy and then added that they would "get the kitchen ready" to do lunch. I took this to mean she would clean it – that it needed cleaning, that she had seen it was dirty – and I felt humiliated and almost changed my mind and stayed. But we needed something to eat and it would seem strange if I would not leave the bungalow. And it had started raining again, a little more than spitting, just as I was leaving, so I was sure they would not go into the garden or anywhere near the air-raid shelter.

Even so, I went there and back as quickly as I could, hoping that Josie would focus on cleaning the kitchen and not go elsewhere, digging about. My bedroom, I think, would be sacrosanct, but I could imagine her doing the bathroom, ignoring Adrian's antiseptic bedroom and heading into the living room. Dusting. Spraying and wiping. Fiddling about, poking her nose in where it was not wanted. Looking in drawers and the sideboard, seeing things, flicking through old local newspapers, wondering why I had kept them. Turning the pages for mentions of myself, or Adrian or her.

Sitting there, trying to make a connection.

To see the thread linking five, six, seven random newspapers.

And asking me about them, curious, pressing – what would I say?

But, quick as I was, Josie had kept herself to the kitchen and I could see and smell the difference when I came in. All of the surfaces looked clean. There was a pile of items stacked in one corner for me to approve for throwing out; mostly out-of-date tins and packets. A lemon scent in the air. She smiled – beamed – at me as I walked in with my carrier bags of shopping, waiting for my enthusiastic thanks. I thanked her as warmly as I could.

She then said she still had the cupboards to do properly and gave me a list of what she called "staples", suggesting I get them next time I went to the local shop or big supermarket, which "would be a lot cheaper". Some were cleaning items, sprays and cloths and so on. Gorilla tape, strong black tape to stick something or other back into place under the sink. I told her we had some rolls of it in the garage somewhere. Sweeteners, flour, eggs, sugar and so on – for "delicious home-made cakes", as she put it. I laughed happily at this and said I'd go and get everything she wanted – anything! – that afternoon.

I saw, in that instant, that wonderful, beautiful moment, how life could be. For years, I had kept my head down as best I could, plodding on in a drab and lifeless marriage with a useless waster of a son. My home, dusty and dirty, slowly falling into disrepair while she laughed and flirted and cuckolded me behind my back, probably many times. And me with little more than half a dozen transgressions over that period. Just to satisfy my natural masculine urges. Now, with Josie, I had a chance to make myself a happy life, one that I should have always had. There is an age gap between us, yes, but these things don't matter when you are in love.

I could so easily fall in love with Josie.

I think I am a little already. Her kindness. Her thoughtfulness. Her beauty.

I wonder if she might be falling for me too. She smiles and laughs and flicks her hair back. As lovers do.

I wander back into the kitchen to ask if I can be of any help, but really to sit at the table opposite the child, who is scribbling, and to watch Josie as she makes our lunch. She is still in Adrian's black T-shirt. Back and forth. Bending over. Showing me little glimpses. Stopping my breath. Standing up. Moving about. She is lithe and athletic, a fine sheen of perspiration on her arms. Despite the rain, now little more than a sprinkle, it is still warm. No longer a heat-wave. But enough to make you sweat after just a little activity.

A quiche. Some salad, lettuce, tomatoes, a mix of peppers that Josie asked for. She asked me to buy some fruits and I gaze across as she makes a salad with them. Chopping and peeling and dicing and goodness knows what this lovely young lady can turn her hand to. I ignore the child, who is still in her dirty pants and seems to be drawing castles and princesses and dragons again. I just let my mind drift away with thoughts of Josie. Happiness is so close, I can almost touch it.

I can imagine how it will be so easily. We live together, on our own, in this bungalow, but it is newly decorated, clean and tidy, with all mod cons. I do not work, I do not need to, and fill my days with writing – something witty and amusing, a novel perhaps, something like *Billy Liar*, which I read at school many moons ago. I've always thought I could write something like that, but better.

I take a morning and an afternoon stroll, to keep healthy, some-times Josie comes with me, and I also continue with my civic duties, informing the authorities of local wrong-doing, undeclared businesses and the like. Josie stays at home most of the time and busies herself with cleaning and cooking and all sorts of things that the ladies like to do. I would drive her to the hairdressers now and then. She could have her nails done too, as a special treat.

The child is not in my thoughts. She is not part of our future.

I am not sure how this will come to pass. But it will.

I will have to work out what to do. It needs careful considera-tion.

I imagine Josie stretched out in the garden, on her back on a sunbed. She is half-naked. It is quiet and peaceful, there is no noise from the road or railway, nor from either side. It is as if we are on our own. I come out of the bungalow, with two carefully prepared drinks. Vermouth and lemonade, with a slice of lemon in each. She sits up, her bare breasts hanging down and a line of hair curling out from the top of her bikini bottoms.

I sit there watching as she sips at her drink. She looks at me and smiles, warm and inviting. I do not move, although the sight of her excites me more than I can say. She finishes her drink, placing it carefully on the ground and stands up. I look up at her breasts, the tautness of her stomach and her long tanned legs. She beckons to me to follow her and, not ashamed of my visible arousal, I follow her back into the bungalow and to the bedroom where she lies back on the bed.

There is a sharp knocking at the door.

Inexplicably, the child jumps down from the table and dashes by me, too fast for me in my breaking reverie. I do not know who she thinks will be there.

She opens the door, I hear voices. I step into the hallway. It is the police.

SATURDAY 29 JULY, 11.59AM

We are sat in the living room, Josie, the child and I, on the sofa. Josie in the middle, the T-shirt riding up so that you can almost see her black lacy underwear. The child on her right in just her pants, her arms clasped across her scrawny chest as if preserving her modesty. I, on Josie's left, am fully dressed and am now hot and sweating because I know how this must all look and that I am close to being undone at any moment.

It is all I can do to sit still.

Seem normal.

I can hear my heart beating, fast and loud.

The two policemen, in their early 20s I would guess, one bearded, one ginger, have acted perfectly normally. Stamping the wet off their boots, shaking themselves down in the porch. Asking politely if they can come in "to have a word".

Sitting in the two chairs opposite. Making eye contact with Josie, studiously avoiding looking downwards. Noting our particulars, our names and all of that. Checking. Cross-referencing later, no doubt.

Expressing no surprise as Josie burbles stuff and nonsense, "Adrian… my boyfriend…" and "We've been changing" and referring to me, with a tinkling laugh, as "Dad-… in-law". I do not see myself as a father to her but, embarrassed, I say nothing. I have more troubling matters to think about right now.

"So," says the policeman with the beard, opening his notebook, and looking up at me, "we're just following up on a routine interview between yourself and Special Constable O'Hanlon… about Mr Philip Rennie, who has been reported missing by his wife."

(Yes, I said nothing untoward in that conversation.)

I nod, not sure how to respond, waiting for him to go on. The options available to me whizzing round my mind, not giving me enough time to think, to ponder, to decide. I am mindful that the other one, the ginger policeman, is watching me.

"We've established that… (he pauses)… from conversations with witnesses… that a relationship exists between Mr Rennie and Mrs Dawn Todd… your wife."

(Present tense, 'exists', so they assume both are missing, probably together, but are still living.)

"They work together as teaching assistants at the school, yes," I answer breezily, with a steady gaze.

The policeman with the beard says quietly, "We've established they were more than that."

(I don't know what to say, really I don't.)

There is a long-ish silence as they wait for my reply. I think fast, deciding whether I should admit it, deny it or feign surprise. All I want is to avoid being forced into giving them a non-existent address or phone number for her. An address or phone number that will, within the day, hours or even minutes, bring them back to my door, asking more questions. I just want them to go away and leave me alone with Josie. My love.

I drop my head into my hands, pretend to be struggling with my emotions. Josie reaches out and puts her hand on my back.

After 20, maybe 30 seconds, I take a deep breath and sit up. "I think they have run away together. I don't know where they've gone."

I can sense Josie and the child looking at me. Not saying anything. The two policemen glance at each other. The one with the beard speaks.

"Special Constable O'Hanlon noted that you say your wife left to visit her sick father on Sunday 9 July... and that she calls you once a week."

"She did... to start with, yes... (I have to take a chance with Josie)... but she has not called for a while."

"Mr Rennie left home on 25 July and was reported missing because he... has... had... mental health issues. He drove his car here, parking it over the road. Nothing has been heard of him since. His mobile phone was left in his car. He took the keys with him. He has not contacted anyone. His debit and credit cards have not been used. He has simply vanished."

(More than they'd normally say, I think. The comments, heavy with suspicion, are designed to tease me out.)

I nod, still not sure how to respond. I know the end is near. Perhaps the end is now.

I want to get up and run, but I would not even get out of the door with these two young, strong policemen here.

I have to calm my nerves, try to speak steadily with casual confidence.

"Do you have any information as to the whereabouts of Mr Rennie... and Mrs Todd?" The policeman with the ginger hair asks. I notice he has a tattoo of a small elephant on his wrist.

(This is the key moment; I have to get this right.)

I am not sure what to say. I cannot risk giving them a false address or phone number just to get them to go. They might sit there and call the number straightaway in front of me and then I am done for.

I could say they were in Newcastle or Edinburgh, somewhere a long way away. I don't have the address, nor a phone number. But that would seem suspicious.

They might ask questions about her. Where she banked. Whether she had taken cash with her. A phone. All sorts of questions I would not know how to answer. If they contact her bank, they could check no money has been taken out by her, nor credit cards used. And what would they then assume?

(Everything is closing in on me, every which way I turn. I am done for.)

Josie sits forward, clearing her throat. I think she is coming to my rescue. She puts her hand on mine as she speaks and it is a comfort and an encouragement to me. I can barely believe what she is saying. She must have overheard the conversation between the special constable, Adrian and me, and then asked Adrian about it, drawing her own conclusions.

"He's heartbroken... he won't explain it very well. He's so upset.

Mrs Todd…" she turns to me with a sympathetic smile, "… was having a relationship with Mr Rennie and they were going to leave together at the end of the school term."

I look at Josie and have no idea where she is going with this. But the look she gives me, of warmth and understanding and love, yes love, reassures me. I do my best to look as sad as I can for the two policemen.

"Mrs Todd then went early because her father, who she had been estranged from, got in touch to say he had terminal cancer. So she went ahead to spend his last few days with him."

I look towards the two policemen and they look at me for confirmation. I nod my agreement. Josie then goes on.

"She came back here to collect Mr Rennie after her father died and they have gone off together. She would not say where, only that they'd be in touch, to sort out matters, once they had settled in. Malcolm… (she gestures towards me)… is heartbroken."

Josie sits back and pulls the child towards her, bending down to kiss her head. My mind buzzes, trying to remember if that all fits in with what was said to the special constable. I cannot be certain but I think that it ties up well. I keep quiet, not sure what to say, but turn my head towards the policemen, waiting for them to speak.

There is a silence.

And it strikes me that these policemen, for all their grown-up beards and tattoos, are simply wet-behind-the-ears, beat bobbies or whatever they call them these days. They are not detectives. This is just a routine matter, not an investigation. They are ticking boxes.

And they are out of their depth.

It occurs to me that, if I take charge, I might be able to get them up and out of here and away, never to come back. I just have to play it right, think quickly. Say the right things. I pause, as if struggling for words, and then speak.

"The last time she called... She called me to say her father had died and that she wasn't coming back... that she was going on holiday with this Philip Rennie... that she'd get back to me in the autumn once they'd returned... She didn't give me a chance to say anything. She put the phone down... I wanted to call her back. But she had withheld the number. I don't know where she is... I don't really know why she left me..."

I dip my head down, put my head back in my hands, and wait for Josie to put a comforting arm around me. She does and I lean into her, my body shaking slightly as if I am fighting off tears. And then I realise. Exactly what I should do. What I should say. I sit up, brush at my eyes and talk on, looking at the policeman with the beard who seems to be in charge.

"I need to find my wife. Talk to her. Tell her how I feel. Can you find her for me? Trace her. And him. So I can talk some sense into her?"

A pause and then he replies. "I'm afraid not, sir. If two adults choose to leave their partners and move away together then legally, unless there's any sign of wrong-doing... evidence of foul play... then it's not a police matter."

"Are you going to trace her, though? Find out where she is?" I raise my voice, tinged with anguish. A poor, broken husband. His heart in pieces. "Could you tell her... I mean... could you at least pass on a message for me? You can do that, can't you? That I... miss her... I want her back."

He shakes his head and adds, as they look at each other and start to get to their feet, "We've one or two more enquiries to make but there's no apparent risk to either of them or the public so it will go up to our superior officer, who'll review the papers and make a decision."

"So that's it, then, you're not actually going to do anything to find my dear wife?" I try to sound as disappointed and as bitter as I can as I stand up.

"As I say, sir," he speaks almost over his shoulder as they leave the room followed by me and then Josie, "it'll be reviewed and we'll get back to you if we need any more information about your wife. In the meantime, if you do hear anything from her, do..." His words are obscured as he goes to pull open the door.

It jams and he stops, looking and noting that it has been damaged. I hold my breath. He mutters something, that I "need to get that fixed", before pulling it harder so that it opens.

They are away down the path.

I watch them go.

And that, I think – no, I know, in my heart – will be the last I see of them.

SATURDAY 29 JULY, 1.22PM

We sat, all now dressed properly, in the living room, with trays on our laps, and ate the vegetarian meal and the fruit salad that Josie (and the child, supposedly) prepared from what I bought at the local Co-op. She had also found some (what must be old) spaghetti in the back of a cupboard and had boiled that and cut it up into little pieces and mixed it in with the peppers and some sort of vinegary dressing. Very tasty it was too.

Josie has been talking quietly to me about why she did not use the (cheese and ham) quiche and how she feels about vegetarianism and films she has seen about animal welfare. I have tried to smile and nod and agree without really listening to the more graphic descriptions of animals being tortured and butchered. When I was young, I did go through a phase of stamping on mice and hamsters to see them burst, but I seem to have become more squeamish as I get older.

I am scared of rats. Have been for years really.

When I was young I tried to stamp on one I had trapped in the corner of the shed. As I lunged, it moved so fast, I missed it.

It ran up my leg, over my shoulder and away. I could scarcely believe it. They have always scared me ever since.

The child now sits in front of the television set and watches something or other that Josie has found for her. It is a film with a dog in it, a Jack Russell, I think it is, and the child likes these dogs apparently and so is quiet for a while. Josie laughed when she saw my TV, saying she had never seen one so big behind the screen and that, if I bought a new one, we could get Freeview, whatever that is, and receive all sorts of channels for nothing. I said I would look into it and I will.

We chatted for a while about the types of film and TV we enjoyed. She named several of what sounded like American shows and I smiled vaguely at the right times about those and something called Netflix. I then opened, and realised the danger as I did it, the cupboard and showed her my collection of VHS tapes. This triggered a giggling fit. I pointed out the *Poirot* and the *Morse* and the *Morecambe and Wise* and *The Two Ronnies* tapes one by one and she said, between snuffles and giggles, that she had not heard of any of them (which I found hard to believe).

I pointed to a box of *Some Mothers Do 'Ave 'Em* tapes and explained it was a very funny programme we might all enjoy.

I was tempted to do a Frank Spencer impression at this point to make her laugh. I do it rather well (and had done it two or three times to great gales of laughter at office parties at Christmas).

But I hesitated and the moment passed. Josie smiled at me and said that we could watch it later. For now, we are both sitting back and watching the dog film on the television.

"Do you think Adey will call this evening?" Josie asks suddenly.

(I knew this moment was coming at some point and can't help think this might prove a tricky conversation. I give her my prepared answer.)

"I don't know. I'm not sure he could do if he lost his phone and can't remember your number."

"But… if he's with your wife… and she called you here… and he's with her… could he not ring me on your home phone? Like she did with you?"

(I pause, not quite sure what to say to that.)

I shrug, "Maybe… he might not have told his mum yet… about you… might not have had a moment… what with his grandad dying. It might be rather insensitive, mightn't it?"

"But he could just ask to use the phone, couldn't he? Even just to see how we all were? A quick call, that's all."

She sits up straighter and I can tell she is thinking about things. Working it all out. Realising something doesn't quite add up. Moving ever closer to the truth.

"What I said for you, to the police. Am I right? Is that how things are? I wasn't quite sure."

(I can handle a conversation but I am not sure what I will do if it becomes difficult, perhaps even dangerous, if she asks too much, probes too far.)

"Pretty much," I answer slowly.

She looks at me and I can see she is waiting for me to explain things more fully.

"Dawn… I think she'd been seeing this Philip Rennie for a while. When her father was taken ill, she went up there. Thought about things. Then she told me about… their relationship… that she wasn't coming back."

"Yes, that's what Adey thought, pretty much. But I don't understand… if the police think this Philip is missing… why don't you just tell them where your wife is and give them her number? Otherwise, they're only going to keep coming back if you're their only lead."

I sigh as if I had explained this a thousand times. "Because Dawn was estranged from her father until recently and didn't know where he lived. He – his wife, I cannot remember which – got in touch with Dawn out of the blue."

I shake my head, suggesting I am frustrated in having to explain myself. That I am disappointed with her for asking. I hope that she will stop this line of questioning. Today was meant to be a happy day, our first perfect day together, and all I get is questions.

"All I know is it's Manchester, or thereabouts, which isn't very helpful. And she withholds her number when she calls. So I've nothing to give the police. If I tell them that, they'd be suspicious."

"Suspicious of what?" she asks and I could curse myself for saying the word. I think she is moving ever closer to the truth of the matter.

I shrug, as if it's no matter. "I don't know. This Philip Rennie disappearance. A missing person. All he's done is leave his wife and stolen mine."

She goes to answer, to say something more, to ask the next question she has in her mind but, as she formulates the words, the child suddenly stands up and knocks over her tumbler of orange squash. Josie jumps to her feet to clear it up and I take the opportunity to take the trays into the kitchen to start tidying everything away. The moment – leading to the end – passes, but I know she will come back at me with more questions soon.

Why did Philip Rennie leave his car by my bungalow two weeks or so after she had left?

Why, as the police said, hasn't he been in touch with anybody since or used any cards? What is he living on?

Why did Adrian go up to Manchester without taking a change of clothes or even taking two minutes just to say goodbye?

What has really happened to her, him and Adrian?

When these questions come, as they will surely do sometime soon, I have to decide what to say. And then what to do as I examine her face, her mind working through my answers, trying to make sense of them, struggling to understand before her ready acceptance of everything at face value turns to doubt and scepticism and, eventually, suspicion. And then what will I do?

SATURDAY 29 JULY, 1.42PM

Josie stands by the kitchen sink, washing up the knives and forks and plates, looking out across the garden. I stand to her right, slightly behind, drying each item that she puts on the draining board and then putting these away in the cupboards.

She has given the child a bag of cheesy Wotsits from her handbag, to keep her quiet while watching television.

I can hear the child chomping away, her mouth open, as she pushes in one Wotsit after the other. I am not imagining it. I hear it clearly.

I do imagine her looking at her bright orange hands when she's finished and wiping them on my settee. The dirty child has no manners at all.

When Josie cleaned and tidied, she found an iron and a nylon washing line, still in its packaging, under the sink and has suggested that I put that up later, when it has hopefully stopped drizzling. I am not sure where I will put it. We used to have a rope washing line across the trees at the end of the garden, but I took that down when I removed them, and the rope, which is perfectly serviceable and could be used again as such, is in the garage.

The nylon washing line lies on the table beside me and I idly read the label: '20-Metre Clothes Laundry Washing Line Metal Steel Core Braided Rope Nylon String'. Quite a mouthful really. 'Nylon Rope With Steel Core' would suffice. I do not know where it came from nor why it was under the sink. I do not recall buying such a thing.

She would often buy random, useless things from catalogues in Sunday newspapers. A rubber safety bath mat. A bottle of tissue mist for spraying on toilet paper. A portable foot spa. Moisturising gel gloves. Dehumidifiers galore. Anything that smelled of lavender; manicure sets, mouthwashes, foot pastes. An endless flow of cheap tat that she would buy for her birthdays and Christmases and then discard, worn out or broken, within six months.

This should have been a sweet and lovely day. Laughs and giggles galore. Falling in love.

Shared confidences. Our heads bobbed and close together, conspiratorially. Two as one.

Instead it's all been sharp and jagged and edgy. That stupid child. Endless questions from Josie, who just won't shut up. I wish to Christ she'd stop talking.

After babbling on about ironing their clothes later and the washing line, the length of the garden, how quiet it is (it isn't) and how we must sit and watch the trains go by when it's dry and bright (what fun), she turns her attention to what, inevitably, is coming next. The air-raid shelter. I had expected these questions and so I am prepared for the conversation.

"Why do you have an air-raid shelter in your garden?"

"Oh, that? It's from the Second World War. It was still here when we moved in over 25 years ago. The previous owner used it like a shed, for storage… We should have knocked it down and filled it in, but it was too expensive… they couldn't get a digger in… We used it for storage at first but everything got damp and musty so it's empty now."

She nods and I can sense she thinks nothing of it, is just making polite conversation. But then she adds, by way of a joke.

"Except for scarecrows!" she laughs, and I am not sure what to say. I am not certain what would be normal. I do not want to dwell on the matter in case she decides she wants to go and look at the shelter right now. Nor do I want to be seen to sharply change the subject, which may seem an odd thing to do.

"Oh yes," I reply. "They've long gone." (Thinking that will be the end of this conversation and that next we will move on to talking about the weather.)

"Lily can't stop talking about those scarecrows of yours. She's convinced she saw them hiding in there from the farmer."

(Go on then, keep talking, sign the child's death warrant, why don't you.)

I smile, more of a rictus grin really.

I titter a little.

I laugh, hearing its falseness in my head.

(I don't know what else to do, I need to play this down, move on, talk about something else.)

"It's all I can do," adds Josie, smiling to herself, "to stop her hiding in the shelter."

(I say nothing as she goes on.)

"When it's stopped raining, could you just open it and let her peek inside? It's the only way I'll get any peace and quiet tonight."

(I do not know what to say or do.)

She puts the last piece of washing-up on the draining board. It is a large and heavy, smoked glass bowl. It was a wedding present all those years ago and I am amazed that it has survived so long without a single chip or crack. I lift it up and wrap the tea towel, now damp from drying, around it. I feel its weight in my hands.

Josie turns and looks at me and smiles. And I am lost for a second.

The look in her eyes is so innocent and beautiful and loving.

And I cannot, while she looks at me like this, do anything to her.

"Maybe," she says, oblivious to my utter torment, "when it's dry, you could go and unlock it and we could play hide-and-seek and sit in the lounge while Lily goes and finds a place to hide. Wouldn't that be fun?"

I smile.

I nod.

I agree.

And then Josie is gone, waltzing happily out of the kitchen to the bathroom, completely unaware that everything has now changed. This is not, nor can it now be, a perfect day. We cannot live happily ever after at all. I know that, if these endless questions and the relentless badgering continue and the hide–and–seek game commences, I will have two more deaths on my hands.

SATURDAY 29 JULY, 2.22PM

Josie and the child are having what they call 'quiet time' in Adrian's room until four o'clock, when we are due to play hide-and-seek if it has stopped its endless on-off, stop-start raining. I can hear Josie telling stories and the child is quiet for once. I am sitting in my room with the newspapers from the living room cupboard beside me on the bed. My diary, which I need to destroy, is on my lap. I am working through the newspapers, from the past five or six years, and am writing a list. To get things straight, in my head. What I have done. Such terrible things.

15-year-old girls, Ipswich.

18-year-old woman, Bury St Edmunds.

43-year-old woman, Colchester.

19-year-old woman, Woodbridge.

It has now stopped raining and the sun is shining and my nerves are all on edge expecting the child to wake up and come running out to play at any moment. I do not know how I will handle that. I need to give it some thought. I pause and add some dates to the list, moving forward from six years to not so long ago, and then write a simple description for each.

Showed myself, made them watch.

Satisfied myself on top of her.

Had sex.

Had sex.

I wanted, from this day forth, to live a happy-ever-after life. With Josie and, yes, with the child, Lily. I have tried to do that. But it is one thing after another with them. It is not going to work out. I must decide what to do. Make a decision and stick to it come what may. In the meantime, I add more to the list in second and then fourth place.

Blonde, 25? Unreported. Touched her everywhere. Wherever I wanted.

Brunette, 60? Unreported. Stopped halfway through (false teeth).

The first incident, six or so years ago, was spur of the moment. They just happened to be passing. I felt ashamed afterwards.

Would never do anything like it again. I lasted a year before I succumbed to my urges one more time. Then 13 months. And so on. I think this last one, a park in Woodbridge where she struggled and fought and almost pulled off my balaclava, will be the last.

I have not done anything like this for a little while now. Not since I was arrested outside the delicatessen. I know now, with the police having my DNA on record, that it is only a matter of time before someone, somewhere, a young rookie policeman with time on his hands, runs it through the main police database. There may be matches. I don't know for sure but suspect there will be. And then they will come for me. If I were to do anything else anywhere, in another park with another woman, it would only hasten their arrival.

Her.

She. The wife. She made me what I became. She turned me away. Spurned me. Forced me to subdue my natural urges until I could last no longer. If it had been a happy marriage, a proper, loving marriage, a physical one, none of this would have happened. And, after everything, she was going to leave me. Take all I owned and more; my self-respect, my dignity, my soul. I do not regret what I did. No, I do not and I never will. I will not apologise for that.

Him.

He. Her lover. I do not know if he was her first lover. Probably not. But he was her last, that's for sure. I saw to that. I did not intend to do what I did. It was not planned. It was not intended. He came round here, uninvited. Strutting about as if he owned the place. Telling me what he was going to do. Speak to the police. I had no choice. To do what I did. It was forced upon me. There is no need to apologise for that.

Adrian.

My twitching, jerking, stuttering son. My useless, unemployable waste-of-space son and heir. I had no plans for him either. But then he stood there, with his hands at his face and his great big 'O'-shaped mouth by the open door of the air-raid shelter. And I did what I needed to do, no more and no less. I regret it, though. I don't know why, but I do.

Baby Todd.

Baby Todd.

So long ago now, near the start of the marriage, that I can barely remember the babies. The screaming, yes. The endless whining. The snuffling, for sure. But I remember little else.

Baby girl.

Baby boy.

The girl had a birthmark, a red rose on her tummy, just above her belly button. As I rested my hand on her tummy, I remember the mark was the same size as the fingernail on my little finger. He, the baby boy, was a nondescript thing. Forgettable.

Flora Beatrice Todd. A stupid name she chose. Like the margarine.

Jonathan Todd. I forget the middle name. Another one she picked.

She gurgled. The little baby. I remember that. The sweetest little hiccupy gurgle. I had forgotten. I used to listen to that funny little noise stopping and starting. It had slipped my mind, that. I am crying now. I don't know why. For the babies, I suppose. And everything else. So much that I have done. So many dreadful things.

Through my tears, I complete my list.

Josie.

Lily.

I look at these last two names on the list long and hard. Considering the options. Thinking things through. Deciding. Planning. Reaching my decision. I then take my pen and strike a line through Josie's name and then another through Lily's. There, I have made my decision. It is done.

SATURDAY 29 JULY, 2.49PM

I have decided that Josie and Lily must go. Back to where they live. Taking their non-stop questioning and endless nonsense with them. To leave me here on my own to live out my days in peace and quiet. It is not what I want in a perfect world. I want love and warmth and a happy little family. But it is the right thing. The only thing to do. I must do it when they wake up, before their hide-and-seek game ruins everything for all of us.

I glance up, at the sound of my bedroom door creaking open. I push my diary and the papers beneath the duvet as casually as I can.

Josie stands there. She looks shocked and frightened.

"Leon's outside. I don't know what to do."

I jump to my feet, reach out and hold her by the arm. "Don't be scared," I say, and then add quietly. "Is he at the door now?"

She shakes her head. "I just woke up and looked out of the window. I've seen him on the other side of the road, at that house with the broken gate. An old woman came out and spoke to him and then closed the door. He went to the next door, the one with the caravan, and rang the bell. No one answered and he's gone in through the side gate."

I move, with Josie, to my bedroom window, and we stand there, side by side, my arm on hers, watching the far side of the road.

Josie points at the house with the caravan and says, "He put his hand over the gate, unbolted it and went in."

I can barely believe what she is saying.

But I smile, nod, and humour her. I think she's been dreaming vividly and has just woken up.

Minutes pass as we wait for him to reappear.

Or not. If she has imagined it in her sleepy state.

Then she adds, a tremble in her voice, "I think he's going from door to door, down that side and then up this, ringing and speaking to whoever comes to the door, and forcing his way in if no one answers."

I go to say, "He's got some nerve to do that." But, as I start the sentence, Leon comes out of the side gate over the road and walks to the pavement. He stops there, a short bull of a man, with his shaved head and tattooed face, arms and legs, and lights a roll-up cigarette that he takes from a pocket of his shorts. He is dressed completely in black, T-shirt, shorts and trainers.

"Oh God," I say involuntarily.

"Exactly," she replies, as she watches him turn to his left and move towards the next house over the road.

Away from us. For the time being.

Until he turns at the bus stop down by where Adrian and Josie got off.

And then works his way back up this side, one by one, and gets to the bungalow.

"You're not going to be able to reason with him, are you?"

"No, what Leon wants, Leon gets. And if he doesn't, he'll destroy it."

"What... I mean... how... why are you with him... were you with him?"

"He was nice at first. Attentive. Paid me lots of attention. And he was different. And everyone seemed to think he was something special."

I nod, to indicate I am listening as I monitor Leon going to the next house and, rat-a-tat-tat, banging on the door.

"Then he turned... wanted to control me, the way I looked, what I wore... once Lily was born, it just got worse. He wanted to... He's a control freak... and the drugs just make him worse... more paranoid."

There is a long pause as Leon waits for the door to be answered. It is opened. Leon steps forward. An aggressive stance. Words are spoken. I find I am holding my breath. Expecting a confrontation, sudden violence.

"He wouldn't hurt Lily, though, surely?" I whisper. "Nor you, as her mother?"

"Oh, he sees himself as the best dad in the world. That's a laugh. He even had her name tattooed on his forehead. Lilly. With two Ls. No one's dared tell him... and yes, he hurts me. All the time. He thinks nothing of it."

"Can you not go to court, get a restraining order?"

She laughs, a bitter sound. "He'd take no notice... it would make it worse... his brothers would just take over, harassing me... then his mates. It would never end. He told me once, if I left him, they'd all take turns with me. It's why I stayed so long. But then he started with Lily..." She tails off.

I hear her swallow.

I don't know what to say.

We watch out of the window.

Eventually, Leon turns away, the door closes, and he moves towards the next house. Again, further down and the last one in sight to us. After this, he will disappear from view for a while.

"He used to make me dress up in front of his mates... and then accused me of cheating on him. Four weeks after I had Lily." She shakes her head. "I broke up with him months ago and he still won't leave us alone."

"What does he do? Does he work?"

We watch as Leon comes away from the next house. No one answers the door. He tries but is unable to open the side gate. He peers through the windows at the front. Then scratches something with a knife into the front door.

"That will be his initials... No, he doesn't have a proper job now. He's done various things... he trained as a bricklayer. But he'd always lose them... fall out with the boss... hit someone... he's been in court so many times. He's been on benefits for ages but does cash jobs for his mates... night clubs, security stuff. Where he can push people about."

And then Leon has gone, out of sight over the road.

Still working his way down to the bus stop. Then across the road and up this side, towards us.

How long? Five minutes? Ten? Five I'd guess. Ten if we are lucky.

"We should call the police," I say. "Anonymously. Just say we've seen someone going up and down, going in and out of the back gates."

She looks at me and almost laughs again but manages to stop herself. "What? A police car racing to the rescue? You'd be lucky to get one turning up tomorrow night... anyway, he's like that with one or two of the police round here (she holds up two crossed fingers). He acts as an informant..."

Her words halt as she sees my look of incredulity. But then she adds, "We need to hide... or go. Me and Lily. He'll be here in five minutes."

I look at her, not sure what to say. Either I answer the door and bluff him that they are not here. Or I don't answer it and he comes round the back gate, forces his way in, snooping in the garage, peering through the back windows and walking down to the air-raid shelter.

"We could hide in the shelter," she says, turning away from the window to go and get Lily.

I look at her.

"Or we could go over the railway tracks and wait until he's gone."

I am not sure what to say.

"Me and Lily could make a run for it back to where we live... and then come back this evening when it's all quiet?" She goes to walk by me, to wake Lily, decide what to do.

I grab her arm, stopping her. It is too late.

I look beyond her, out of the window, and she turns back to follow my gaze.

Leon must have crossed the road earlier than expected and is now walking up the path to the front door.

SATURDAY 29 JULY, 3.01PM

We hear Leon opening the porch door, stepping inside, stamping his feet.

We stand there looking at each other.

The doorbell goes, then the aggressive, rat-tat-tat, 'answer the door now', knocking.

"Lily," whispers Josie.

The child, in Adrian's room, woken by the knock-knock-knock, will be sitting up, rubbing her eyes, wondering what woke her, looking around for Josie.

Getting up off the bed, she will come running out into the hall-way.

He will see her, start shouting and then break the front door down.

Grab the child and then Josie before yelling at them to "Wait there" before turning on me with his knife.

Josie holds my gaze and raises her left hand to her mouth, making a "ssshhh" gesture, then lifts her right hand too, fingers crossed.

There is a long silence. From the road, neighbours, the railway line. The world has stopped turning in this instant.

There is no noise from Adrian's bedroom. Is she awake, the child, pit-patting her way over to the door?

I hear another sudden stamping of feet in the porch. Wait in agony for Adrian's bedroom door to be opened.

"I go… to the door?" I whisper, half-stating, half-asking.

Josie shakes her head. "Wait," she mouths and then puts her hands to the side of her head and mimes the child sleeping. And does the finger-crossing gesture again with both hands.

"I go if she…" I whisper and do a walking gesture with my fingers.

She nods.

The doorbell goes again. He holds his finger on it and it ding-a-ling-a-lings artlessly through the bungalow, on and on, for ever and ever.

Josie shakes her head, a look of despair.

Then it stops and the knocking starts again, bang, bang, bang, bang, bang.

Loud.

Angry.

Insistent.

There are stirrings from Adrian's room.

I move towards the bedroom door. I have to be quick, getting to the front door before the child appears.

Josie grabs my arm. "No. Wait," she whispers urgently.

Another unbearable silence.

Leon, angry and impatient, standing in the porch.

The child, half-woken and turning in her bed, to be woken fully at the next round of furious ringing and knocking.

Josie and I, tense and straining, holding our nerve until the instant we need to make a decision.

That next ring or the next bang will be the end of us.

The child up and running.

And we will be facing down Leon, knife in hand, in the hallway.

I start counting.

1... 2... 3...

I don't know why.

... 4... 5... 6... 7...

It calms me a little I suppose.

... 8... 9... 10... 11...

Any moment. God help me.

There is a sudden scuffling noise from the porch and we hear the porch door being slammed shut as Leon walks away. So loud that it seems to echo down the hallway, shaking the walls of the bungalow.

"Mummy?" A thin, uncertain voice from Adrian's room.

The child, just woken, is calling, almost plaintively, for Josie.

Josie opens my bedroom door carefully and peeps out up the hallway. She crosses the hall in two or three steps and steps into Adrian's bedroom.

Not a second look back at me.

I stand there, suddenly realising that I am bathed in sweat. A reaction to the terror of facing this brute of a man and the blessed relief that he has gone.

I move into the hall and follow Josie into Adrian's room.

It is dark as the curtains are almost fully drawn. But I see Josie sitting on the bed, her arms around Lily. The child is half-asleep, still drowsy. Josie is soothing her, keeping her still and quiet. Calm. Then she looks up at me and speaks, in a hesitating, low voice.

"Leon's walked by the window.

"He's just opened the back gate.

"He's gone into the back garden."

SATURDAY 29 JULY, 3.06PM

I cannot breathe properly.

The moment of truth is now.

It was not meant to end like this.

If he is in the back garden and looks through the window, he will see the child's things in the living room: her Peppa Pig toy, her scribbled drawings.

The door to the kitchen is unlocked.

He will be inside the bungalow in little more than a minute.

I move out of Adrian's bedroom, down the hallway and into the kitchen. I know what I have to do. Try to do anyway.

Dear God, he is in the garden, his back to me, facing the air-raid shelter, which has caught his attention.

He walks towards it. Then stops, looking.

I have no choice about what to do.

I don't know how I will manage it.

I reach for the biggest knife from the rack on the side by the fridge. Tuck it into the waistband of my trousers in the small of my back. Move it slightly to the side so I can walk comfortably with it there.

I stand for a moment, willing myself to step into the garden, feeling sudden, dreadful movement inside my stomach and lower down; a reaction to the fear I feel for this horror of a man.

It occurs to me that my best, my only, chance of survival is to walk out and tell him they are inside, that he should come and take them, somewhere else, anywhere but here. That I want no part of this, it's all my son's doing, and I just want to be left alone and not have anything to do with this anger and fury and madness.

But I see Josie's innocent face. The child's eyes.

For all I have done, I doubt I can let this man have them, to go back to whatever hell they have had to endure for so long.

I think there must be some other way.

I know that if I go for him with the kitchen knife, he is likely to overpower me, take Josie and the child and maybe then come back and stab me repeatedly in anger. My life over, ended in the next few minutes.

If I were to kill him, what next? Josie would call the police and then where would I be? It would all be for nothing. It strikes me, a forlorn hope, that, if I were to kill him, there is a chance that Josie might conspire with me, agree to…

Leon turns and sees me watching him from the kitchen.

I wave as if I am expecting him. I don't know why. Instinct I suppose.

I step outside as he walks towards me. I speak, my voice cracking with fear.

"Have you c… come about the shelter?"

He stops and looks at me like I am an idiot, as if it is perfectly normal to come into someone's back garden without so much as a by-your-leave and not have to explain yourself.

"Shelter?" he laughs, more of a sneer. "No. I'm looking for…"

He takes his phone out of his back pocket, presses buttons, scrolls through the screen with his thumb.

Up close, with his tattoos and piercings and a ring through his nose, his face has a look of bovine stupidity. But there is a sense of barely suppressed anger and he is clearly strong and itching to fight. I fear him. He could brush me aside so easily if he knew they were in the bungalow.

"… them two." He shows me a photo of Josie and the child, much as they look now, in bed together. Josie has pulled the duvet up to her shoulders, to cover her nakedness. All I can see of the child is her face, maybe a touch chubbier and less defined than it is today.

"No," I answer firmly, shaking my head. I then maintain eye contact, as warm and as friendly as I can, and, puzzled, I ask as a normal person with nothing to hide would do, "Who are they, your family?"

He breathes out heavily. "Wife and kid. The whore left me for some cunt. The old woman across the way says he lives here. Some big fucker."

I step back, try and look as shocked as I can. Not by his words but for the suggestion they might be here. Thinking fast, I surprise myself with my own invention.

"No, not here. I lived here with… my husband… Roger… but he passed on a while back and I am in mourning for him."

"Fuck's sake," he mutters under his breath.

"Roger had a nephew who came to visit for a while. He was quite tall. Six foot and more. He left a month or two ago after Roger passed away."

He shakes his head, as if he cannot believe what he is hearing. This brutal pig of a man. He sighs heavily, clicking his phone off and putting it back in his pocket.

"What about the neighbours?" he says, demands really. Like he owns the place.

"Oh," I reply. "Peter and Lynn, that side, a middle-aged couple. A blonde woman, I forget her name, Shannon I think, with two young girls over there." I point towards the garden gate. As if he might take the hint and go.

"Fuck." That's all he says.

I have no idea what to say to that so I fall back on my HMRC training and say nothing. Wait for him to go on.

He turns around to face the shelter and says, close to conversationally. "What the fuck's that doing there anyway?"

I could stab him now.

In the back, six or seven times. I feel a surge of desire to do it.

Put paid to him once and for all. Then Josie and the child could go home and I could live out my days here in peace. My only real chance of happy-ever-after.

But he turns to face me, a look of contempt on his stupid, in-bred face. And I do not think I could pull the knife out from behind me fast enough to slash across his throat in one clean, smooth move so that he would drop lifeless at my feet, spurting blood from his fat, bulging neck.

I would most likely drop the knife as I brought it round from behind.

Or he would see it. And know. And be quicker than me, drawing his own knife, and I would look down to see it sticking in my stomach as he pushed by me into the bungalow.

"It's an old air-raid shelter that's been there since the war. We never knocked it down and filled it in. So it just sits there, really."

"I'll fill it in for you, piece of piss, that."

(For God's sake. Just go.)

"No," I reply. "You'd need a digger and we can't get it round the back. The drive's too narrow."

(I need to get him to go because, at some point, Josie will think he must have left and will appear suddenly at the kitchen door.)

"No," he says ("Naa-aah"). "Me and my brother could do that in a couple of days with wheelbarrows."

(I don't know what to say to this stupidity, honestly I don't.)

"I'd rather not, not now. Thank you all the same. I'm not well. Need my peace and quiet… please."

(Go now, right now, before Josie appears.)

He shrugs as if to say "Your loss, m-a-a-ate" and turns to the gate.

As he opens it, he stops and reaches into his back pocket and pulls out a small card, which he hands to me. It has his name and mobile phone number on it along with the phrase, 'Building Servces'. The 'i' is missing.

"If you see the bitch, text me."

I nod, pleased to see him leave.

"There's a reward. In cash."

I nod again, moving him towards the drive and away.

"The slut stole almost ten grand in cash from me last week and I want it back."

SATURDAY 29 JULY, 3.43PM

The three of us are now back in the living room. I know there is, at the back of the cupboard, a box of draught pieces and a board and so I take these out, thinking it might be a good way to keep the child busy and distract them both from wanting to play hide-and-seek. Josie starts explaining to the child – very, very slowly – how to play draughts. I sit quietly, patiently, with a gentle and encouraging smile on my face.

Josie and the child sit on one side of the board on the floor.

I am on the other.

It is going to be hard going I think. Very hard indeed. With this difficult child.

It begins well enough with the child seeming to understand how to play the game, nodding and smiling as Josie explains what's what one more time. The child has a little go herself in a simple game of just a few pieces with Josie. She 'wins' and is then ready to play a proper game against me.

So we start, the child and I, and I am playing properly for there is no point in playing any game unless you try to win – Monopoly, Cluedo, KerPlunk, whatever. I am not a believer in letting children 'win' all of the time. It is one of the (very many) reasons why children turn out to be so self-obsessed and have such issues with mental health these days; they all think they are the centre of the universe and cannot handle it when they find out they are just a tiny speck of nothing.

Josie asks about Leon and what he said. "Did he suspect?"

I summarise what happened. She gives me an admiring look. I do not mention the stolen money but I notice, for the first time, that Josie keeps her bag close to her even when she does not need it.

I idly wonder what I would do with £10,000 in cash, a nice little windfall, that.

The child doesn't understand how to play draughts at all and is getting angry very quickly. She has quite a temper. I do not say anything and just sit here calm and relaxed as ever as she huffs and puffs as I push my pieces about, and scowls whenever I take one or more of her pieces off the board. She folds her arms theatrically.

Josie leans forward and says, to the child, that they should play as a team against me. "Team Lily," she says, "will beat Grandad!" The child seems to like this idea and looks at me with a know-all smirk that I would rather like to wipe off her face. But I press on to win the game. It will teach her an important lesson in life.

"What will he do next?" I ask, and mouth "Leon" as Josie looks at me.

"Never give up," she replies. "He'll break into our home soon, if he hasn't already. Sitting there in the dark all night, waiting for us to come back. Stewing in his own juices, getting angrier."

"What will you do then? About clothes? You can't stay here forever," I add, as an afterthought.

She thinks for a moment as she points to a draught and shows the child where to move it. "I've a little money. Maybe tomorrow, you could drive me somewhere, Colchester perhaps, and I can buy some clothes to keep us going."

"You've nowhere else to go?" I ask as I move a draught to counter Josie. I don't know why I say it.

"We feel safe here because no one knows we are here." She looks at me and smiles and then adds, "Thank you… once Adey is back we will find somewhere else to live. Maybe Bury or Colchester. Somewhere further out where we won't bump into Leon."

The child moves a piece, nonsensically.

I do not reproach her.

Just jump the piece and take it. The child looks at me angrily.

"It's looking nice out again," says Josie, suddenly turning her head to look towards the garden. "And drying out. I don't think it's going to be as hot as it was. Just warm. For the rest of the summer. We can have picnics!"

I nod. I know where this is going.

"When we've finished this," she says, "we must play that game of hide-and-seek." She drops her voice and almost mouths the last three words but the child hears her and stands up, kicking the board away with her foot.

"Lily!" admonishes Josie, but laughing, as if it is the funniest thing in the world.

The child stands there, with her excited beaming face, clapping her hands.

I am on my knees, picking up the pieces, putting them into the box, folding the board, tucking everything away in the cupboard. Deciding what to do.

The three of us now stand in the living room, facing each other. Josie is smiling and happy and I cannot help but feel a surge of warmth for her. The ridiculous child is clutching herself. Between the legs. Nervous with excitement. I am standing there, a moment of quiet desperation, my thoughts churning over in my mind. Damned, whatever I do.

"I'll just take Lily to the toilet," says Josie, breaking my thoughts.

I follow them out, watching as they go into the bathroom, shutting the door behind them. Walk into my bedroom. To gather my thoughts. To bring myself to do what has to be done.

I gaze out of the window, lost in my mind for the moment. I know I should really try to get them to go. But, with Leon out there, they won't. And they will want to stay until Adrian returns. And he's never coming back. If I tell them he's stopped in Manchester or wherever, met someone else, what then? They might want to stay a little longer but I don't think I want them to. Not now. I just want to be left alone. In peace. In safety.

But then there's this £10,000 in cash.

I need money and I could drip out that sort of sum for quite some time.

You know, it might make all the difference to my life.

I turn, as I hear Josie come up behind me. Unexpectedly, she rests her chin on my left shoulder and I tense for a second as I can smell her scent and feel her close to me. I imagine her breasts brushing against my back. And then I relax, come close to enjoying the moment. I could almost turn and hug her. I could kiss her. But I know that if I turn, I will be in love with her forever and won't be able to do what I must do.

We stand there like that in silence for what must be 20 to 30 seconds.

I hear her sigh and I can smell her sweet breath. I wait for her arms to slip around me as if we were lovers. And, if she does that, I know I will be doomed.

She goes to speak but then stops and points out of the window. Somehow, I had not noticed the two women, one about 50, the other maybe 25, taping an A4 sheet of paper to a lamp post a little way down on the other side of the road.

It is his wife and daughter, I believe. Putting up 'Missing' posters for him.

We watch as they move to the next lamp post, still over the road but a little closer, and start taping a sheet of paper to it.

And I wonder how long it will be until they get to the lamp post just outside here and whether they'll know the significance of the bungalow in front of them. And what will happen if they do.

SATURDAY 29 JULY, 4.09PM

I contemplate the two women, one older, one younger, but clearly mother and daughter, working together with their envelopes and posters and sticky tape. They are slow and patient – methodical, even – in what they are doing.

There is a grim kind of fascination watching them work.

I am in the eye of the storm, the maelstrom all around me.

I will, at any point, be swept away by it all.

Slim and blonde and tidy in their blue jeans and white T-shirts; hairdressers or beauty therapists by the look of them. Studying them, I am not sure what he saw in her, dumpy and old before her time. I think it must have been love, whatever that might be.

"Why do you think he left the car here?" asks Josie suddenly, stepping back from me. "Of all places. He must have been coming here, surely?"

I turn my head slightly towards her and shrug with calm indifference. "I don't know. I think she must have come back and fetched him."

"Why, though? Why didn't he drive to the station to get a train to Manchester… or drive himself up? Why just abandon a nice car like that?" A pause before she adds, "It doesn't make sense… and why has he not used any money? The police said."

I shrug again, realising she is thinking things over. Believing it all automatically at first. Now trying to make sense of my nonsensical story. Soon to have doubts. And then, eventually, piecing it all together. The truth of the matter.

The two women finish taping a poster to the lamp post over the way. They step forward as an old man walking his poodle goes by them. They hand him a poster. He takes it reluctantly. Looks down at it. Looks up at them. They seem to be pleading with him. He shakes his head a little, tries to hand the poster back. Moves by them. I observe and assess as they talk between themselves for a moment, deciding what to do next.

I feel that these women are relentless.

That they will go on and on.

Until they have uncovered the truth.

Josie starts talking again. "Will Adey be with them, do you think? Your wife and Philip?" (Philip!)

I shake my head, shrug, as if to say, I don't know. I just want her to shut up.

I need to think about these women and what they are going to do. They worry me.

"He'll call tonight, Adey, I know he will. It's not like him to go off so suddenly without a word... saying goodbye. He's... well... a bit clingy, actually. I'll ask him then... I will ask him if Philip will at least contact his wife. She must be beside herself with worry."

I nod my reply, as if agreeing.

Distracted by her incessant babbling.

I need to keep a close eye on what's going on outside.

The two women are now moving up the road, on the other side, towards the next lamp post. I imagine they have posted these wretched posters from the bottom of the hill and are now going to the top, one lamp post after another.

They will then cross over and come down this side of the road, working their way back to the bottom across from where they started. Then, all being well, they will go away and leave me in peace.

That's what I hope. And pray.

I just need them to be gone.

Away from here as soon as possible.

"When will she come back, do you think? For the bungalow? For her half-share?" Josie prattles on, seeming to think she can say anything, this woman. That she has the right to ask these personal questions. On and on. Whatever comes into her mind. It angers me, but I stay calm as I reply.

"They won't come back," I say steadily, "not now they're together. It's mine. This bungalow. It's all paid for."

I think for a moment and then continue.

"I'm just fine. I get a small pension, paid into my bank account, enough to tick over." I pat my pocket and add, "I need to get some cash out of the ATM later. We could have fish and chips if you like."

I then think a little longer and finish my words.

"I'm just going to enjoy the rest of my days here. I'm going to see out my time quietly… with my books and papers… writing my letters and…"

"How can you be sure she won't come back?" she interrupts, laughing and then adds, "she'll want some money from the bunga-low… once they've run out."

I don't answer her. Ignore her.

Instead, I carry on looking out of the window.

Watch what is happening there.

I see the next-door neighbour, the young trollop with the screaming girls, walking up from the right, the girls following behind her. She stops as she gets near to my gate and puts down the bags she is carrying. She stands upright for a second, then arches her back before saying something to the girls and bending forward to lift the heavy bags again.

I watch the younger Rennie woman, who has taken the enve-lope full of posters and the tape and is walking up the other side, moving out of sight as she continues taping posters to the lamp posts. She will reappear in five, ten minutes.

I note the older woman taking a handful of posters out of the envelope. She is now crossing the road and is approaching the next-door neighbour, who puts down her bags again to exchange greetings. I can imagine what they are saying to each other.

The trollop studies the poster. Thinks for a moment. Shakes her head.

The older woman looks up and down the road. Asks another question.

The trollop nods her reply. Then turns and points to my bungalow.

The older woman looks across as I step back sharply from the window. Josie stands there unmoving and says to me, "She's seen us." As if I didn't know. There are more words between the trollop and the old woman and then the trollop turns to go with her children following along behind.

The older woman waits until they have gone, glancing towards us once or twice as she does, and then looks back up the road where the younger woman has disappeared out of sight. She tucks the posters under her arm and reaches to take a mobile phone out of her pocket.

"Do you think she's calling the police?" I ask Josie, speaking as slowly and as calmly as I can.

Josie laughs. "Why would she do that?" I'm not sure what to say.

"Hang on," she replies, "let me go and talk to her." And, before I can stop her, she is out of the room, down the hallway and at the front door.

"Hello..." she calls out, "... Mrs Rennie?"

The woman, about to start pressing buttons on the mobile phone, looks up and I can see her mouth the word "Yes?"

Now hell and fury is walking up the path and into my bungalow.

SATURDAY 29 JULY, 4.16PM

"Mr Todd?" she asks as I move and stand in the hallway facing her as she comes through the porch.

Josie steps to one side.

"Yes," I reply, as calm and as mannered as I can be before the onslaught.

She moves forward, three, four, five paces, and stops just in front of me. I can barely breathe. Am holding my breath. Then she says, "I'm Carol... Philip's wife," and she puts her arms around my back and pulls me towards her in a hug, her face next to mine, almost touching.

I don't know what to do.

An unexpected turn of events.

I can feel her body close to mine, just the slightest space between us.

"There, there," I mumble, not sure what else I should be saying. "It's okay, come and sit down."

We move, the three of us, into the living room and Josie takes an armchair while the woman and I sit next to each other on the sofa. She puts the posters on the carpet and then reaches out and holds my hand, pulling me towards her again for another embrace. She struggles with her composure. I feel hot and flustered by this sudden turn of events. I am not sure what to do. Eventually she sits back, reaches for a tissue from her pocket and wipes her face and nose.

"You poor man," she says. "I know how you feel."

I nod, twist my mouth a little as if I am close to shedding tears.

"I'd wanted to come and see you... once I heard... about Philip... and your wife. Di, one of the teaching assistants, knew you lived here but I wasn't sure which one it was... your neighbour pointed out where you lived."

"It's been a great shock," I manage to say in a crackling voice. "Very upsetting. To have gone off like that."

"This isn't the first time," she says, her head slightly bowed. "He did something like this a few years ago. When he worked at his last place... with someone there. A younger model."

I nod, and smile slightly, encouraging her to go on.

"He worked at… well, it doesn't matter. He said it was a midlife crisis. I agreed to take him back if he sorted… well anyway, that's how he came to be working at the school… as a teaching assistant."

"I see," I add, not really sure what else to say.

"He wanted a complete break. A fresh start. He could have done better. He was qualified. Well qualified. But it was what he wanted to do, work with young children. To inspire them." She laughs and goes on, "We've struggled you know, with money. Quite a step down, money-wise. And now he's gone. But he'll be back when her money runs out, you watch."

Josie and I look at each other.

She looks puzzled. At the woman's assumption that my wife was a rich woman. Had money. That they are living on that.

She goes to speak but stops at the slight shake of my head.

"I'm not being funny," says the woman in a sour voice. Then she pauses, and laughs, a cynical, angry sound. "But… I've seen a photo of your wife in one of his jacket pockets… I can't think why else he would leave me for her."

I nod, realising suddenly that, if she believes this, she will be no trouble to me. That she will just go away. Sour and bitter but no more bother.

I had expected angry, demanding questions in an ever- louder voice. Why has he left his car over the road? Why has he disappeared? Why hasn't he spent any money? Used his cards? Vanished without trace? The final, screeched question, "Where is he?" preceding a call to the police.

"This man," she'd say, "knows something."

"He has a terrible secret."

"You need to find out what it is."

I thought that she would never let up. She would hound me.

Follow me. Watch my every move. Until I gave in and confessed to what I had done. That I had killed my wife. Him too. And my son. Such awful crimes and so many others. But she has no idea. No idea at all.

I look sad and smile gently as if I agree with her.

"Do you know where they are? We've been putting up posters, offering a reward. We've been hoping someone might know where they are so I can find him and speak to him. To sort things out – the money, at least."

I see Josie watching me, waiting for my reply.

"I don't know," I answer. "But if you leave your phone number I will give you a call if my wife gets in touch."

The woman sighs, exasperated, as if I am expected to sort things out for her.

"It's on this," She says, passing me a poster. I look at it. The close-up photo of his stupid face in the middle. 'Missing' above. 'Philip Rennie' and 'Reward £500' and her mobile phone number below it. Like a lost dog.

"I could do with a reward," I say, trying to sound cheerful, to lighten the mood.

"I don't want him back. Not this time. But I do want to speak to him to sort everything out. I want a divorce."

She goes to say something else but her phone makes a jin-gly-jangly noise.

I look at her face as she studies the phone, holding it further away as if she needs glasses, and then swipes the screen. It is a hard face. And she is older than I had first thought. I do not think she is as nice and gentle as I assumed. I believe the earlier warmth, the hugging, the sniffing, the wiping of eyes and nose, was just part of an act to win me over.

"Hello? Yes... darling, I'm at 56... the bungalow with the... yes, come down."

She swipes the screen again the other way and looks at me and then Josie for the first time, "My daughter, Amy... the posters were her idea. Just in case," she said, in a humourless voice "... I wish he had been murdered... or thrown his stupid self under a train."

We sit there together, quietly, patiently, for what must be two or three minutes. Avoiding eye contact. Smiling vaguely. Waiting for the daughter to arrive. God knows why.

There is the sound of a door opening. We all look up. To smile at this Amy. Instead, the child, Christ, she'd slipped my mind, walks into the room.

She is holding my wife's red and white scarf in her hand. Serious-faced, she walks over and gives it to Josie.

SATURDAY 29 JULY, 4.26PM

Josie takes the scarf and looks at it and smiles and says, "Oh that's lovely, Lily, is it for me?" Then she wrinkles her nose and lifts the scarf up and adds, "Oh Lily, it's really smelly, where did you find it?"

I have stopped breathing.

My heart is beating so fast and so loud everyone must be able to hear it.

I flush red hot.

The old Rennie woman looks at Josie and says, "I can smell it from here." I'm not sure that she can, but I don't doubt it stinks of damp and mould and maybe even worse than that. Blood. Decay. The smell of death.

A nightmare of a moment.

I cannot speak.

Do not know what to do.

I hold my breath as Josie folds the scarf neatly and places it by the handbag at her feet. The moment passes, although I know there are more to come. Josie goes to pull the child closer to her but she wriggles free and stands there, her back to me, facing Josie.

"Look at you, Lily," she says, "you're all covered in dirt, and your hands. Show me your hands."

The child puts her hands behind her back, as awkward as ever.

"Show me your hands now, Lily." Josie speaks in a firmer voice and I fear what the child is going to do. Turn and run back to the shelter, with Josie chasing after her, two, three, four steps behind? Then what will I do?

The child puts her hands out towards Josie.

"Lily, your hands are filthy, what have you been doing? Digging a hole to Australia?" She laughs and adds, "Go to the bathroom straight away and wash your hands and face… and don't look so serious."

The child turns, her face solemn, and she glances towards me as she leaves the room. I can see from her expression that she has uncovered my secret. I sit and watch, helpless and unsure what to do, with Josie and this Rennie woman with her mobile phone in front of me and the daughter about to join us.

I am trapped.

It is like being in a nightmare where everything is happening around you. And you cannot do a thing about it.

I cannot move.

I hear the porch door opening, then the front door, which must have been left unlatched by the older Rennie woman, who came in last behind Josie and me. I hear the footsteps of the young Rennie woman passing the child in the hallway and then she is standing in the doorway, a younger version of the hard-faced mother.

The mother stands up and gestures to the daughter, "This is Mr Todd, the husband of the woman Daddy's gone off with." She then waves a hand towards Josie and says, "And this is his daughter… I'm sorry, I didn't catch your name."

In that instant, I think Josie is going to introduce herself, correct the 'daughter' reference, and give the younger woman her chair before going off to the bathroom to speak to Lily. Instead, she just smiles widely, gives her name, and then points the younger woman to the other armchair. We all sit there facing each other.

"Are you well, Mr Todd?" asks the older Rennie woman, suddenly. "You seem to be sweating rather much."

They all watch me as I take a handkerchief from my pocket and mop my brow and face.

"I… I'm alright, thank you." I can hear the stutter in my voice. It sounds strangely strangled. They look at me as if they expect me to say more.

"I… (I try to swallow, I cannot help myself, but my throat is dry)… I am okay." I cannot add any more as my voice, my attempt to speak sentences, will betray my collapse.

The older Rennie woman speaks to her daughter, almost as if Josie and I are not here, "Daddy and… Mrs Todd… have gone away together… as I said… and Mr Todd has promised to call us when he hears from his wife."

The younger woman turns to me and I nod.

It is all I can do.

I am almost speechless and I realise how this must look but I cannot seem to do anything else.

"Do you have any information, Mr Todd?" the younger Rennie woman asks. "Where they are, where they've gone… do you know what they are doing?"

Josie interrupts my attempted answer, "We know no more than you, I'm afraid. They've just run away. Left us all in the dark. Do you know anything?"

The younger Rennie woman answers, a trace of sarcasm in her voice, "We don't know anything, only what the police tell us. We haven't even got the car back yet. It's why we are putting up posters."

She holds the poster towards Josie and then says, "It comes to something when the only way to find your father is by putting posters on lamp posts... like he's a lost cat."

The older Rennie woman laughs, a cynical noise.

Josie smiles, a touch of sympathy on her face.

I try to smile as well, but I am distracted by a sudden noise.

I can hear the kitchen door being opened. I think it must be Lily. I do not think she went to the bathroom. I did not hear that door closing, nor taps running, or the toilet flushing. I think she simply went back out to the air-raid shelter, hurried down the steps and slid in under the door, having already pulled off the rotted, broken pieces.

And now, having dug around, she is coming back into the bungalow. It scares me, the thought of what she will have in her hands this time, and whether it will be something that these Rennie women will recognise as belonging to him. Then what will I do, as the older Rennie woman, her face in shock, taps out 9... 9... 9 on her mobile phone?

I sit here, in as calm and relaxed a pose as I can.

Inside, I think I am about to die. My heart will stop, just give up on me.

The sweat streams constantly down my face and I think my face must be ashen.

Lily comes into the living room and I turn to look at her. Her hands are just as dirty as they were and there are thick marks of mud on her clothes where she has slid into the shelter. She has her right hand outstretched, her fingers clenched into a fist around something. I think it may be a button off Rennie's jacket, or shirt, or cardigan; my mind has gone blank and I cannot recall what he was wearing.

Lily stands in the middle of the room, as if she knows she has an audience and that they are all watching her. She holds her hand out like a magician who is about to reveal a complete £20 note that she took from an audience member some time earlier and cut into so many pieces.

I want to reach out and snatch whatever it is from her hand. But I cannot move at the crucial moment. I cannot even speak. Nor scream. I think my heart is about to beat one final time and will then stop and I will simply fall, dead, as I hit the carpet, in front of them all.

Lily opens her hand.

I cannot see what it is, something gold and shiny. A button from Rennie's coat, I think. Or maybe something of Adrian's? Either way, the game is up.

"Oh Lily," says Josie and pulls her forward to hug her.

The child drops what she was holding on the carpet and I see what it is. A clean and bright £1 coin. I do not know where she found it; from the floor of the shelter or from someone's pocket. Hers. His. Adrian's. I find myself breathing in great gulps of air. Try to steady myself. Appear and act as normal as I can.

"Well," says the older Rennie woman getting to her feet. "I think someone needs a bath… We must be going… Thank you, Mr Todd… for your time."

There is an awkward moment as I struggle slowly to my feet, the young woman even reaching out her hand to take my elbow to steady me. I stand facing the two Rennie women and Josie, who seems to be distracted by something Lily is saying to her.

"You really don't look very well, Mr Todd. You should have a lie down when we have gone and see a doctor if you're not feeling any better this evening."

I try to smile, a warm and reassuring, 'don't-worry-about-me' kind of smile, but it comes out as more of a grimace, I think. I can feel the sweat still pouring off me. It is all I can do to act normal. The most I can do is just stand here. After a second or two of further awkwardness, and I note Josie does not look at me, I raise my right arm carefully and gesture them towards the door.

This time, as they say goodbye, there is no theatrical hug or pretence of kindness or emotion. These two hard-faced women simply want to know where he is for financial reasons. They want money, plain and simple. There is no love in what they are doing. We shake hands, the four of us and the older Rennie woman smiles down at the child by way of goodbye.

I follow them to the door, Josie and the child just behind me whispering to each other again and we all stop as we get to the porch. The two Rennie women step outside and then turn and speak to me.

"We'll put the rest of the posters up," the younger woman says.

"Down as far as the supermarket," adds the older woman, finishing the sentence for her.

I nod, smile, go, just go.

"Keep in touch," says the older woman. "Call us when you hear something. You've got our number, on the poster."

Go, for God's sake, go now.

"Have we got your number, Mr Todd? So we can call you if we hear first?" the younger woman checks.

I shake my head. Shrug. They have to go. Now.

There is a searching for a pen in the older woman's handbag. A torn-off corner of a poster. My landline number written in a shaking hand. Is that a one or a seven? A seven. A dash is added through it. Final farewells.

I hope to God I will not see them again.

That they will eventually give up the search.

Accept that he has gone forever.

I stand, smiling, as they move down the path and to the gate, then go right and walk down the hill. Neither of them acknowledges my presence, politely waiting there.

I turn to speak to Josie, to say something about Lily and the scarf and the coin, some kind of explanation, but neither she nor the child is standing behind me any more. The hallway is empty. They have both gone to the air-raid shelter.

Composing myself, I walk down the hallway and move towards the kitchen. I now know what I have to do. What I should have done already. I have to go into the kitchen and get a big, sharp knife from the rack on the side.

And kill Josie.

Then the child.

That is the only way that I will – at last – live happily ever after.

SUNDAY 30 JULY, 2.19AM

I have been lying here all night.

On my back, gazing up at the moonlight.

I think it must be 2 or 3am and, for once, all is quiet.

I can hear traffic from the road at the front of the bungalow but the noise is low and sporadic and I hardly notice it. It does not bother me at all.

The railway line at the back of the bungalow has been silent for hours. I ponder whether, with the heatwave and then such relentless rain, a train has been derailed, blocking the line. If so, the line may remain silent for days.

The neighbours, to both sides, have not made a sound at all. No late-night singing or revelry. They have gone to bed without even a single noise. It makes for a peaceful night. The world is fast asleep. Except for me.

I am in the air-raid shelter.

I am bound and gagged and my feet are roped to a large metal ring in the wall.

The moonlight comes through a crack in the door.

The last thing I remember before waking here is hurrying into the kitchen and seeing Josie standing in the doorway from the garden. I recall her face. Horror. Shock. Disbelief. I knew there could be no reasoning with her. None at all. There was no room for debate. She must have gone straight to the shelter and seen the bodies. Adrian. Her. Him. Then pushed Lily into the garage and come back to confront me, to protect the child. Frantically telling her to stay hidden in the garage; a real-life, live-or-die, game of hide-and-seek.

I moved towards the knife rack. Because of all that had happened, I was not as fast as usual. But my hand was almost upon it.

She stepped forward quickly and raised her hand above her head. I noted a very strange expression on her face; her eyes were full of madness and her teeth were bared, like a wild animal's.

She was holding a huge spanner from the garage and I saw it coming down towards my head. It all seemed to happen in slow motion.

The next thing I remember was waking up here on my back

with a constant pain above my left eye and what felt like dried blood down that side of my face. Something soft, such as a sock, had been pushed into my mouth and black tape she must have found later in the garage was wrapped round and round my head covering my mouth. It took me a few minutes to control my overwhelming sense of panic and urge to scream.

I can only breathe slowly and carefully through my nose.

One of my nostrils makes a slight whistling noise. I worry that my nose may become blocked over time.

And then I will not be able to breathe at all.

The rest of the black tape, and she must have used all of the rolls in the garage, has been wrapped around my body from shoulders to feet. I am encased. I have tried very hard, several times, to flex my muscles against the tape to try to break it or at least loosen it so that I might free a hand, or even a finger or two. I have not succeeded. There is no give at all, no sense of movement. I am trussed up tight.

The front of my trousers is damp.

I have wet myself.

I know that I will soil myself soon.

I have also been tied up with rope, the same rope that used to be a washing line and that I had kept in the garage in case it came in useful one day. It has been cut into three pieces: one loops round and round my torso, another around my legs and the final one attaches my feet to a steel ring in the wall. I do not know what it is nor why it is there but I wish it wasn't.

I have managed to leverage myself a little to push myself, by my feet, away from the wall to see if the ring will break free or at least loosen a little. But there is no movement at all. All I have been able to do is to roll over, with some effort and several attempts, so that my face is in the moonlight.

The thin shaft of light keeps me sane.

I could not bear to be in total darkness.

Everything around me would scare me to death.

I try not to look at the corpses too often. Her face, sagged and collapsed and decomposing, is towards me and she would not like to be seen like this. She was always very particular about not being seen without her make-up on. Now, she does not even have a proper face.

Her body is obscured by his body, his back to me. I have noticed that he is – was – wearing a hair piece. I had not spotted it before. It has come loose and hangs there in mid-air, half stuck to his scalp. I see coins from his pocket on the floor and am pleased, though that may not be the correct word, that the child came in with one of those rather than the wig.

Adrian's body is sprawled on top of them as if in a playground game of bundle. He looks almost normal as if he could actually still be alive. In truth, other than her ghastly, rotting face, they are no more than a mass of torsos, arms and legs at awkward angles.

And smells. By God. The stench of the abattoir. It takes all of my powers to stop myself gagging and vomiting, choking to death on my own sick.

And there are noises. Slight and rustling and occasional. Rats. Nesting. Within the corpses.

My imagination only, I think. My fears surfacing. The light allows me to see, to keep watch, to calm my rising panic.

I do not know what the morning will bring. Josie and the child may have simply gone and left me here. She could disappear, at least for a while, with £10,000 in cash. If so, I am doomed. I cannot free myself. If, over time, the tape and ropes loosened slightly, I would by then be too weak and sickly to break free. Even if I could loosen the tape at my mouth, what could I do?

Call out?

The neighbours coming here?

The police called?

It is possible that, having seen what is in the shelter, and having regained her composure overnight, Josie might simply call the police in the morning. Show them the diary left in my room. Tell them where I was. It would save my life. But I would spend the rest of it locked up in a cell. Would that be better than this? I do not know. It would be a life, of sorts.

But would Josie call the police?

Questions and investigations?

Leon and the missing £10,000 in cash?

Josie and the child could just stay there in the bungalow. They would be safe from Leon. With the bungalow paid for, and bills that could be settled as they went along, £10,000 would go a long way. Josie knows Mrs Todd won't be coming back to make a claim. Neither will Mr Rennie. Or Adrian. No one will ever come knocking on the door. I think Josie and the child might just do that. Yes, that is what I believe.

So I will remain trussed up in the air-raid shelter.

In the heat and the rain.

With the corpses.

Waiting for the rats to arrive and discover me.

One way or the other, I will die here.

This is the end.

AUTHOR'S NOTES

My first novel, *Sweet William*, from Contraband, an imprint of Saraband, was published in November 2017. A man, Raymond Orrey, escapes from a psychiatric unit to snatch his son, William, from foster parents and to go on the run to start a new life together in the south of France.

In some ways, this was a simple book to write – its linear narrative going from 'A', the psychiatric unit, to, or at least towards, Z', the south of France. In essence, it's a manhunt – the age-old story of an innocent man on the run, although I subverted it a little bit by having a flawed and damaged lead character. I told most of the story from inside Orrey's head – a mix of anger, love and madness – and then aimed to crank up the tension by having him running away with an increasingly sick child with Type 1 diabetes.

With this second book, *Mr Todd's Reckoning*, I wanted to write something more ambitious and complex, layered, back and forth, while still retaining the same characteristics as *Sweet William* – mainly, the story unfolding from inside the mind of the lead character. I also wanted to set the story in one main location, over a short period of time, and with a growing sense of claustrophobia and tension. Most important of all, I wanted to try to present a character who was exactly the same at the start as he was at the end but to change the reader's perception of him over the course of the book.

The initial idea, of the father and son in a bungalow story, came to me two to three years before I started work on the book. I wrote the first, 'snip, snip' scene in the middle of 2015 and then put it aside until I had a plot to go with it.

It's well-documented that my eldest son, Michael, suffered from depression and anorexia and spent time in hospital and The Priory because of it. I wrote a memoir, *Dear Michael, Love Dad*, published by Hodder in 2016 and 2017 followed by another memoir, co-authored with Michael, called *Out of the Madhouse* for Jessica Kingsley Publishers in 2018. Michael's fit and well and happy now – his turnaround has been remarkable and I am very proud of him – but when he came back to live in the family home in May 2015, things were bleak and it was touch and go for a while.

That first scene – 'snip, snip, snip' – was based on Michael preparing his evening meal and me sitting close by. Michael was just minding his own business, getting his tea ready and was oblivious to the fact that I was there, feeling hot and bothered, listening as he snip… snip… snipped… long pause… snip, snip snip… snip… snip, snipped his way through his vegetables.

So I wrote that first scene and thought there was a potential story here – a father and son forced to live together, the son appearing to have some serious issues but supported by a kind and decent father; although things were perhaps not quite as they seemed.

I began thinking about this book after finishing *Out of the Madhouse*. The idea I had was that the son would drive the father mad with his constant, twitching presence. The father would then kill the son in a sudden rage and spend the rest of the book trying to deal with that on various levels: emotionally, practically etc. That's how I planned to start and where I intended to go with it.

I always feel slightly deflated when I read about well-known writers plotting a book from start to finish, knowing exactly what will happen when and doing several drafts before they get it all just so. It's not how I do it. I write the first scene, agonise and tweak it, sit with my head in my hands thinking I can't do this, write the next scene, agonise and fiddle a bit more and so on. What this means is that my book sort of evolves as it goes along and what seemed like a good idea when thinking about things seems less so when I have begun writing.

I also used to read about successful writers who said their characters kind of 'took over' when they wrote and they had to go where the characters went. I always thought that was a load of twaddle. I was wrong. When I started writing creatively, I found that, by getting inside the character's mind and imagining myself in that setting, the book does sort of write itself in that you think 'yes, he'd do that', 'no, he'd not do that', 'that's how he'd react' and so on. When I got stuck into this book, everything pretty much fell into place and went where it wanted to go.

As I started writing, the father began as a sort of skewed version of me and the son was a twisted version of Michael. As it progressed, and I got more into it, the characters became completely fictionalised, but lived as real people in my mind and ended up bearing little or no comparison to Michael or me.

I like to see the setting in my head when I write. The bungalow – shabby, rundown etc. – is based on my late mother's and stepfather's bungalow in Windmill Lane in Rustington, West Sussex. I should state that it was a nice and clean and well-presented bungalow, but it always seemed so small to me. They moved from a biggish house on the outskirts of London and downsized to the south coast as many do. I was always struck by how cramped the place was whenever we visited. As there were two of them and five of us – Iain, Tracey, Michael, Sophie and Adam – I guess that wasn't so surprising. But that squashed-in feeling stuck with me.

I moved the bungalow in my mind near to where I live in Suffolk. I wanted it to be anonymous, out of the way, overlooked, neither in Ipswich nor in Felixstowe, where I live. It's sort of in-between. If you live this way and drive into Ipswich from Felixstowe, I imagined it up by Sainsbury's at Warren Heath, on the left, as you approach St Augustine's Church. If anyone working for HMRC lives thereabouts, apologies – it's just a coincidence. We used to have friends, Wendy and Nick, who lived opposite and, whenever we visited, the road always seemed noisy and it was hard to get your car in and out. So that sort of fitted in well.

The other locations mentioned in the book – the railway line behind the bungalow, the Co-op, the park in Ipswich, the theatre in Felixstowe – they are all real enough but have been slightly re-imagined in my head. The Spa Pavilion is there on Felixstowe seafront, and very nice it is too, but the wooded area where Rennie parked his car would be harder to find nearby; I saw it in my head as being up near the Grove woods a mile or two away.

The heatwave! I set the story during a heatwave as it helped to add to that ever-increasing sense of suffocation and tension in the bungalow. Many readers will assume, naturally enough, that I wrote the book in the summer of 2018 when it was blisteringly hot, day after day, week after week. It was, in fact, a coincidence. I actually finished writing at the end of May 2018. I then had a bit of a read and an edit through June and sent it to Saraband on 2 July 2018.

Finally, the names of the characters and the last thing to fall into place – the title of the book. The father was always going to be Malcolm and his son Adrian. The names just suited the characters I saw in my mind so well. As for the title, it started off as

Mr Somebody's Secret – the 'Somebody' surname being that of a tax inspector who carried out a random tax investigation on me many years ago. He was a nice guy and it all went well enough but his unusual, and really rather lovely, surname stuck in my head. His surname would have been just perfect but, not unreasonably, it might have been an issue further down the line; especially when doing local publicity.

I then ran through a list of names that occurred to me for various reasons as being potentially suitable – Simkins, Stenning, Halliday, Hyde, Vine, Hunt, Laight, Hurst, Hulton, Joyce and more – before settling on 'Todd', an anonymous, short and blunt English name. I then changed *Secret* to *Reckoning* because of its dual meaning – the book kind of started with one meaning and then sort of ended, rather neatly, with the other.

Iain

Iain Maitland
www.iainmaitland.net
twitter.com/iainmaitland

AUTHOR'S ACKNOWLEDGEMENTS

I'd like to thank ...

Saraband, for publishing *Mr Todd's Reckoning*. You have been wonderful from start to finish.

Sara, I always wanted you to publish this and I'm so glad you did.

Ken, great cover!

Ali, for copy-editing the book so brilliantly. You made it a better book.

Craig – love the blurb.

Barbara and Paul and Chris for your quotes and all you lovely bloggers for your reviews.

Tom, an excellent proof-read.

My fab agent Clare, for the literary stuff and for staying calm as I bounced off the walls.

Will at Stillwater Books – and Linda, Alison and Dennis – for the book launch.

Tracey, Michael, Sophie, Adam – my family. No-one will recognise you in *Mr Todd's Reckoning*. But you're all in here - as you are, one way or another, in everything I do.

ABOUT THE AUTHOR

Iain Maitland is the author of *Dear Michael, Love Dad* (Hodder, 2016), a moving book of letters written to his son, who suffered from depression and anorexia, and co-author (with his son) of *Out of the Madhouse: An Insider's Guide to Managing Depression and Anxiety*. Iain is an ambassador for Stem4, the teenage mental health charity, and talks regularly about mental health issues. A writer since 1987, he is a journalist and has written more than 50 books, mainly on business, which have been published around the world. His first novel, *Sweet William*, a thriller, was published by Saraband, in the Contraband imprint, in 2017.